ENDING IN DEATH

By P.B. Barry

Copyright © 2016 P.B. Barry

Cover Design © 2016 John O'Mahony

All characters and events featured in this work other than those clearly in the public domain are entirely fictitious and any resemblance to any person living or dead, organisation or event, is purely coincidental. Any mistakes are the author's own.

This novel is not a police procedural and all the workings of the *Garda Siochana*, the Irish police force, are pure invention. I hereby apologise to all members of the *Garda Siochana* for taking such liberties. I also apologise to the people of Co. Kerry for using their beautiful county as a setting for my story.

The Sergeant Alan Murray Series:
DEATH IN A LONELY PLACE
ENDING IN DEATH

Also by this author writing as Peggy O'Mahony:
LOVE AT A LATER DATE
LOVE AT CLOSE RANGE

Writing as Peggie Biessmann:
SPATE OF VIOLENCE

Chapter One

Penny Wallace paused at the landing window on the first floor of Ballyamber House and looked down at the front garden spread out below. Her eyes followed the gravelled driveway to where it curved gently round the tall rhododendron bushes before disappearing from view. The old woman, Agnes O'Toole, was standing there in the shadows staring up at the house. Penny could see the tails of her shabby raincoat flapping gently where the hefty mountain breeze caught them. She tried to ignore the sudden shiver which travelled from the base of her neck to the bottom of her spine.

'Ignore her,' Penny's husband Gregory had said on many occasions over the past few weeks. 'She'll get tired of trying to intimidate us and give up.'

Penny wasn't so sure. Since they had come here to Ballyamber House she had heard stories about the magical powers of Agnes and the O'Toole clan and the inadvisability of crossing them. Mrs Quinn who came to help with the housekeeping three days a week told hair-raising tales of destruction and ruin brought on by one of Agnes' curses and although Penny laughed at them, she still felt a faint trickle of fear run through her whenever Agnes came and stood at the bend in the driveway and stared at the house, something which happened nearly every day.

'I suppose you heard about the row over Ballyamber House?' Mrs Quinn said to Sergeant Alan Murray as they both stood in line at the check-out of the local supermarket in Ballyamber village.

'A row over Ballyamber House?' Murray looked surprised. 'I heard it was sold to some millionaire or other and that he's been doing it up. So what's the row about?' In his position as head of the local garda station in Killglash, most of the village gossip was relayed to him by one means or another, but he had not heard this particular story.

Mrs Quinn was only too delighted to have found someone who didn't know about it already. Her position as housekeeper at Ballyamber House gave her a certain status in the village and she did not let it interfere with any loyalty she might be supposed to show her employers. 'Well,' she said, 'as you said, the place was sold last year to a man by the name of Stanley Wallace. He came over from London to have a look at it and he got a smart architect fella to come down and run the place. Agnes O'Toole is hopping mad over it.'

'Agnes O'Toole! Why? Did she want the job of architect?'

Mrs Quinn did not crack a smile. Murray's sense of humour was often lost on the villagers. 'You know where Agnes lives,' she said. 'The O'Toole's were tenants of the Ballyamber estate – it was a colossal big place and Agnes's great grandfather was a coachman I believe - and when the old owner died he left the O'Toole family the cottage at the entrance to the avenue. Agnes said that Stanley Wallace came to see her. He wanted to buy the cottage off her and tear it down or make a fancy guest lodge out of it or something. And he warned her about trespassing. There's a right of way past Ballyamber House even though it's never used nowadays.' Mrs Quinn shook her head, her tightly curled hair almost bouncing in indignation. 'As if the house wasn't big enough to sleep twenty people or more without building a lodge. Anyway, Agnes says she's not selling and she won't put up with being denied right of way.'

'If she doesn't want to sell then that should be the end of it,' Murray said mildly. Without knowing the details of the right of way he did not intend to comment and be misquoted by Mrs Quinn the next time she talked to anyone about it. Right of way, the right to travel over a neighbour's land, was very important to country dwellers and many a legal battle had been fought over it.

'You'd think so,' Mrs Quinn sniffed. 'Agnes says they're putting her under pressure. That architect fellow Donlon has been calling on her as well as Stanley Wallace. I wouldn't cross Agnes if I was them. She's been heard saying she's going to put a curse on them if they don't leave her alone. She says they should go back where they came from.'

Murray gave a short laugh. 'Put a curse on them. The lord be merciful!'

Mrs Quinn pursed her lips. 'You could never trust them O'Tooles,' she said with another shake of her head. 'I remember when my son Danny killed Agnes' cat – he ran it over when he was on his motor bike, sure he couldn't help it, it ran out in front of him. She was hopping mad. She told him he'd never have luck for it. And sure enough about a week after it happened he had an accident and broke his leg. He was out of work for nearly six months and it wouldn't surprise me if Agnes hadn't put the evil eye on him.'

'Well,' said Murray, 'we can only hope that Agnes keeps her cats away from Ballyamber House.'

'So, Cinderella, how are you liking the country life?' Rod grinned mischievously at his sister as he strolled into the small salon of Ballyamber House.

Penny paused in her task of filling one of the heavy cut-glass vases with a bouquet of gerbera which she had purchased that morning in Killglash. 'It takes some getting used to,' she admitted. 'But of course it's very peaceful and Gregory loves it all.'

'Does he?' Rod stuck his hands deep into the pockets of his jeans and began to pace up and down the room. 'Did he ask *you* if you loved it? I'll bet he didn't. Greg is always going to do what Daddy says, isn't he?'

Penny gave her brother an appraising look before she answered. 'Greg and Stanley get on very well. There's nothing wrong with that. They've made you very welcome.' She could have added that her father-in-law had also paid for the six weeks of treatment for his alcoholism which Rod had received in a private clinic.

Rod snorted. 'I don't need Stanley Wallace's charity.'

'He's just trying to be helpful,' she said. She arranged the flowers to her satisfaction and placed the vase on the small table near the window, taking a few paces back to admire the effect. 'It's amazing how flowers brighten up a room. It makes me think that spring can't be very far off.'

Rod did not appear to be listening. He stopped his pacing and came up close to his sister. 'Tell me, what you do you think of the new wannabe Mrs Stanley Wallace? Quite a little go-getter isn't she?'

'Sophie seems quite nice,' Penny said, aware that her voice lacked conviction. 'Stanley is crazy about her.'

Sophie Winslow was an aspiring actress whose very minor supporting role in a recent television series had just come to an end. She had arrived from London last night with an unbelievable amount of luggage. To Penny's disgust both Greg and Rod had rushed around offering assistance like two over-eager puppies. At dinner that night the three men, Stanley, Greg and Rod gave her all their attention, leaving Penny to sit and fume in silence. To add to all the other vexations, Sophie had ordered her breakfast in bed and Mrs Quinn's expression spoke volumes as she had climbed the stairs with a laden tray this morning. It was not a very promising start to Sophie's stay.

'And she's crazy about Stanley's money.' Rod gave a short laugh. 'It wouldn't surprise me if she persuades him to marry her. That would make a dent in the Wallace fortune wouldn't it? Old Gregory might not get as much as he hopes.'

Penny shrugged. 'I doubt if that will be a problem,' she said. 'Stanley has made provision for Greg long ago. Besides, he can do what he likes with his money.'

'As long as Greg does what Daddy wants, I expect he'll get his share-out in good time.'

'Rod, don't you think you're being a bit overcritical? You're a guest here in his – our home and you've been treated with nothing but kindness. I think you'd have to admit that. And besides, it's Stanley's life and if he's found the woman he wants to marry, well good luck to him.'

'And is Gregory Wallace the man you thought you married?'

Penny was silent. Rod could sometimes surprise her with his depth of insight. Difficult he might be, but she knew that they shared a bond of deep affection. Ever since they were children she had kept an eye out for him and he had loved her unconditionally in return. His question had hit the exact sore spot.

Gregory and Penny had fallen in love when they met on holiday in the south of Spain. Penny had started work as a receptionist in a modest London hotel and her first holiday abroad was spent with friends on the Costa Blanca. It had been a chance meeting on the beach, he had cut his hand on a piece of broken glass and she had offered her services in cleaning the wound - which wasn't very deep

- and supplying him with a plaster. Gregory was immediately smitten by Penny's blonde good looks and sexy figure and they were married within twelve months of meeting. The Wallace family were aghast. Penny was "nobody" as Stanley Wallace told his son at least three times a day, conveniently forgetting his own humble beginnings. Gregory should be able to do much better for himself, he reasoned. Penny came from a working-class background, had not been to university, and had a brother who was an alcoholic. But Gregory remained surprisingly stubborn and in the end his father gave in. Penny was acknowledged as his son's wife and treated with cold politeness and ignored as often as possible.

'That's a silly question,' she said briskly in answer to Rod's remark. 'Gregory and I are very happy.'

'Are you?' The look Rod gave her was grave. 'I think you're starting to fall for Stanley's star architect. I saw you laughing with him the other day. You never laugh like that with Gregory – not that anyone could. He's such a wet blanket.'

She felt the colour come into her face. 'Now you're being absolutely ridiculous.'

'I wish I were, dear sister. What a pity you didn't meet Steve Donlon before Gregory snapped you up. Although, I suppose your paths wouldn't have crossed, would they? He only works for the super-rich and we've never been in that category, now have we? Not even in the slightly rich category if you think about it.'

'Penny,' said Gregory's voice from the doorway. 'I've been looking for you.' How long he had been standing there they could not tell. He walked further into the room, glancing from one to the other of them. 'Sorry, am I interrupting a tête a tête? I was looking for that list of guests we made out for Sophie's birthday party. I think you had it last?'

'I might have left it in the kitchen,' Penny said. She watched his expression, alert for any indication he could have heard what Rod had said about her liking Steve Donlon. 'I was going over it with Mrs Quinn to make sure we have enough bed linen and towels for the guests. We'll probably need to stock up –'

'Yes, yes, all right,' Gregory cut her short impatiently. 'No need to make the five-times tables out of it. Father wanted to see it. He's thinking of adding a few more names now that most of the rooms in the East Wing are decorated and we can accommodate a few more guests. He turned as if to leave the room then turned back again to address Rod. 'Are you planning on being here for Sophie's birthday party on Saturday or do you think it better if you keep away from temptation?'

'I wouldn't miss it for the world.' Rod said.

Chapter Two

'That was delicious,' Murray lied as he put down his knife and fork and wiped his mouth with a paper napkin.

Nicola Ryan beamed at him from across the table. 'I'm glad you liked it,' she said, 'there's nothing like a roast beef dinner on a Sunday.'

Murray returned the smile although his jaws were aching slightly from the amount of chewing necessary to battle the roast beef. Clearly Nicola had put the joint in the oven much too late. The roast potatoes had been hard in the middle and the gravy lumpy (Murray was a gravy fan and liked to trickle it generously over his roast vegetables). If his hostess had tried to produce the least appetising Sunday dinner in Ballyamber, she had succeeded.

'Strawberries and cream for dessert.' Nicola rose from her chair and began to clear the table. 'No don't get up,' she told him. 'Vanessa will give me a hand.'

Murray took a sip of Sauvignon Blanc – that at least tasted good – and watched in a bemused fashion as Nicola and her daughter removed the dinner plates.

Nicola was his new neighbour. She and her teenage daughter Vanessa had moved into the cottage next to his over a month ago but owing to his irregular hours he had not seen much of them until now. He wasn't sure if he welcomed a new neighbour. It was difficult getting used to someone else living in what he still regarded as Elena's cottage.

Elena. The thought of her caused him to catch his breath. He had thought she was his soul mate, the one person who could make him get over the disappearance of his wife Sheila on Ardnabrone all those years ago. He'd even proposed to her, damn it all! And then the unthinkable had happened. A group of hill walkers had found a plastic water bottle with the name "Sheila" just legible in black letters on the side. Murray had been on duty and he could still remember the shock that had run through him when he saw his wife's handwriting – barely legible after so much exposure to the weather - on the half empty bottle. The hikers told him they had found it near a place known locally as the Devil's Spout. An extensive search of the area revealed no further clues.

The finding of Sheila's water bottle, one she always carried with her, had devastated Murray. Over the years he had tried to come to terms with his wife's disappearance, to accept the fact that she might never be found, that he would never know what had happened to her. This discovery was like a tap on the shoulder by an icy hand. He could not go through with the planned wedding to Elena. He needed more time, he reasoned. Who could blame her, therefore, that while telling him she understood, she had moved to London and had cut all ties with him?

The cottage had stood empty for a long time but whatever hopes he had entertained of Elena changing her mind and returning to Ballyamber had been dashed when Nicola and Vanessa moved in. Now he was going to have to get used to new neighbours and he did not relish the idea.

He had the weekend off, the weather was stormy and wet as befitting early March in this mountainy area, and he had been dozing by the fire yesterday afternoon when Nicola called on him. 'I was wondering if you'd like to have Sunday lunch with Vanessa and myself tomorrow?' She had sounded a bit unsure of herself, almost as if she expected him to turn down the invitation. 'That's if you're not engaged elsewhere,' she'd added.

'No, I'm free. I'd be delighted.' He had in fact bought himself a ready-made heat-in-the-oven meal at the local supermarket. When Elena lived next door they had often cooked together – he made a very good chicken curry and Elena was able to produce a tasty meal from a few basic ingredients at the drop of a hat. Often they had sat and drank hot toddies by the fire afterwards and talked and talked. He still missed those times more than he cared to admit.

Nicola served the strawberries and cream. He caught her watching him with a wary expression on her face, trying to gauge his mood. The village gossips had no doubt been talking to her about him. Did she know about Sheila's disappearance? he wondered. Or had someone mentioned his romance with Elena to her? Women loved things like that, he reflected. They seemed to think it was romantic.

'You're settling in well here in Ballyamber, you and Vanessa?' he said in an attempt to be sociable. He could not recall much of what she had told him about herself when she first moved in. It had been a busy time for him with two families in Killglash fighting each other and causing numerous public disturbances in the course of a long-time feud.

'It's very quiet, of course.' Nicola admitted. 'I was lucky to get the part time job at the hotel in Killglash and between that and giving massage and reiki, I keep afloat. Vanessa loves school which is a huge relief. She's settled in very well. She loves animals and wants to be a vet so being allowed to help at Mitchell's veterinary clinic and getting a bit of money for babysitting for them now and again is just perfect for her.'

'I'm glad to hear it.'

'Have you ever had your fortune told?' Nicola asked as she placed three coffee mugs on the table and proceeded to fill them.

'Mum,' Vanessa said, rolling her eyes towards the ceiling. 'No one believes in that rubbish any more.' She had hardly spoken throughout the meal, answering Murray's enquiries about school and what she thought of living in Ballyamber with the minimum of information. With her long blonde hair, heavily made up eyes and full, sulky mouth she looked older than her fifteen years, or so Murray thought but then, he reminded himself, with no children of his own to judge by, this could well be how all young teenage girls looked these days.

'It's not rubbish.' Nicola smiled at her daughter. 'And people do believe in it. Look at how popular horoscopes are!'

'What do you use, Tarot cards or a crystal ball?' Murray raised an eyebrow at her.

Nicola laughed, tossing back her auburn hair from her face. 'I use playing cards.' She turned to her daughter. 'Vanessa, be a darling and get me the pack I bought last week.'

Vanessa gave an exaggerated sigh but did as she was told, returning to the table with the pack of cards which she laid down in front of her mother. 'I'm going to my room,' she said, 'I'll leave you to it.' She picked up her mug of coffee and left the room.

'Vanessa was out late last night doing some babysitting for the Mitchells in Killglash,' Nicola said. 'I expect she's a little tired today. I do like to insist that she's home before midnight – the Mitchells always drive her home in good time - but last night was an exception.'

Murray drained his coffee cup – it was surprisingly good coffee, the best part of the meal – and searched frantically in his mind for an excuse to make his escape. An afternoon of fortune-telling was not on his list of favourite ways to spend a Sunday afternoon.

'Now,' said Nicola before he could marshal his thoughts. 'I'm going to count out fifteen cards and put them face down on the table. You pick five of them and I'll tell you what's in store.' She laughed suddenly. 'Of course it's all just a bit of fun.'

Murray obediently picked the five cards. Nicola Ryan was an attractive woman, he thought suddenly. Not beautiful nor even conventionally pretty. But there was something engaging in her wide-mouthed smile and in the way her eyes sparkled with enthusiasm as they did just now.

'Let's see.' Nicola turned over the first card which was the deuce of spades. 'You will get a letter.' She turned over the next two cards, revealing the queen of hearts and the ten of diamonds. 'The letter will be from a woman and will have something to do with money. Now for the last two, they will make sense of these other three cards.'

Although he didn't have the slightest bit of faith in it all, Murray found his pulse quickening and leaned forward slightly. 'I can't wait,' he said with a laugh intended to lighten the atmosphere.

Nicola looked at him, her face set in concentration. Slowly she turned over the last two cards revealing the ace of spades and the joker. There was a moment's silence. When she spoke her voice was grave. 'The ace of spades means death, the joker means mischief of some kind.' She paused again, studying the five cards. 'I shouldn't have done this. It's not good.' She gathered up the cards hastily and mixed them into the rest of the pack. 'You mustn't mind me, Alan. I'm sorry.'

'No need to be sorry' Murray said. 'I don't believe for one minute that a pack of cards can tell the future.'

'Good.' She stood up from the table. 'Would you like another coffee?'

He had intended sloping off home but that would probably appear like a reprimand after the fortunate telling, so instead he relaxed in his chair and allowed his coffee cup to be replenished and accepted another piece of coffee and walnut cake from Gleason's supermarket.

He had not taken more than two bites of the cake before his mobile rang. He dragged it out of his jeans pocket and checked the display.

It was Garda Jim Flynn, his second-in-command at Killglash garda station, who was off duty like himself.

'Alan, I've just had a phone call,' he said. 'A body was found on the side of the road near Agnes O'Toole's cottage. No details as yet. I'm on my way up there.'

'See you there in a few minutes.' Murray replaced the mobile and stood up. 'I'm afraid you'll have to excuse me,' he said to the startled Nicola. 'It looks like the ace of spades has come up trumps.'

Chapter Three

Murray looked down at the body of a young girl lying in the water-logged ditch, her body sprawled untidily. Her long blonde hair lay in wet strands across her face. He took in the rain-sodden clothes, the dark green anorak and blue jeans, the heavy walking boots, all of which seemed to point to her being a climber of some sort. From where he stood he could see the cord around her neck which had presumably been used to strangle her. He felt the slow burn of anger grow inside him. Having solved the murders of three young women from the village a few years ago, he had hoped never again to be confronted with another murder scene.

'Do we know who she is?' He directed the question at Flynn who came to join him.

'Not yet,' Flynn shook his head. 'No ID on her of any kind.'

Murray took one last look at the girl's body then turned away to make room for the forensics team.

'Who found her?'

'Len Higgins was driving down the road and saw something in the ditch. He was looking for a sheepdog pup which had run off out of his yard he says and he thought he saw something move in the ditch there. He rang Killglash garda station straight away.'

Murray knew Len Higgins, a farmer who lived about two miles from Ballyamber village. He was a quiet man, not given to gossip or wild exaggeration. 'Something moving in the ditch? I wonder what that could be?' He looked back at where the girl was found.

'It could be the hood of her anorak,' Flynn said. 'That gusty wind might have caught it.'

Murray grunted. Flynn was probably right. In any case they would learn more when the scene had been thoroughly examined and the coroner had made his report on the time and cause of death. Something else was puzzling him. 'No one has reported her missing? Someone must be wondering where she's got to, surely?'

'No one's reported anything yet, I just checked before you arrived,' Flynn said. 'It's early days though, especially if she went climbing or hiking on her own.'

'Climbing on her own? That would be unusual and foolhardy.' Murray stood for a moment and took in the scene, impressing it on his memory: the lonely stretch of road, the withered bracken wet from the night's rain, the looming presence of Ardnabrone mountain in the background. He was reminded sharply of the legend that Ardnabrone claimed three lives every year. He might not believe such superstitions and yet standing there looking at where the dead girl lay and with Nicola's fortune telling still fresh in his mind, he felt a sudden chill run through him.

'Well, we'd better leave Forensics to it and start asking some questions, Jim.' He glanced in the direction of Agnes O'Toole's cottage which was only about a hundred metres away. 'I'm surprised Agnes isn't poking her nose out to see what the gardai are doing here.'

The two men walked up to Agnes' cottage and rapped on the door. It was opened after a minute or two by Agnes. She was a small, skinny woman with tanned leathery skin, her frame somewhat bent now with arthritis. Her pale grey eyes looked the two officers up and down.

'Has there been an accident?' A wave of her hand indicated the scene on the roadside. 'Them drivers are always speeding round that bend. Young Foley, Gerald Foley's youngest son - you know that lad that went to Limerick to work? - he landed in the ditch only last weekend, going like a madman.'

'I heard about that,' Murray nodded. He could have told her that not only was Gerald Foley driving too fast but a breathalyser test had revealed that he was well over the legal limit and in a fair way to losing his driving licence. 'Can we come in Agnes?' he added as she did not make any move to invite them inside. 'We promise to scrape our shoes.'

'I'm afraid the place is in a mess,' she said but she did open the door wide enough for them to enter.

The cottage was a three room affair with the kitchen serving as living room and dining room combined. A door led to the two bedrooms at the back. Agnes had apparently been ironing as was evident by the ironing board and a basket of clothes in the middle of the room and Agnes hastily moved them out of the way. Murray looked about him, taking in the massive oak table and matching chairs and the two neat armchairs one on each side of the open fire. His practised eye also noted the state-of-the-art television set and the modern kitchen cupboards. Agnes might only have her modest pension to live on, as she was forever telling the villagers, but it looked as if she spent it very wisely. One thing was certain, the kitchen and its furnishings did not fit with the somewhat forlorn exterior of the cottage. Maybe she had frightened a few people into giving her money to stop her putting a curse on them. He wouldn't put it past her, he thought, as he and Flynn took their seats around the table.

Agnes started to fill the kettle at the spotless stainless steel sink. 'Ye'll have tea?'

'We won't keep you long, Agnes,' Murray said hastily. 'We just wanted to know if you heard anything last night? Did anyone call on you, a stranger asking the way maybe?'

Agnes switched on the electric kettle and stood with her hands on the back of one of the chairs which gave them the opportunity to see the black rims under her fingernails. She furrowed her face in thought. 'Last night? T'was stormy, that wind kept me awake for a while. I didn't hear anything out of the way – not with that wind blowing. But then my hearing's not as good as it was. Dr O'Reilly is always telling me I should get a hearing aid, don't you know?'

'Did you happen to see any strangers around the place in the last few days?' Flynn asked. He had pulled out his notebook and now reached for the ballpoint he kept in the top pocket of his uniform.

Agnes frowned at him. 'Strangers? Tourists you mean? There's good bit of traffic on that road. Mind you, there was a lot happening last night up at Ballyamber House. Some kind of party going on, I believe.' Her eyes narrowed. 'What happened out there? It wasn't an accident at all, was it?'

'The body of a young woman has been found nearly on your doorstep, Agnes,' Murray said. 'At the moment we don't know anything about her. We were just wondering if you'd heard or seen anything that might help us find out who she is.'

Agnes crossed herself, her mouth open in amazement. 'A young woman? Murdered? God protect us!'

'A party at Ballyamber House,' Murray said thoughtfully as he and Flynn retraced their steps to where Murray had parked his car. 'I wonder if our young victim was one of the guests.'

'Seems likely,' Flynn said, adding after a moment, 'if someone was missing you'd think they would have noticed by now.'

'Good point, Sherlock. I'm going to talk to the Wallace family. I'd like you to coordinate things here. I'm hoping that by tonight someone will be sobbing their hearts out in Killglash garda station and telling us he didn't mean to do it.'

Chapter Four

Penny suppressed a sigh as she checked off on her little desk calendar just how many days were left until the big house-warming party which Stanley Wallace was planning next month. If it was anything like the surprise birthday party for Sophie Winslow last night she wasn't sure she could bear it. She had hated every minute of Sophie's party. Originally planned as a small intimate gathering, it had mushroomed into a much bigger affair, requiring a great last minute effort on her and Mrs Quinn's part to have all the available bedrooms ready. She felt that her father-in-law wanted to show off the house even though there was still an enormous amount of work to be done on the place. It was important to him to prove to everyone that he had not made a mistake by buying such a huge place in an out-of-the-way location. Thankfully all the guests had now left except for Sophie Winslow. Stanley's glamorous girlfriend was proving even more insufferable than she remembered her from their few encounters in London.

'How sweet of you, Stanley, to throw this wonderful party,' she had cooed at the beginning of the evening, slipping her arm through his and smiling adoringly up at him. The guests were just starting to appear in the large dining room – one of the rooms which had not yet been re-decorated – and Sophie turned to Penny, her expression one of barely concealed pity. 'I can see you've done your very best, darling', she'd said and she might as well have added "but never mind". Penny, as conscious as anyone of the shabbiness of the room, had gritted her teeth in silence. If she had had her way, there would have been no party for Sophie's birthday and no guests invited to Ballyamber House.

But maybe that was not the most infuriating thing about Sophie's party. Infinitely worse was that Gregory seemed completely bowled over by his prospective new mother-in-law. He followed her around like a lapdog looking for approval and seconded everything she said. Penny's marriage to Gregory might be something of a disappointment – failure was too harsh a word she sometimes told herself – but at the same time, it was no great consolation to see him paying attention to another woman right under her nose. He had always been his father's puppet but up until now she had never had cause to think him unfaithful to her in either thought or deed and it was not an endearing prospect. Even Rod, usually so loyal to her, seemed to be falling under Sophie's spell while pretending to laugh at her behind her back. And then there was that business between him and Stanley Wallace at the party, which was too embarrassing to think about.

Her gloomy thoughts were interrupted by Mrs Quinn's knock on the door. 'Sergeant Murray is downstairs wanting to talk to you.'

'Sergeant Murray? The police? What does he want?'

'There's something going on down at Agnes O'Toole's place,' Mrs Quinn said. 'I can see the flashing lights of the garda cars and there's an ambulance as well. Must have been an accident or something.'

Penny stood up reluctantly. She loved this little room on the first floor of the East wing which had been converted into an office for her. It was a place she could escape to whenever things got her down. Originally Stanley Wallace had wanted to use it as a dressing room for the bedroom next door but this would have involved knocking a door into the adjoining wall. In the past the room had been used to store bits and pieces of furniture which were no longer in use. It was Steve Donlon who had seen its potential as an office for Penny. Once it had been brightened up by a coat of paint, she had picked out an ancient writing desk and chair from the old schoolroom on the second floor, had added a bookcase which she found in the attic and completed the comforts of the room with the addition of a sofa which had stood in the main hall downstairs but was showing signs of wear and tear. She spent a lot of her time here safe from the rest of the family, reading and writing emails to her friends on her laptop with overly enthusiastic news of her life at Ballyamber House. (They in turn wrote to her of how envious they were, how romantic it all sounded and assured her they would come and visit just as soon as the house could accommodate them).

Her only visitor apart from her husband was Steve Donlon, the architect, who occasionally wandered in to chat to her about his plans for the house. Without him she would have known very little of what the design plans were except what she gleaned from mealtime conversations between her husband and his father. If she were honest, she did not really care. She considered Ballyamber House as a temporary residence only and she looked forward to the day that she and Gregory could leave and return to their comfortable apartment in Kensington. If Stanley decided to marry Sophie Winslow and continue living here so much the better, she reasoned. That would leave them free to return to London and start living their own lives without her overbearing father-in-law looking over their shoulders. Gregory, however, saw things differently, as she was coming to realise. To him Ballyamber House was an ideal family home where they could all live together.

Penny found Alan Murray seated in one of the deep comfortable armchairs which had been drawn up to the fire in what was known as "the small salon" which overlooked the rear garden. She introduced herself and after they had shaken hands she took the armchair on the other side of the fireplace.

'I'm sorry to disturb you on a Sunday afternoon,' Murray said. 'I just need to ask you a few questions, if I may.'

'Please go ahead, Sergeant. Mrs Quinn said something about an accident on the main road?'

'Not an accident I'm afraid, Mrs Wallace. We found a body near Agnes O'Toole's cottage.'

Penny's hands flew to her mouth, the blood draining from her face. 'Agnes O'Toole is dead? My god, I didn't think –' she broke off and stared at the sergeant's impassive face.

'Didn't think what?' He hoped she wasn't going to faint or collapse into hysterics. Certainly her reaction was interesting. Why did she automatically assume it was Agnes?

Penny swallowed hard, fighting for control. She had been about to say that despite the enmity between Agnes O'Toole and her father-in-law, she didn't think Stanley Wallace would have actually harmed the old woman. 'I'm just so shocked,' she said, aware that she sounded anything but convincing. 'Agnes is – was such a character.'

'She still is,' said Murray, still in that same mild, pleasant tone. 'We found the body of a young woman. As yet we have not identified her but we expect to be able to do so shortly.'

'A young woman?' Penny clasped her hands tightly in her lap and tried to calm herself. 'But how – I don't understand.'

'Neither do we – yet. I take it that none of your guests is missing? I believe you had a big party last night?'

'N-no. I mean, yes we had a lot of visitors. But they've all gone, except Sophie that is.'

'Could you let me have a list of names and addresses and when they left here exactly? This is just routine, you understand.' He gave her that smile which usually ensured wholehearted cooperation from its recipients. 'It would be a big help to us right now.'

'I'll need to talk to my husband, he'll have all the details, the addresses and everything. He's gone to the airport with my father-in-law and Sophie Winslow. They're seeing off the last of our guests. My brother Rod has gone out for a drive somewhere.'

'You're on your own in the house today?'

'Yes, I was very tired after the party so I decided to stay at home. There's only me and Steve here.'

'Steve?'

'Steve Donlon. He's helping my father-in-law to do a make-over of Ballyamber House.'

'He's staying here in the house?'

'Yes, it's easier if he's on hand. He has been away in Spain for the past few days. I gather there was some problem with a project he's involved in over there, but he came down a day or two ago. He stays here while he's working on the house.'

'Can you tell me a bit about who is actually living in the house at the moment.' Murray got out his notebook.

'As I said, the guests have left, except for Sophie Winslow. She is staying with us for a few weeks, I think, as guest of my father-in-law. There's my father-in-law, Stanley Wallace, my husband Gregory and my brother Rod and Steve Donlon.'

Murray finished making notes. 'That's all? No one else stayed over?'

'All the guests went away today. We had around eight people staying, they were all friends of Sophie Winslow or of my father-in-law and they came for the weekend only. There was a birthday party for Sophie last night.' A thought occurred to her and her hands flew to her mouth. 'We had to get in some help from Killglash. Oh my god, this girl, could she be one of the catering staff?'

'Who did you have to help out?'

'It was a woman from Killglash, Mrs Colbert and her daughter and daughter-in-law. I think their names are Katherine and Mary.'

Murray nodded. 'I know the Colbert family,' he said. 'It was not one of them. This girl is a stranger.' He paused a moment before continuing. 'What I came to ask is if you observed anything unusual at any time over the past few days. A stranger hanging around, a car parked where it wouldn't normally be. Anything like that.'

Penny felt a faint nagging pain of worry start up in the pit of her stomach. She remembered Rod's appearance all too clearly at the end of the night when she was serving a very late supper to the weary guests. He had looked as if he had just dashed through the rain and it was not until then that she realised he had been absent from the party for some time – just how long she could not say. She had danced nearly every dance, owing to a slight imbalance in the number of men and women guests, and had been too preoccupied to notice what her brother was up to. There was no need to mention this to Sergeant Murray, she reasoned, it could surely have no bearing on the murder of a young woman, and yet, she felt that pain in her stomach.

'I can't say I've seen anything unusual, Sergeant,' she said after a moment's thought. 'Steve and my father-in-law and my brother Rod collected all the guests from Cork airport on Friday. It was supposed to be a surprise party but of course it was hardly that as all the guests were here the day before. They all had other commitments this coming week so they left again today.' She looked at him anxiously. 'What do you think happened to this girl? Do you have any idea who could be responsible?'

'We've only just started our enquiries.'

'It's frightening to think something like this happened right on our doorstep. Ballyamber is such a peaceful place, or so I've always thought.'

Obviously Mrs Quinn had not yet told her that three young women from the village had been murdered a few years ago, Murray thought, or she would not have used the word "peaceful" so easily. Something was slightly off-key about the interview but he could not put his finger on what it was. People reacted differently to shocking news, he knew, especially when it concerned something that had happened on their doorstep. And yet, there was something there, something lurking in the background which was making her wary of him even if she now seemed more relaxed.

'What time did the party finish on Saturday night?'

He thought she looked slightly wary again, as if trying to guess what information he was looking for.

'It was late. Around two o'clock in the morning I should think. I didn't actually check the exact time. I served everyone soup and sandwiches in the big salon and then we all went to bed. I was so tired I fell asleep straight away.'

'The party was held where exactly?'

'We used the large dining room. It's the only room which could accommodate so many people at present. There's a lot of decorating going on in the other rooms. We had dinner first and then Rod and Greg cleared away the tables and chairs and we had a sort of disco which Steve Donlon took charge of.'

'Were all the guests present all the time?'

'Why, yes of course they were. It was Sophie's birthday!'

'You're sure of that? No one slipped out at any stage?'

She hesitated, biting her lip. 'No, I don't think so.'

'Would you have noticed if someone had slipped out?'

'Well, I might notice but really Sergeant I think that everyone was there all of the time. Certainly all the guests were present when I served the soup and sandwiches. I can vouch for that.'

'When you say all the guests, does that include your brother Rod and Steve Donlon?'

Penny's eyes widened. 'Rod? You surely don't think he had anything to do with – with that girl?'

Interesting reaction, thought Murray. 'Was he there when you served the soup and sandwiches?'

'Of course he was. I remember him chatting to Sophie.'

'I see.' It was too early to come to any conclusions, Murray knew, but it was obvious to him that she was hiding something or thought she was hiding something to do with her brother Rod. He decided to leave it for now. 'I'll be back to talk to everyone. If anything occurs to you in the meantime, I'd be grateful if you'd let me know.' He handed her a card with his mobile phone number. 'Everything you say will be treated in the strictest confidence.'

He stood up to signal that the interview was at an end. 'I'd like to talk to Steve Donlon, please.'

Steve Donlon came hurrying into the room with a grave expression on his face. Somewhere in his early forties, he was of medium height with a stocky figure. He was dressed in brown corduroy trousers and a grey and blue checked shirt inside a lambswool sweater which made him look more like a country squire than an interior designer. Murray noted the affectionate way Donlon patted Penny's arm as she left the room having shown him in.

'You're working on the restoration of Ballyamber House, is that correct?'

'Yes, that's right. I met Stanley through a mutual friend and he told me about his difficulties in upgrading the place. Ultimately I think he'll want to make a hotel out of it. I can't see him living here permanently. The place is too big for a family home unless you have a very big family which Stanley does not. And of course he does dabble in the property business quite a bit.'

'There is a bit of trouble between himself and Agnes O'Toole about right of way and wanting to buy her cottage, I hear.'

'Yes, Mrs O'Toole is proving a bit stubborn. Stanley has made her an excellent offer for that cottage. He intends hiring a manager for Ballyamber House and Mrs O'Toole's cottage would be a very suitable place for him to live.' Donlon spread his hands in a deprecating gesture. 'As for the right of way. Well, we can't deny it's there even if never used. In the old days, farmers drove their cattle along the main road and took a short cut to their farms via that lane next to Ballyamber House. It's overgrown now. The old family farms have been sold and the lands all amalgamated and no one uses it any more. Not even the estimable Agnes O'Toole. She's just being awkward with her talk of fairy trees and what have you.'

Murray nodded to himself. Right of way was still a big issue in parts of the country especially as very often the old rights of way were not held in writing and were merely handed down from family to family. But this all had nothing to do with why he was here.

'Tell me about the party last night.'

'It was a surprise birthday party for Sophie Winslow. I expect Penny has already told you that. There were eight guests, all friends of Sophie's and Stanley's. I didn't know any of them, they were mostly from the London theatre and business world. I helped collect them from the airport on Friday. Rod and I drove most of them to the airport at some ungodly hour this morning as they were all catching early flights. Stanley and Sophie are driving the remaining two couples this afternoon. Greg has gone with them, as I expect Penny has told you.'

'None of them came by car?' According to Agnes there had been a lot of coming and going but that was probably an exaggeration. Or had she heard the car which had possibly been involved in the murder of the young girl? He made a mental note to question her again on that point.

'No, they all flew in on Friday. Stanley said it would be easier for everyone if we collected them at the airport. It would save them trying to find Ballyamber. We're a bit off the beaten track here, I think you'll agree. It all went very smoothly.'

'Did any of the guests leave the house before or during the party?'

Donlon thought for a moment before answering. 'I doubt it. Stanley showed them round the gardens on Friday when they arrived but then it started to rain. And as you know yesterday was so wet and stormy you wouldn't put a dustbin out.'

'So all the guests were present in the big dining room during the party? You're sure of that?'

Donlon shrugged his elegantly clad shoulders. 'About as sure as I can be. I was helping entertain the guests, keeping the music going. There was dancing and chatting, people moving about as they do at parties. Why? Was somebody missing?'

Murray decided to ignore the question. 'You say you and Rod had an early start this morning. Did you see anything unusual like a parked car or someone hanging around on your travels to and from the airport?'

Donlon shook his head. 'No, I'm afraid not. We left pretty early, around half past seven I think, and as far as I can recall we didn't meet a single vehicle on that road. Nothing remotely suspicious. But I'm a stranger in these parts so I might have missed something.'

Chapter Five

'Let's go through what we've got so far.' Superintendent Stephen Coyle, known to them as 'Percy' because of a former fondness for the expression 'per se', looked around at the officers seated at the table. It was the next morning and Coyle, their immediate superior, had summoned every available officer to attend this meeting at Killglash police station.

Flynn obediently read from the notes he had made as information had come in during the course of the previous afternoon and evening.' Cause of death is most probably strangulation. A post mortem is being carried out this morning. We'll have a better idea of the time of death after that, at the moment it's estimated that the body lay there all night. With all that rain and storm it's going to be hard to find anything significant. No ID on the victim, no mobile phone, no purse or shoulder bag. At this moment in time we do not know who she is nor where she came from.'

'So we have the body of a young girl found by the side of the road nearly 24 hours ago and we still have no idea how she got there nor who she is.' Percy made it sound as if they had all been slacking in some way.

'So far no one has come forward to report her as missing,' Murray said, careful not to show his irritation at Percy's remark. 'We'll be checking out the hotels and B&B's in the area. If she was a climber then she will most likely have been staying locally and she won't have come back to her lodgings last night. She might have left her passport at a B&B or at least we'll have her name and when she booked in.'

'Hmm.' The frown on Percy's face did not lift.

'I spoke to Penny Wallace and to Steve Donlon at Ballyamber House immediately after I'd been to the scene,' Murray went on. 'They had a party on Saturday night and guests were being ferried to and from the airport on both Friday and yesterday. According to what they told me, the guests never left the house, none of them came by car, and nothing suspicious was seen by either Penny Wallace or Steve Donlon. Agnes O'Toole also claims not to have heard anything out of the way. But we're only at the start of the investigation,' he added.

Percy's mobile pinged and he excused himself and left the room only to return a minute later. 'I have to go or I'll be late for my next meeting. You'll keep me informed, Alan?'

When he had gone Murray went through a plan of action for the day with his staff before heading off to attend a court hearing where he was due to give evidence on a particularly brutal assault case. It was a long day – in the end the case was adjourned for two weeks - and he was tired and depressed by the time he returned to Killglash garda station. Flynn was there, seated at his desk and tapping away on his laptop. Murray put his head round the door. 'Anything new?'

Flynn looked up. 'Long and Foley aren't back yet,' he said. 'They were visiting all the B&B's in the area. It's a big job, especially with some of those places being spread around the countryside.'

'I've been thinking.' Murray said. 'Who springs to mind when we think of a young girl being murdered?'

'Harold Brannigan,' Flynn answered promptly.

'My thought exactly.' Murray consulted his watch. 'We might as well go and have a word with our good friend Harold. He should be home from work by now.'

Many years before Harold Brannigan was convicted of the murder of a young girl in Dublin and given the maximum prison sentence. Upon his release he had come to live in Ballyamber in a dilapidated old cottage left to him by his maternal grandmother who had been a native of Ballyamber. The villagers had all been up in arms but over the years they had learned to accept his presence, avoiding any contact with him as much as they could. He lived quietly and unobtrusively and Murray had never received any complaints about his behaviour. The most damning fact about him was that he had never proffered a motive for the killing, refusing to speak about it to anyone.

Brannigan's cottage was set in a maze of little by-roads which criss-crossed the area and which were full of potholes.

'What amazes me is why Stanley Wallace moved here from a city like London and bought that old house in the middle of nowhere with that big black mountain for company,' Flynn said with feeling as they bumped their way along in low gear. 'Talk about the back of beyond.'

'You're losing your romantic streak, Jim.'

'Just as well. There's no one down here to try it out on.' Flynn gave a mock sigh.

Murray smiled to himself. Although Flynn often spoke disparagingly of Killglash and environs, Murray suspected that he enjoyed life down here in the lonely Kerry countryside. A run-in with Percy (which neither of them was prepared to discuss) ensured that for the present he was not going to be promoted and transferred to another area, something that Murray was grateful for. He enjoyed working with the younger man. They both knew what to expect from each other.

'I'm wondering about Penny Wallace and that Donlon fellow,' Murray said, changing the subject. 'They were on their own at Ballyamber House yesterday. She decides she's not well enough to go for a jaunt with the rest of them and her brother Rod clears off somewhere but she stays behind with Donlon. Something tells me they like each other more than they should. At least Donlon fancies Penny. I'm not so sure about her feelings for him, she was very cool, but then women are hard to read.'

'You reckon Donlon fancies her. Really?' Flynn looked interested. 'She's a good looker is Penny Wallace. I've seen her once or twice in Killglash. She could have her pick, I'd say.'

'I suppose that includes you, does it?' Murray grinned at his subordinate. 'I'd stick to less elegant ladies if I were you. You'd be boxing well above your weight with Mrs Penny Wallace.'

Flynn rolled his eyes to show he was not amused. 'It's an interesting idea, though,' he said. 'All these rich people having affairs on the side. Maybe our victim was mixed up with someone from Ballyamber House.'

'I'm not even going to try and guess about that for the present,' Murray said as they pulled up in front of Brannigan's cottage.

Harold Brannigan opened the door to them, blocking it with his bulk.

'What do ye want?'

'Can we come in for a minute?' Murray asked in a mild tone. 'It's a bit cold and damp out here on your doorstep, Harold. We're appealing to your mercy.'

Brannigan hesitated then opened the door and admitted them to his kitchen. Murray had not been here since he investigated the murders of three local women some years before. Nothing had changed as far as he could see. In contrast to Agnes' cottage, Brannigan's place was meagrely furnished and badly in need of re-decorating. The daily newspaper lay on the table folded back at the racing page, next to it a mug of tea stood beside an overflowing ashtray. Murray and Flynn pulled out battered wooden chairs and sat down at the table without being asked. As Murray had once observed to Flynn "You can't expect too much. Harold's education didn't involve finishing school in Switzerland."

'What do ye want?' Brannigan repeated. He stood glowering at them, his back to the fire which was just starting to give out some heat. Clearly he had not been home long.

'Just a quick chat, we won't keep you.' Murray leaned back in the chair causing it to creak in protest. 'The body of a young girl has been found up at Agnes O'Toole's place. It looks like she's been murdered. It must have happened some time on Saturday night or the early hours of Sunday morning. We were wondering if you'd seen anything on your way to work or anyone hanging around in the area over the weekend.'

Brannigan's thick black eyebrows met over the bridge of his nose as he absorbed the information. 'The body of a young girl? Who was she? Someone from the village?'

'She's a stranger,' Flynn put in. 'We don't have all the details yet.'

Brannigan stuck his hands deep into the pockets of his dirty overalls. 'Why would I have seen anything? I go about my business.'

'I know that,' Murray said quickly before Flynn could make a comment. 'We're asking everyone the same question, Harold, not just you.'

'I went to work at half past seven on Saturday morning.' He was still frowning. 'I was asked to do a bit of overtime. So I cycled over to Gleason's supermarket and left me bike there like I always do and Matt Thomas picked me up and we drove to work. You know I work on that building site over in Killglash?'

Murray nodded. He did indeed know all Brannigan's movements. 'What time did you cycle home on Saturday evening?'

Again the black beetling eyebrows came together in a frown. 'I dunno. We finished around five o'clock. T'would have been around half past five or six, I'd say.'

'You pass Agnes O'Toole's place, don't you? Did you see anything out of the way?' They would have to wait for the coroner's report to get the estimated time of death, Murray thought, but it didn't do any harm to tick as many boxes as they could.

Brannigan shook his head. 'I saw nothing. I stayed at home on Sunday and watched the telly.' He withdrew his hands from his pockets and folded his arms across his broad chest, looking pointedly at them. 'Is that all you want to ask me?'

At that moment the front door opened and a man came into the kitchen. He stopped short just inside the door and for a moment it looked as if he would turn around and leave as quickly as he had come. He was small and wiry with a scraggy white beard, his white none-too-clean hair, equally scraggy, flowed down over his coat collar.

Himself and Brannigan exchanged glances and there was a moment's silence before Brannigan spoke. 'This is Ginger Ford.' He gave a nod of his head towards the two men. 'The gardai from Killglash. A young girl's body was found this morning they tell me.'

'I haven't seen you before,' Murray said pleasantly. His eyes took in the other man, the shabby jeans and jacket and the surprisingly smooth skin of his hands. 'Ginger Ford, is it?'

'I'm a friend of Harold's,' Ginger said. 'I came down a few days ago.' He looked from one to the other of them. 'What's this about a girl's body?'

'When did you arrive here at Harold's?' Flynn produced his notebook. 'Can you give us your full name?'

Ginger looked at Brannigan who threw up his hands in a gesture which seemed to say "they never leave me alone" as clearly as if he had spoken the words out loud.

'My name is Peter Ford,' Ginger told them. He gave an address in North Dublin. 'Harold and I grew up together,' he added. 'I'm a lorry driver by trade. Self employed.'

'The body of a young girl was found on Sunday morning near Agnes O'Toole's cottage and we're trying to find anyone who might have seen something suspicious in the last few days, especially on Saturday evening and the early hours of Sunday morning.'

'Agnes O'Toole's cottage,' Ginger said slowly, 'that's that place just outside the village, near the entrance to Ballyamber House, isn't it?'

'All we want to know is if any of the two of you saw anything at all suspicious on Saturday night or in the early hours of Sunday morning.' Murray looked at Ginger. 'Harold went to work on Saturday so you were here all day on your own. What did you spend your time doing?'

Ginger scratched his head. 'I wanted to put some money on the horses so I got a newspaper in the village to check what was running. After that I drove to the bookies in Killglash and then I came back to the village and had a drink and a sandwich in the pub and watched the racing on the television while I was waiting for Harold to come home from work. You can ask them at the pub if I was there or not.' He hesitated then added as if explanation was necessary. 'I did the same today. I'm just back from Killglash.' He pulled a wad of betting slips from his jacket pocket and waved them at the two officers.

'You were working today, Harold?' Murray enquired.

'Just like every Monday,' Brannigan said.

There didn't seem to be much point in pursuing the conversation, Murray thought. Brannigan would keep information from them just for the hell of it. They would check out both men's stories as a matter of routine. He signalled to Flynn and they both stood up.

'Thanks lads,' he said. 'You've been a great help. If you remember anything or see anything strange, I'd appreciate it if you'd let us know.'

There was no answer from either Brannigan or Ginger.

Murray nodded towards the ashtray. 'I see you're smoking very exotic stuff these days, Harold. Muratti. Haven't seen one of those in years. I'm glad that you've enough money to spend on expensive cigarettes, the job must be paying well.' He looked from one to the other of the two men. 'Or are they Ginger's brand?'

'Got a present of a few packs,' Ginger Ford said smoothly. 'The fella said they fell off the back of a lorry.'

'Bunch of losers,' Flynn said with feeling as they walked down the path to the car.

'A slippery customer our Ginger,' Murray said. 'I wonder what he's up to down here.'

'I never heard of that brand of cigarette you mentioned, Muratti was it?'

'You don't see them very often. My guess is you'd only get them in a specialist tobacco shop or online. I can't see them being very popular.'

'If he got them for nothing, I expect he doesn't mind.'

'The only question I'd have on that head would be where would Ginger meet someone who was driving a lorry-load of them?'

Murray's mobile rang as they turned onto the main road on their way back to Killglash garda station. The voice on the other end identified himself as Dan Foley, one of the officers who was checking out the local hotels, hostels and B&B's.

'Alan, I think we've found the Bed & Breakfast where our victim was staying. The Emerald B&B in Ballyamber village.'

Chapter Six

'I'll bet you were surprised that Stanley didn't announce his engagement to the beautiful Sophie at her birthday bash.' Rod grinned at his sister as he spoke. 'I thought that was the whole idea of having all that gang here for the party.' He had joined Penny in the kitchen where she was putting the finishing touches to the evening meal. There was an appetising aroma of herbs and roast meat.

'I *was* a bit surprised.' Penny straightened up from the oven where she had been checking on the chicken roast and turned troubled eyes on her brother. 'But Rod, what does it matter? It's his business after all.' Rod was acting so strangely this last day or two she thought uneasily. She had hardly seen anything of him since the party on Saturday night. Was he about to relapse yet again and start drinking? It was all too quiet for him here in Ballyamber House. That was assuredly why he sneaked away as often as possible, why he had left the party on Saturday night without anyone noticing except herself. Her thoughts went back to the visit from Alan Murray and his questions regarding the body of the young girl found so close to the house.

'You heard about the body of a girl being found down at Agnes O'Toole's cottage?' She wondered as she spoke why he had not mentioned it. Surely it was dramatic enough to be the focal point of every conversation? Stanley and Greg had been full of it when they and Sophie returned from seeing off the last of the guests on Sunday night.

'Of course I heard it, who hasn't?' Rod pulled open a drawer and aimlessly inspected the contents – it contained the cutlery - before closing it again with a clatter. 'I heard she wasn't a local girl. They believe she was a tourist, a hiker. Probably her boyfriend did it. You're not scared are you?'

'It's disturbing to say the least.' She gave a little shiver. 'I most certainly do not want to be alone in this house until they find the person who did it.'

'Right, yes, I see what you mean. I expect we had all better be careful if it comes to that.'

'The police were here,' Penny said, watching his face for a reaction. 'They were asking if I'd seen anything unusual. I told them I hadn't. Neither did Steve. They said they'd come back in a day or two and talk to everyone.'

Rod pulled a face. 'What are we supposed to have seen, eh?'

'They said anything out of the ordinary – a stranger in the area or a strange car driving around.'

'A stranger? We're strangers here ourselves. How would we know who's who?'

'You left the party on Saturday night and drove somewhere, didn't you?' She was half afraid to ask the question and equally afraid of what answer she might receive.

'Why do you ask?' He stuffed his hands into the pockets of his designer jeans. Rod might be out of work and, according to himself, was currently penniless but his clothes were always of the expensive variety.

'I saw you coming home again when we were all having late supper,' she said, regretting suddenly that she had brought up the subject.

'Yes, I drove off in a bit of a huff. Stanley was being his usual unpleasant self and I'd had about enough of him and the whole caboodle of his friends. Sorry – I should have asked if it was OK to take the car. I was only away an hour or so.' He had the grace to look slightly embarrassed. 'I just needed to get out for some fresh air, it gets a bit claustrophobic here with stuffy Stanley at the best of times.'

'Where did you go?' Penny took out the roast and began to arrange the potatoes around it, giving the task all her attention. The thought crossed her mind that if Rod found living here so boring he did not appear to be doing anything to remedy the situation such as searching for a job, at least as far as she was aware.

'I drove to Killglash and stopped at McDowds – oh, I didn't drink anything in case you're worried. Can't say I wasn't tempted though. I don't suppose anyone at the party missed me anyway, did they?'

'And you really didn't see anyone hanging around Agnes O'Toole's cottage?' She paused in the act of spooning fat over the potatoes.

'I just told you I didn't,' Rod made an impatient movement with his hands. 'Why are you quizzing me? Are you doing police work now?'

'I'm not quizzing you. A young girl was murdered practically on our doorstep. It's worrying that something like that could happen here.' She knew him of old and knew now that he was hiding something. But what? It might not even be important. Rod liked to play games. His alcoholism had made him secretive but she had hoped that the therapy he had undergone would have helped him to cope better, to interact more with people.

'Don't worry sister dear. I'm sure we're all safe as houses. No one would dare interfere with Stanley Wallace.' He turned and walked swiftly out of the kitchen before she could think of a reply.

Chapter Seven

It took only a few minutes for Murray and Flynn to reach the Emerald Bed & Breakfast which was located in a lane off the main street of the village just a few short steps away from Gleason's supermarket. Garda Dan Foley was waiting for them at the front gate.

'According to Mrs Flaherty, a young girl booked in for a few days and she didn't show up for breakfast this morning,' he told them. 'I haven't got any farther than that. I thought you'd like to be present when we did the questioning.'

'Good work, Dan.' Murray stood for a moment taking stock of the place.

The Emerald was a bungalow with a built-on extension for guests. The yellow washed walls and dazzling white window-frames and doors gave it a cheerful look. The front garden was neatly kept with tubs of tulips and daffodils dotted about the stone paving. Altogether it was a place to gladden the eye of a tourist looking for reasonably priced accommodation.

Murray had never been inside the building although he knew it very well by sight. It was owned by Sam and Thea Flaherty, a middle-aged couple who were both natives of Ballyamber village. Sam Flaherty owned a small sheep farm and his wife managed the bed and breakfast.

As they followed Thea into the big kitchen he wondered what had made the girl decide to stay here. If she didn't have transport of any kind it was hard to see how she planned to get around, unless of course she was depending on meeting other climbers who would give her a lift. Killglash would have been a better choice, given that there was a bus service to Tralee which operated three times a week in the tourist season. Had she planned on meeting up with someone? At least now they would learn who she was, he thought in relief.

They took seats around the kitchen table and Thea Flaherty insisted on serving them all mugs of tea before she was ready to sit down herself and tell them about her young guest.

'She rang me about a week ago and said her name was Maike Bloem and she was looking for a double room for a few nights.' Thea's hand shook as she toyed with her teaspoon, betraying her shock at the discovery that her guest might have been the victim of a murder. 'When she arrived, she said her partner had been delayed but that they'd pay the full price for the room. She was a lovely girl. Bright and bubbly. Loved Ireland. Said her family came here several times before to do a bit of climbing but usually stayed around the Killarney area.'

'Did she give the name of her partner?' Murray took a quick sip of tea then put down his mug, stifling the craving for a cigarette.

'No, she didn't. But as long as I had her name and an address I didn't mind. People get delayed, it wouldn't be the first time. As I told Dan, she didn't show up for breakfast yesterday morning. I wasn't too worried about that. These young people do their own thing, as they say. They meet up with someone like themselves and if it gets late they stay over with them. That's happened one or twice before with young people I had staying.' Thea looked anxiously around the table. 'I heard something about the body of a young girl being found but I didn't put two and two together and then Dan called.' Her voice trailed away.

'What address did she give you?' Flynn asked the question.

'I wrote it down in my reservations book. She had to spell it for me.'

She half rose from her seat but Murray put out a detaining hand. 'We'll get to that in the minute. Can we see her room?'

'Of course.' Thea led them via a side door into the extension at the back of the building where the guests' rooms were located. Maike's room was at the end of the corridor. Thea produced a key and then stepped back to allow the three men to enter.

It was a pleasant room, decorated in shades of pale blue which were echoed in the bedspread and floral curtains at the big windows. A small table and two chairs, a built-in wardrobe and a little bedside table on each side of the double bed made up the furniture. Maike's rucksack was parked by the window, a pair of jeans was flung over the back of one of the chairs.

Murray opened the door next to the wardrobe and inspected the ensuite bathroom. Used socks and underwear had been bundled up and tossed in a corner of the shower. A toothbrush and toothpaste together with a few cosmetic items and a hairbrush were all where they should be. Powerful indicators that Maike had intended to return here on Saturday night.

'Alan, look at this.' Flynn had opened one of the drawers of the bedside table and pulled out a passport.

'It's our victim all right,' Murray said as he examined the photo. 'Maike Bloem of Zandervoort in The Netherlands. Her twenty first birthday would have been next month, the fourteenth of April.' He turned to Thea, who stood in the doorway watching them, her face pale with fright. 'We'll have to cordon off this room, I'm afraid, and come back and search it.'

'Whatever you want. What will happen about the other guests? They're all out at the moment.'

'We'll have to talk to them, too,' Murray told her. 'In the meantime, let's see what information she gave you.'

'No sign of her wallet or mobile,' Flynn said in a low voice to Murray as they returned to the kitchen.

'Could have been a robbery.' Dan Foley suggested. 'Maybe someone gave her a lift and panicked when she screamed.'

'Why would anyone consider a backpacker worth robbing?' Murray objected. 'I'm more interested in this partner who didn't show up. Something fishy about that.'

Thea had misspelt Zandervoort when she had written down the booking and there was no street address only the number of what was presumably her mobile phone and her credit card details. But at least now they had the name of a place and could contact the Dutch police who would be able to establish her identity and locate her next of kin. Perhaps she had already been recorded as missing.

'You said she'd been to Ireland before,' Flynn said as he jotted down the few details which Thea had written into her reservations book. 'Did she say when was the last time she was here?'

Thea wrinkled her forehead. 'I can't remember if she said. You know how it is, you chat to all the guests but you only remember so much of what they tell you.'

'And she didn't know anybody around here?' It was Flynn still asking the questions.

Thea shook her head. 'She didn't say, as far as I can remember.'

'Did she appear worried or upset about anything?'

Thea considered this for a moment then shook her head again. 'No, not that I noticed anyway. I was serving breakfast, we had another family staying. They're regulars. Fitzsimons is the name, they're from Dublin and they come down here a couple of times a year. I heard them telling her they were only doing a short climb because they were going back to Dublin that evening and she said she'd join them if they didn't mind and could they drop her afterwards at McDowd's pub in Killglash. All the climbers meet in McDowd's. She knew about that. The Fitzsimons said they'd give her a lift but of course they'd be going on to Dublin after their walk. She seemed to think there'd be no problem in getting back to Ballyamber that evening.' She wrinkled her forehead for a moment. 'I think she said she was meeting someone there. I wasn't paying too much attention because I wanted them to finish their breakfasts so that I could get started on the rooms. We had more people coming, you see.'

A thought occurred to Murray. 'Do you happen to know how she got here in the first place? Was someone with her on the day she arrived?'

'She got a lift from Dolores, you know Dolores, she works as a cashier at Gleason's supermarket. She met her by chance when she went to the tourist office in Killglash. Dolores' sister works there, you see, and Dolores was visiting her. She was on her way to Ballyamber so she offered her a lift.'

*****

'At least we know why she was where she was,' Murray said addressing the team at the early morning briefing next day. 'It's only a short walk from where she was found to the Bed & Breakfast. So what it boils down to is this. Maike booked a double room at the B&B but her room companion didn't turn up. We're assuming this was a boyfriend but it could be a girl. We have no way of knowing until we learn more from the police in Zandervoort. At breakfast on Saturday morning she arranged to go climbing with the Fitzsimons and asked them to drop her off at McDowds pub in Killglash. It will be interesting to see who saw her in the pub and also what the Fitzsimons have to say about what time they dropped her off.'

'She seems to have come here without any means of transport so whoever was supposed to share the double room would most likely have a car,' Dan Foley said.

'Good point,' Murray nodded. 'The question is: who was she going to meet? They should be getting worried by now. Or they should be showing up at the Emerald Bed & Breakfast looking for her. So far this hasn't happened.' He turned to Flynn who had been in touch with the *politie* in Zandervoort. 'What do we know about the girl so far, Jim?'

Flynn opened his notebook and leant over it, resting his elbows on the table. He had been at the station since early morning – Holland being an hour ahead of Killglash – and had made copious notes according as the information came in from Zandervoort.

'Maike Bloem is twenty-one years old, she comes from Zandervoort, that's a town on the coast in the province of North Holland,' he said. 'It's near Amsterdam. She has one brother and two sisters all older than her. She was studying at Amsterdam University of Applied Sciences for an international bachelors' degree in business and languages. She lived at home in Zandervoort and travelled by train to the university.' He glanced up from his notes before continuing. 'Her parents will be coming here. They should arrive tomorrow.'

'Did they know who she was supposed to be meeting up with here?' The question came from Dan Foley. Dan was a family man with two daughters not much older than the victim.

'At the moment, the answer to that is no, they didn't. She had a lot of friends they said but as far as her parents and siblings are aware she wasn't in a relationship. The Dutch police will be interviewing her friends and digging up more background but that will take some time. The Bloem family are respectable middle class people, her father works as an accountant for a firm in Zandervoort, her mother is a kindergarten teacher also in Zandervoort. Maike has never given them any sort of trouble.'

'Do they know that she was most likely hitchhiking on her own?' Murray asked.

'This wasn't mentioned.' Flynn referred to his notes. 'They thought she was with a group of friends. Apparently, they spoke to her on Friday afternoon and that was the last conversation they had with her. She promised to contact them again in a few days. They weren't unduly worried when they didn't hear. Mobile phone reception can be erratic in the mountains. She's a seasoned traveller, they said, not likely to take risks of any sort.'

'And yet people can be very naïve about Ireland, especially down here in the country,' Murray said. 'Dolores' sister offering to give her a lift to Ballyamber might make her think that everyone she ran into was just as helpful. If she accepted a lift from a stranger on Saturday night, I feel that might be the key to what happened to her.'

He paused while the officers took in all they had heard. When there were no questions he continued. 'Her mobile phone and her purse are still missing. As far as we know she had both these items with her when she left the B&B.'

'So it might have been a robbery,' Dan Foley said, patently still clinging to his original idea.

Murray shrugged. 'Could well be but I don't think that's very likely. Would it be worth it to kill a backpacker for a mobile phone and whatever money she might have in her purse? I doubt it somehow, unless she was flaunting banknotes in McDowd's. Right now we have absolutely no idea. Priority is finding the mobile and her purse. We don't know where she was killed, for a start. We have to contact each and every person she spoke to since her arrival.'

He waited while Flynn updated the chart on the wall with the information they had to date and the team scribbled in their notebooks. 'Harold Brannigan's pal Ginger Ford needs to be investigated,' he went on when he had everyone's attention again.' And we'll need to verify their stories of where they were. The only trouble is that if Maike was murdered in the small hours of the morning, everyone will have been at home in bed and it'll be hard to prove they weren't if we have no witnesses or any other kind of evidence.'

There were gloomy nods in response to this remark. 'What about Agnes O'Toole?' Garda Gerald Buckley asked. 'She probably sees everything that goes on in a ten-mile radius.'

'There was a party at Ballyamber House and she says cars were coming and going until around eight or nine o'clock,' Flynn said. 'After that she claims the stormy wind kept her awake for a bit but then she went to sleep and didn't hear or see anything suspicious.'

Murray assigned the various tasks to his team. 'We have our work cut out, lads,' he said, 'but I know you'll all do your best.'

When the briefing was over and the officers had left the station on their various assignments, Murray stepped out into the back yard to have a cigarette while mulling over what information they had in hand. He felt tired suddenly and the all too familiar depression swamped him for a moment. Maike's parents were on their way to Ireland and the prospect of meeting them was a grim one. Elena had once or twice suggested to him that he should give up police work and he had laughed at the idea but faced with another murder in Ballyamber he was no longer so sure that he had the stomach for this kind of investigation, especially when the victim was a young girl on the brink of life. He took a deep breath and squared his shoulders. He'd get the bastard responsible for Maike's murder, he promised himself, no matter how long it took, no matter how many sleepless nights it cost him. He stubbed out his cigarette, squared his shoulders and turned back into the station building.

Flynn was waiting for him. 'It's going to be a busy week,' he said with relish as he shrugged into his overcoat.

'Plenty of late nights at your desk. You're going to have to disappoint a lot of the fair sex for the next while, Jim.'

Chapter Eight

'I'm glad we decided to do this,' Steve Donlon said, pulling his chair a fraction closer to Penny's. 'I never get to see enough of you.'

They were enjoying a pub lunch of chicken sandwiches and a glass of lager in Waterville, a picturesque village on the Ring of Kerry tourist route. They had taken a walk on the nearby beach despite the blustery conditions and were now thawing out in front of the open fire.

Early that morning Stanley and Gregory Wallace had gone to Dublin to attend a trade fair at which one of Stanley's companies had a stand. There was to be a dinner with prospective clients in the evening and Stanley had invited Sophie to accompany them. The plan was to stay overnight and come back late the next day. Penny had decided not to go with them at the risk of upsetting Gregory. She knew that Sophie would upstage her at the dinner and besides she had no desire to witness her husband still behaving like a love-struck calf whenever Sophie showed him any attention.

Rod had also declined to accompany them. 'I'll keep my sister company,' he'd said and although Sophie protested that she needed him to show her round Dublin while Stanley and Gregory were busy, he had stuck to his decision.

'You are so mean,' Sophie had pouted.

'I'll give you time to miss me,' Rod laughed. The remark earned him a black look from Stanley Wallace who was plainly annoyed at Sophie's open flirting with Rod.

Penny was secretly glad to see them off. She felt like a child who has been given an unexpected school holiday. The two days they would be away stretched invitingly before her. She wanted to do something special, something for herself. Before she could make any plans, however, Donlon had approached her with the suggestion that they do some exploring.

'I've hardly seen anything of the country around here,' he said. 'It's not much fun looking at it on my own. We could do the Ring of Kerry and have dinner somewhere on our way home. It will give me some fresh ideas about celtic designs for the library.'

'I don't really know my way around here,' Penny had said, her heartbeats quickening at the thought of a day in his company. He was the most charming man she had ever met. And if that wasn't enough, his evident value for her company and for her opinion on some of his plans for Ballyamber House practically made him perfection personified. She was on the brink of falling in love with him she half admitted to herself.

'I do have a road map.' Donlon smiled at her.

'But what about Rod? We can't leave him on his own.'

'No problem. He's more than welcome to come with us.'

Steve's tone was perfectly polite but something in his air suggested that he did not altogether welcome the addition of a third person to the party.

When approached, however, Rod waved a dismissive hand. 'No, no, you two go on and enjoy yourselves while the cats are away.' His grin was almost malicious. 'I've got other fish to fry. That is provided I can borrow your car, sister dear.'

'Of course you can borrow my car.' Penny felt a twinge of guilt at how much she was looking forward to this day out alone in Steve's company. 'Are you sure you'll be OK? There's leftover salad in the fridge if you get hungry. Maybe we can arrange to meet for dinner in Killglash?'

'Don't worry your pretty little brain.' Rod had patted her on the head as he spoke, as if she were a small child and he the elder brother. 'And don't worry. I don't plan on doing any drinking. I've been dry for over six months now and I don't intend lapsing, in case that's what you're worried about.'

Penny was in high spirits when she and Steve set off soon after breakfast. It seemed a very long while since she had done anything so spontaneous. Their drive had taken them through some of the finest scenery in the country and for the first hour or so Penny was taken up with admiring the vista of mountains and lakes with Steve supplying information from the tourist guidebook he had taken with them. When they reached the halfway point at Waterville they had taken a walk on the windy beach and it seemed the most natural thing in the world for Steve to put his arm around her, pulling her close to him. It had started to rain, big cold drops falling on them suddenly and they had made a run for it to the pub, laughing like two teenagers and Steve had kissed her on the lips just as they reached the door.

'I bet you say that to all the girls,' she said now in answer to his remark. 'I've seen you flirting with Sophie Winslow, you know.' Keep it light, she told herself. Since Sophie's arrival at Ballyamber House she sometimes thought that the way they fell into easy conversation looked almost as if they were old acquaintances.

'Sophie?' Donlon raised his eyebrows. 'She's a lovely person, I'll grant you that. And she keeps Stanley sweet. You're not jealous are you, sweetheart?'

'Me? Jealous? Why on earth should I be?'

Steve put down his empty beer glass and reached for her hand, clasping it in both his own. 'Do you think Gregory knows how I feel about you? I saw him watching us when we danced at the party on Saturday night.'

Penny felt a thrill like an electric current run through her whole body. 'He's never said anything to me,' she said, aware that her voice was breathless. 'In any case, we might have danced together at the party but there was nothing – 'she broke off and swallowed hard before continuing. 'There was nothing for him to see.'

'But maybe he felt something between us. You feel it too, don't you?' Donlon had lowered his voice to almost a whisper even though there were only a few customers ranged around the bar who were more interested in their own concerns. 'I wouldn't have stayed around if I thought you and Gregory were happy together. But you're not, are you?'

'No - I don't know.' She withdrew her hand gently. 'I don't know how I feel, Steve, if I'm honest.'

'I think you do know.' He tilted her chin so that he could look directly into her eyes. 'You're a beautiful woman, Penny. You deserve some happiness.'

Her lips trembled and she felt the tears well up in her eyes. Part of her wanted to surrender, to be encircled in the warmth of his embrace but something held her back and that something was fear. Fear of Stanley Wallace's wrath.

Chapter Nine

Murray emerged from his cottage in Ballyamber to a bright sunny morning. It had rained heavily during the night but the brisk wind had carried off the clouds and Ardnabrone looked serene and inviting. It also looked close at hand which as he knew only too well was a sign that more rain could be expected later in the day. He stood for a brief moment and looked up at the mountain as he did on most mornings when the rain didn't drive him to his car at a sprint.

'Good morning Alan,' said a voice from the doorway of the neighbouring cottage. Nicola Ryan was standing there clad in a threadbare dressing gown, her wet hair falling over her shoulders. 'Could you give me a lift into Killglash? I haven't got my car today. I had to hand it in yesterday and it won't be ready until this afternoon. I meant to ask you last night if I could get a lift with you but then you got home so late, I didn't want to bother you. On top of that I overslept this morning,' she added with an embarrassed laugh.

'Sure. No problem,' Murray said. He hoped she would not take long although in his experience women took forever to get ready. He was running late as usual and Percy was coming in this morning to discuss the latest developments on the Maike Bloem case. He would not appreciate it if Murray showed up half an hour after everyone else.

'That's very kind of you. I'll be quick I promise.' She disappeared inside the cottage.

Murray lit a cigarette and settled down to wait. Nicola, he was beginning to realise, was somewhat chaotic. There was no sign of Vanessa, presumably she had taken the school bus which collected the children at Gleason's supermarket every day. There were not many schoolchildren from the Ballyamber area. Rural Ireland was bleeding its youth to the cities and to immigration. There was precious little opportunity for them down here. He was debating lighting another cigarette when Nicola appeared looking miraculously chic in a navy blue costume, her hair drawn into a chignon at the nape of her neck.

'Thank you so much,' she said as she settled in the passenger seat beside him. 'Without a car you're really lost in the country.'

With his eye on the dashboard clock, Murray started the engine and they moved off promptly. He was really going to be very late at this rate and giving his neighbour a lift was hardly a legitimate excuse. He could just imagine Percy's reaction. He debated giving Flynn a quick call to say he was on his way but then decided against it.

'A terrible thing about this young girl that was killed,' Nicola said. 'Is there any hope of finding the person who did it? I worry about Vanessa walking home from the bus stop.'

'I can understand that people are worried,' Murray said. 'We're working flat out on it, as you can imagine.' He paused then went on. 'I think you said that Vanessa was in Killglash on Saturday night doing some babysitting for Mitchells? What time did she get home?'

'I'm really not sure. I had a migraine and took some painkillers which make me quite drowsy. I heard her come in but I'm afraid I didn't check the time.'

'I'll have a word with the Mitchells. I'll want to speak to Vanessa, too,' he added.

'I'm sure if there was anything to tell she'd have mentioned it to me,' Nicola said, sounding slightly piqued.

Murray glanced at her. Women and their reactions to things were often a complete mystery to him. Aloud he said 'I'm sure you're right. I'd have expected John Mitchell himself to contact us if he had anything to tell us. Everyone knows we're looking for witnesses.'

There followed a strained silence which Nicola finally broke. 'I hope you didn't mind about the fortune telling on Sunday,' she said. 'It was really only a bit of fun, as you know. Just a bit scary the way the cards came up.'

'I don't believe in fortune telling or séances or anything like that.' Murray gave a short laugh that had no amusement in it. 'On the other hand, if they help to solve a murder case, I'm all for it.'

'I read somewhere that the police used mediums sometimes. But I suppose you don't have much call for that down here? I did hear that there was a series of murders in Ballyamber not too long ago.'

'Yes, we solved that without the aid of fortune telling.'

She glanced at him then stared straight ahead again. 'Would you like to come to another Sunday lunch if I promise never to tell your fortune again?'

Murray hesitated, not sure what he wanted. She was an attractive woman and he was lonely since Elena had moved away. But, and it was a big but, he did not want to get involved in another relationship. How to stay friendly without giving her any encouragement? A downright refusal of her invitation would be churlish to say the least. He decided to tread a cautious path. 'I think it's my turn to cook,' he said. 'How about you and Vanessa coming to me? I do a reasonable chicken curry or a casserole if you'd prefer that.'

'That would be lovely. Vanessa and I both like curry, provided it's not too hot.' There was the ring of happiness in her voice.

'Sunday lunch time, then, if that suits you?'

'Perfect.' Her smile lit up her face

'I'll drop you at the hotel,' Murray said, conscious that he was now half an hour late for his meeting. Five more minutes were not going to make any difference, he thought, as he joined the traffic on Killglash's main street.

Murray took a seat beside Percy and Flynn in the incident room with a mumbled apology.

'Glad you were able to join us,' Percy said with heavy sarcasm. He nodded in Flynn's direction, 'let's start the briefing.'

'The coroner's report tells us that Maike was strangled with the cord which was around her neck. Time of death is put at between eleven p. m. and around three or four a. m. the next day. She wasn't killed where she was found. We still haven't been able to find either her mobile or her wallet.'

'What *have* we been able to find out?' Percy interrupted.

'Garda Lynch is still interviewing the people who were in McDowd's on Saturday night,' Murray said. 'It will take a bit of time to find them all. The barman might remember her and maybe even have seen who she left the place with but it turns out that he's off for a few days. He's gone to London to be best man at his cousin's wedding and won't be back until tomorrow. We spoke to Agnes O'Toole, and also to Penny Wallace and the architect staying at Ballyamber House, Steve Donlon. They all claim they had never seen Maike before. And they saw nothing suspicious on Saturday or Sunday.'

Gerald Buckley supplied the next part of the report. 'I spoke to our colleagues in Rathfarnham. They interviewed the Fitzsimons who stayed at the Emerald Bed & Breakfast. The Fitzsimons gave a statement to the effect that Maike went on the Ardnabrone mountain walk with them and they dropped her off in Killglash afterwards. That would be around half past four. She made one call on her mobile, they said. She told them her boyfriend was meeting up with her in McDowd's.'

'The boyfriend hasn't shown up, I take it?' Percy addressed his question to Murray.

'At present we don't know who Maike intended meeting up with,' Murray said. 'She didn't give a name to the B&B when she booked.'

'I called to Ballyamber House this morning,' Flynn put in before Percy could pounce as he liked to pounce on matters he felt were not being attended to correctly. 'All the family were out. Mrs Quinn, that's a local woman who does the cleaning, said that Stanley Wallace and his son Gregory went to Dublin on business and their other guest Sophie Winslow went with them. They're not expected back until some time tomorrow. Mrs Wallace and Steve Donlon had just gone out, she said, as had Mrs Wallace's brother Rod Kirwin.'

Percy raised his bushy black eyebrows. 'Sophie Winslow? Is that the actress?'

Everyone looked at him in surprise. Up until now no one had considered Sophie in this light, indeed none of them had every heard of her before.

'My daughter follows these soaps on television,' said Percy, speaking defensively although there was just a slight blush on his cheeks. 'I believe Sophie Winslow had a small part in one of them but don't ask me the name of it. My daughter read somewhere that Sophie was visiting in this area and of course she was very excited about it. I didn't really believe the story to tell you the truth.'

'She's Stanley Wallace's current girlfriend, I understand,' Murray said. 'She's on our list for interviewing of course but she's obviously low priority.' He did not want this to develop into a discussion of actresses and soap operas which would lead them nowhere. In his opinion it seemed unlikely that Sophie Winslow had any connection to a Dutch hiker. He nodded at Flynn to indicate he should continue with his report.

'The Dutch police have come back to us,' Flynn said. 'They're an hour ahead of us in Holland so they were fairly early – lucky I was here to take the call, in fact.'

There was a small ripple of amusement from the others although Murray did not join in it. Jim Flynn trying to be the dynamic detective again, he thought sourly.

'They've been talking to Maike's family and friends.' Flynn paused to refer to his notes again. 'Her best friend, her name is Rianne Visser, told them that Maike had broken up with her boyfriend around two months ago. It seems he was abusive. They're looking into his current whereabouts and they'll get back to us.'

'Do we have a name for him?' Percy enquired.

'Thijs Bakker,' Flynn said. 'I spoke to a Sergeant Ilse de Jong at Zandervoort police station and she's to get back to me when they find out more on him.'

'Sounds like he might be a candidate,' Percy observed.

'She seemed pretty sure that she was meeting up with a boyfriend in McDowds,' Murray observed. 'At least that's what she told the Fitzpatrick's. If we could get a hold of her mobile phone it might answer a few questions for us.'

'I'll put the word out to the press. We might get lucky and someone finds it or knows about it.' Percy checked his watch and stood up. 'I'm meeting again with Maike's parents later on today. I'll do my best to reassure them that we're doing all we can. We're only at the start of things. I'll leave you to it gentlemen. Keep me up to date and remember, no talking to the media. We don't want to frighten the tourists.'

'What's your take on it now, Alan?' Flynn asked as they went back into Murray's office when the briefing was over. 'Reckon the ex boyfriend is the one?'

'Maybe.' Murray reached for his jacket which hung over the back of his chair. 'Only thing I'm wondering about is how she got to Agnes' cottage. Someone gave her a lift. But would she take a lift from an abusive ex boyfriend who presumably followed her to Ireland?'

'Women do strange things,' Flynn observed. 'He might have met her and told her he'd reformed and wanted her back and she might have believed him. It happens all the time. Ilse said they were together over four years according to Maike's friends.'

'So it's Ilse now is it.' Murray gave the ghost of a smile. 'You'll be getting tulips from Amsterdam before we know it.'

Flynn rolled his eyes. 'Very funny, Alan. I wouldn't say no if Percy wanted to send me over there to do a bit of research, mind you.'

'Percy authorise a trip to Holland? I wouldn't bet my best notepad on it, Jim.'

Chapter Ten

Penny turned over and groped for her little travel clock which she kept on the bedside table. Beside her Steve Donlon murmured something in his sleep and pulled the covers more tightly round him.

The hands on the clock pointed to ten minutes past eleven. Penny sat up with a jerk. She nudged the sleeping Steve gently. 'Wake up! It's late and Mrs Quinn is probably downstairs. We don't want her gossiping about us.'

Steve muttered something and clawed at the bedcovers once more before turning on his back and opening an eye. 'What's going on?'

Penny smiled down at him, remembering their night together – they had made love for most of it and had only fallen asleep a few hours ago. 'Darling, we have to get up! It's after eleven o'clock.'

'Get up? I don't think so.' Steve rubbed both eyes and then reached for her, pulling her into his arms. 'I can think of something better to do than get dressed.'

'No, really,' Penny pushed him away. 'Mrs Quinn is Ballyamber's biggest gossip. If she ever finds out that we spent the night together everyone from the postman to the bank manager will know about it.'

'You're probably right.' Steve planted a kiss on the top of her head and reluctantly swung his feet onto the floor. 'I'd better get back to my room.' He picked up his clothes where he had thrown them last night. 'Do you think Rod knows? What time did he come home?'

'I have no idea,' Penny said. 'I didn't hear him come in.' She slipped out of bed and donned her dressing gown, pushing her feet into her slippers, hurrying now.

Steve grinned at her. 'I suppose we were otherwise engaged, weren't we?' He tossed his clothes back onto the floor and took her in his arms again. 'It's so hard to leave you Penny when all I want to do is to make love to you all day.'

Penny responded as passionately to his touch as she had last night, lost in the excitement of the moment, her fear of discovery thrown out of the window. Only the here and now mattered, the feel of his body against hers.

Afterwards they lay together in a close embrace. 'We have to do this more often, young lady,' Steve said, his mouth against her hair. 'There must be a way of spending a weekend together. Come to London with me for Easter. Pretend your visiting your girlfriends. What do you say?'

'Oh Steve, I don't know! What if Stanley Wallace found out?' It did not seem strange to either of them that her husband Gregory's reaction was not her first thought.

'We won't get found out, darling. Not if we're careful.'

'Stanley would make my life such a misery, I know he would. He never wanted Greg to marry me in the first place. He'd be delighted to have an excuse to part us.'

'Don't worry so, darling. If we played it right no one would know.' He smiled at her. 'Just think of it! A whole weekend to ourselves in London.'

He sounded so calm and matter-of-fact that for a moment she felt safe and reassured. But only for a moment. He had barely finished speaking when the bedroom door opened and Gregory Wallace walked in.

'Still asleep darling?' he asked then stopped abruptly as he took in the two figures on the bed.

Chapter Eleven

'I hope that our friend Rod Kirwin is at home to us,' Murray said as they mounted the steps to the front door of Ballyamber House.

'As you know I checked him out.' Flynn pushed the button beside the door as he spoke. 'He worked for an advertising agency in London for a few years after finishing university. He lost the job last year. The company went out of business a few months later so he'd most likely have been made redundant. He has an alcohol problem and he's been in and out of clinics ever since.'

Murray had already been briefed on all of this but he had found in the past that when information was repeated it was sometimes possible to focus on a fact that had been overlooked initially. He therefore stored Flynn's comments away at the back of his mind to be brought out and compared with whatever information Rod Kirwin might divulge about himself. Flynn was a good cop, as Murray had often acknowledged and they made a good team. He could only hope that the younger man would remain at Killglash as his second in command. There was always the fear that Killglash garda station would be swallowed up by amalgamation with another area which would open up several career prospects to Flynn. Percy, their boss, had managed to forestall any plans for closure of Killglash but the threat lurked in the background.

It was a few minutes before Mrs Quinn opened the door to them. She showed them into the small salon on the ground floor which Murray remembered from his previous visit.

'I'll tell Mr Wallace you're here,' she said and hurried out of the room.

'She's very quiet,' Flynn observed as the door closed behind her. 'She's usually full of talk.'

The door opened before he could say any more and Stanley Wallace came into the room. He was an imposing figure, tall and broad-shouldered, with a shock of white hair, he seemed to fill the room with his presence. The blue eyes beneath the thick white eyebrows were shrewd, and just now watchful. When introductions were over he gestured towards the sofa and matching armchairs grouped round the fire.

'Please sit down. What can I do for you gentlemen? But before we get started perhaps you'd like some tea or coffee?'

'No, thanks,' Murray said before Flynn could answer. 'We're here to talk to you about the murder of the young Dutch tourist,' he went on as he took a seat in one of the armchairs leaving Flynn to perch on the edge of the couch.

Stanley took the chair opposite to Murray and looked from one man to the other. 'Yes, Penny told me that you had been here the day the body was discovered. I'm sorry that I haven't been available up until now. A terrible business and right on our doorstep. Most shocking. How can I help? What would you like to know?'

'Could you tell us where you were that night?' Murray took stock of Wallace as he asked the question, trying to read the body language of the man.

'We had a party here on the Saturday night and some guests stayed over. We – that is Penny's brother Rod, Steve Donlon and myself – drove them to Cork airport on the Sunday to get return flights to London. I'm sure you've been told all this before.'

Murray thought that underneath his calm exterior Stanley was fighting hard to appear calm and collected. It might have nothing to do with their enquiries but anything out of the ordinary was worth noting at this point in the investigation.

Flynn took over the rest of the interview, asking routine questions and requesting a list of the names and addresses of all the guests who had stayed at Ballyamber House over the weekend. He did not reveal that they had already requested this of Penny Wallace but as yet not received. Stanley was nothing if not cooperative and by the time they had finished interviewing him he appeared to have himself completely under control.

'We'd like to speak to your son, Gregory, next.' Murray said when Stanley prepared to leave them.

Gregory Wallace was of about the same height and build as his father, his thick brown hair falling boyishly over his forehead. His was a face that women would find handsome, Murray thought, but the chin was weak and the mouth a little too full for firmness of character. Murray had heard the village gossip about Gregory's failure in various business ventures and his humiliating position as assistant to his father who left him very little do in the business. It never failed to amaze Murray where the gossips got their information and he took a lot of what he heard with a pinch of salt, but for the most part the villagers take on people and situations was surprisingly accurate.

Gregory reiterated his father's offer of tea which both men again declined and they got down to the matter in hand. It seemed that Gregory had very little information to offer. No, he had not seen anybody acting suspiciously nor had he heard anything out of the ordinary. He had not left the house on Saturday night. 'Of course not,' he said in answer to Flynn's query on that head. 'We were entertaining guests. Why on earth should I want to go out?'

'Where is your bedroom, front or back of the house?' Murray enquired.

'Penny and I sleep at the back, as does my father. Rod uses the guest room at the front in the East wing and Steve has the bedroom next door to him. The bedrooms have all been newly decorated except for the one Steve uses,' he added as if this needed explanation.

'Can you hear the traffic on the road from the front rooms?' Murray asked.

Gregory shrugged his shoulders. 'I don't really know. I've never noticed it but then it is a quiet road, really. That horrible old woman Agnes O'Toole should be able to hear anything on that road. Have you asked her?'

Flynn made some noncommittal comment and shortly afterwards the interview was over and Gregory was free to go.

'Sounds like they're all blessed with good sleep or good sleeping pills,' Murray said in a low voice to Flynn as they waited for Rod Kirwin. 'I wonder if our friend Rod is a sleeping beauty with a bad memory like the rest of them.'

Chapter Twelve

Penny's hands were still shaking as she stepped into her little office on the first floor. She would never forget the expression of shock on Gregory's face when he had discovered Steve and herself in bed a few short hours ago nor his anguished cry of 'Penny!' as if he could not believe his eyes.

Infinitely worse was the appearance of Stanley Wallace, who had heard his son's raised voice as he prepared to enter his own bedroom two doors down. He had come striding down the corridor and stopped in the open doorway.

'What the hell is going on here?' He bellowed, his face red with anger. He quickly took in Penny sitting bolt upright in bed with the covers pulled up to her chin and Donlon lying by her side. 'You!' He almost spat the word as he stared at his daughter-in-law. 'I might have guessed you'd be up to no good the first chance you got!'

There was a moment's silence in the room. Penny could only stare at her husband and her father-in-law. Her mind was paralysed. She could not have said a word if her life depended on it. She would gladly have thrown herself out of the window if by doing so she could simply disappear.

'Give us a minute to get dressed and we can talk about this.' Donlon's voice shook slightly, betraying the fact that he was not as calm as his words. 'There's no point in making a scene here.'

'I'd like to know what you think you can explain,' Stanley Wallace snapped. 'I want you both out of my house within the hour.' He turned on his heel and stamped down the corridor, closing the door to his bedroom with a thud.

Gregory still stood there, his eyes darting from his wife to Steve Donlon. Finally, making a visible effort, he addressed Penny. 'I'll go and see my father.' With that he turned and left them.

Donlon hopped out of bed and scooped up the clothes he had left lying on the floor.

'It'll blow over, don't you worry,' he'd said. 'I'll have a word with Stanley when he's calmed down and he'll be able to speak to Greg about it and clear things. I wonder what made them come back from Dublin so early,' he added. 'They must have started out at the crack of dawn this morning.'

Now, seated at her writing desk in the relative peace of her little office, she tried to sort out her thoughts and feelings. What would happen between herself and Gregory? That was the question which kept going round and round in her head. She had not seen anyone since the scene this morning. While dressing she had heard voices in the corridor which she recognised as Gregory speaking to his father. She had been too scared of running into them to go downstairs for breakfast and now she felt light-headed and sick to her stomach. She badly wanted to know what had transpired. Had Steve already approached Stanley? What had been said between them? And most important of all, had Steve left the house? Was she going to have to face the music alone?

There was a tap at the door and Mrs Quinn put her head round it. 'Ah, there you are, Mrs Wallace.' Her sharp eyes took in Penny's white face. 'The gardai are here talking to people. They're looking for Mr Donlon, they want to speak to him when they've finished with your brother. Do you know where he is?'

Penny shook her head. She wondered how much Mrs Quinn knew or guessed about what had happened this morning. 'I've no idea,' she said.

'His car is still there so he can't be very far,' Mrs Quinn gave her another curious glance. 'I'll see if he's in the back garden. Mr Wallace was talking about putting up a greenhouse there so maybe he's gone to look at the layout of the grounds.'

'Yes, try the back garden.' Penny wished the woman would go away but at least now she knew that Steve was still here. A thought occurred to her. 'Have the gardai spoken to my husband?'

'They've talked to him and to Mr Stanley,' Mrs Quinn said. 'I don't think they've got very far on finding out who killed that poor little Dutch girl. T'is a scandal that something like that should happen here in a small place like Ballyamber.'

'What about Miss Winslow? Have they spoken to her?' Penny wondered what Sophie's take on all of this would be. At the party the other night she and Donlon seemed to be getting on like a house on fire, she recalled, but obviously Sophie would be on Stanley's side on this.

Mrs Quinn gave her an odd, appraising look. 'Sure Miss Winslow stayed in Dublin,' she said. 'Mr Gregory told me that she's having interviews for a new soap that's going to be filmed there.'

'Oh, yes, of course, I forgot.' Penny was under no illusion that the house keeper believed her.

'Well,' said Mrs Quinn, 'I don't blame her for wanting to stay away from Ballyamber what with all that's going on. That poor young girl, to be killed like that, and right on our doorstep.'

Penny had heard Mrs Quinn's views on the murder several times before and was determined not to hear them again. She cut in before Mrs Quinn could get started on her lamentations. 'Is my husband downstairs?'

'I met him just now when I was looking for you. He was on his way to talk to Mr Stanley in the library.'

The library was a large airy room at the front of the house which currently did not house many books. It was a favourite room with Stanley who spent a lot of his time there enjoying the view of Ardnabrone mountain from the big windows and no doubt dreaming of all the illustrious guests he would invite there in the future.

Penny nodded. 'I expect the gardai will want to talk to me as well,' she said. 'They're talking to Rod now, I think you said?'

'That's right.' Mrs Quinn nodded. 'They haven't asked about you,' she said before adding: 'I was just going to make them a pot of tea and I thought yourself would like a cup as well. Mr Gregory said you had a migraine and needed rest.'

'I'm much better, thank you. In fact, I'll come downstairs with you,' Penny said. She was suddenly alive with curiosity to find out how her brother's interview with the police had gone.

Chapter Thirteen

'So, Rod,' Alan Murray said pleasantly, as the young man took the seat opposite him which had just been vacated by Gregory Wallace. 'Can you tell us a bit about yourself.'

Rod Kirwin was tall and slim and like his sister had blonde hair and dark brown eyes but there the resemblance ended. Whereas Penny had a pleasant expression, her eyes lighting up when she smiled, Rod looked as if he did not smile too often, the brooding eyes and thin line of the mouth giving the impression of someone who was very dissatisfied with life. Murray took in the designer jeans and sweatshirt and the discreetly expensive wristwatch. Whatever problems Rod had had in the past, it seemed he was not doing too badly money-wise. Out of the corner of his eye he could see that Flynn – highly fashion conscious – was also eyeing Rod's wardrobe with interest.

Rod gave them a brief summary of his age, previous occupation and touched slightly on his alcohol problem.

'I'm a few weeks out of rehab,' he said and from his tone he could have been talking about having spent a few weeks away in the South of France or some other fashionable hotspot. 'Penny and Greg have kindly asked me to stay with them until I get myself sorted out.'

As Flynn had already given Murray all the details, there were not many questions open on that head.

'You know why we're here,' Murray said. 'The body of a young girl was found near Agnes O'Toole's cottage on Sunday and we are anxious to talk to anyone who can help us with our investigation. What did you do over the weekend?'

'There was a party for Stanley's girlfriend, Sophie Winslow, on Saturday night,' Rod said. 'I didn't actually know any of the guests, they were mostly friends of Stanley's and a few people from the entertainment world. Everyone thought Stanley was going to announce his engagement to Sophie on the night of the party but he didn't.' Rod grinned suddenly. 'In fact, there was a bit of a kerfuffle because he thought she was paying more attention to me than to him.'

'What do you mean by a kerfuffle?' Murray asked. He had no trouble in recognising that Rod could be irritating especially with that smirky smile on his face.

Rod shrugged his shoulders. 'Stanley was shouting at Sophie and threatening me. His usual way of dealing with anything that doesn't suit him.'

'How did he threaten you?'

'Oh, theatrical stuff but all bluff, of course. I'm a good-for-nothing leech and he'd throw me out of the house, that sort of thing.' Rod glanced from Murray to Flynn and back again, his face darkening at the memory. 'He likes to keep me up to date on all he's doing for me so that I'm truly humbled. And I expect he wanted Sophie to know what an ungrateful beggar I am.'

'What happened next? He threatened to throw you out. When did this happen? During the party?'

'Sophie and I get on like a house on fire which I expect doesn't suit him. Not surprising, after all, she's much nearer my age than Stanley's.' He gave another of his malicious smiles. 'We had about two dances together I'd say when he interrupted us and asked if we'd come into the library with him. He was pretty insulting and I took a swing at him, if you must know.' Rod looked down and examined the backs of his hands.

'You hit him?' Murray had not noticed any marks on Stanley Wallace when he had spoken to him this morning. Rod's knuckles were also without any evidence of physical contact.

'I didn't actually hit him. He was too quick. Sophie started crying and begging us to stop. Which is what we did.'

'And then?' Murray prompted when Rod was silent.

'Then we went back to the party and no one was any the wiser.' Rod hesitated then looked directly at Murray, his dark eyes flashing with remembered anger and humiliation. 'To be honest, I wish I'd punched him in that arrogant face of his.'

Murray debated pursuing the topic then decided against it. Whatever undercurrents were present among the residents and guests of Ballyamber House it was unlikely they had anything to do with the murder of Maike Bloem.

'Let's leave that for now,' he said. 'Can you tell us if you left the party on Saturday night at any stage?'

There was a moment's pause before Rod spoke. 'Actually, I did leave the party after that row with Stanley. I needed a bit of fresh air.' He hesitated then went on. 'I drove into Killglash and stopped off at McDowds very briefly. I usually stay away from pubs but I just needed to calm down, I suppose.'

Flynn handed him a picture of Maike Bloem which her parents had provided to the police in Zandervoort and which had duly been sent to Killglash garda station. 'Did you happen to see this girl in McDowds?'

Rod studied the picture carefully. 'This could be the girl I spoke to. She said she was Dutch or Danish. I don't think she told me her name or if she did I don't remember it. She was with a group of hikers, some of them were locals I believe, and they were planning to do a walking tour next day unless the weather got worse.' He wrinkled his forehead. 'If I recall correctly, they said something about Mangerton Mountain. Walking isn't my thing, so I lost interest in the conversation at that point.'

'Was she with someone in particular, a boyfriend?' Murray's gut feeling told him that Rod was not telling the whole truth.

Rod shrugged. 'I didn't notice but then I only had a few words with her while I was getting a drink at the bar.'

'Did she appear worried in any way?' This from Flynn who had been making copious notes.

'I really couldn't say. To me she seemed to be having a great time.'

'Can you tell us when you arrived at McDowds and when you left?' Again it was Flynn who asked the question.

'Yes, I can – more or less. I must have got there some time after ten o'clock, nearer half past ten, I should say. I had a drink of orange juice at the bar and I left again at around eleven or thereabouts. I wasn't really checking the time.'

'Was the girl still there when you left the pub?' Murray asked.

'Again, I didn't take any notice. I wanted to get back to the party. I knew my sister would have been worried if I didn't show up again.' He waved an expressive hand. 'That's what happens when you've been on the booze, people expect the worst.'

Chapter Fourteen

'What did you think of Rod Kirwin's explanation about meeting our victim at McDowds?' Murray asked as he and Flynn returned to their car.

'Rod is hiding something for sure. I'll have another look at what we know about him but as far as I recall he has a drink problem, was in rehab, came out a few months back and his sister took him under her wing. We don't know anything more than that.'

Flynn settled himself behind the steering wheel and waited for Murray to take the passenger seat before he went on. 'It seems a bit strange that he'd leave the party and go to a pub for an hour or two especially considering his alcohol problem. It would have been more logical to go up to his room for an hour to cool off.'

'That's exactly my take on it,' Murray said. 'Jim, me lad, you've passed Paper One on Looking for Clues – the Ballyamber version of it anyway.'

'Have I missed something?' Flynn enquired suspiciously.

'I don't know,' said Murray. After a moment's silence, he went on: 'We'll be passing Agnes O'Toole's cottage. Agnes has a lot of expensive stuff in her kitchen, like that big new television which I couldn't afford I'm sure, not to mention the other bits of furniture. Where does she get the money for all that? She might have won on the lottery, of course, but I'm sure if she had she'd be boasting about it and telling us all that it was thanks to some magic she'd worked. I wonder what she's up to. I think we'll pay her a flying visit.'

If Agnes was surprised to see them again so soon she gave no sign of it. They refused her offer of tea and Murray broached the subject in a roundabout way.

'I'm looking for a table like this for my cottage,' he said, tapping the oak table at which they sat. 'It looks like it might cost a fair packet, though. Do you mind if I ask you what you paid for it?'

Agnes stared at him, obviously taken completely by surprise at the question. It was the first time Murray had ever seen her at a loss for an answer.

'I bought it in a closing down sale in Kenmare,' she said after a full minute's thought. 'A fella I know got it for me at a bargain price.' She cast her eyes around her well-furnished kitchen and then went on. 'There was a lot of stuff going really cheap so he bought it for me.'

'Very obliging of him. Maybe I should talk to him.'

'He's a fella I did a favour for a long time ago, I cured a pet dog of the evil eye for him. I think he moved away.' Agnes spoke quickly, her eyes darting from Murray to Flynn and back again. 'The furniture store is closed down now. This fella wouldn't be much help to you. He's not from around here, so you wouldn't know him' she added as if that settled the matter.

'I suppose you paid a few grand for all this stuff?' Murray gestured with his hand to include the whole room.

'I've saved all me life,' Agnes said virtuously. 'What else would I do with me money? I don't go anywhere. It's not against the law, is it, to save your money?'

'They haven't made it an offence yet,' Murray said with half a smile, 'but don't be putting ideas into politicians' heads.'

Flynn had been fingering his notebook during this exchange, now he addressed Agnes in his most respectful tone. 'We've been admiring how well your garden is looking. I suppose you get help with that, do you?'

A look of what could be relief passed over Agnes' face. 'A nice fellow from Killglash does it for me,' she told them. 'He cuts the grass and everything. He works up at Ballyamber House as well.'

'What's his name?' Flynn asked, still in that same respectful tone.

'Ian Creedy.' Agnes said promptly. 'He's Liam Creedy's son,' she added with a glance at Murray.

The name Liam Creedy gave Murray a shock. Liam Creedy and his brother Darragh were enthusiastic mountain climbers and his wife Sheila had often gone on trips with them. They were part of the group she had planned to team up with the day she had gone missing.

'Thanks Agnes,' he said in as neutral a tone as he could manage. He was aware that Flynn was looking at him curiously. 'We'll need to talk to him at some stage. When was he here last?'

Agnes wrinkled her already lined forehead. 'He came the week before the party and planted a few things for me and tidied the place up. He cut the grass, too, even though there's not much growth at this time of year.'

'And you haven't seen him since?' This from Flynn.

'No, sure there would be no need for him to come here. I pay him as soon as he does the work.'

'Has he been up at Ballyamber House?' Murray asked.

'I saw him a few times tidying up the gardens but I don't know what goes on at that house. That fella Stanley Wallace shouts at me if he sees me anywhere near it. I have the right of way, though,' she added. 'That's been there for hundreds of years and it'll take more than Stanley Wallace to change that even with all his money.'

'I've been meaning to tell you,' Flynn said as they set out on the drive back to Killglash garda station. 'I put out the word on anonymous tip offs about anything suspicious last Saturday night. There was one phone call. It said something about lights being seen up in the woods near Ballyamber House a couple of times but not lately.'

'Lights in the woods.' Murray whistled through his teeth. 'I wonder. Could be a poacher but what would he be doing in the woods? Our sheep rustlers are out on the mountain as we know only too well. Any hope our tipster will call back?'

'I doubt it.'

'We'd better organise a search of the area, see if we can turn anything up. At the rate we're going, Jim, our to-do list is getting longer than the housekeeper's at Buckingham Palace.'

Chapter Fifteen

When Murray and Flynn had left, Penny went in search of Rod but learned from Mrs Quinn that he had driven off in her car. The police interview must really have upset him, she thought, at the same time feeling a flash of anger that he had not asked her permission to use the vehicle. Fearful of bumping into Stanley Wallace, she retreated to her little office but found she could not settle to anything. The lonely hours ticked slowly by. Once she thought she heard footsteps upstairs in the attic and wondered if Steve Donlon was up there with Stanley. She knew there was some project afoot to renovate the rooms. Hunger finally drove her downstairs. She had half hoped, half feared running into Greg but she encountered no one.

She was half-heartedly eating a bowl of soup in the kitchen when Steve Donlon appeared.

'There you are! I've been looking all over the place for you.' He pulled her to her feet and into a tight embrace. 'Penny, darling, I'm so sorry about this. What a mess!'

'What's going on?' She whispered, clinging tight to him. 'Have you spoken to Stanley?'

'I had a quick word before he and Greg went out today. He hadn't calmed down at that point. The upshot is that I'm going back to Dublin, at least for the time being. My guess is that when he's thought it over, Stanley will behave like a man of the world and have me finish my work here.'

'You're going back to Dublin now?'

'Yes, as soon as I've packed. I just came to say goodbye for the present.' He kissed her gently on the lips. 'Bear up, darling. I'll ring you as soon as I can. It'll all work out, you'll see.'

Night settled over Ballyamber House. Penny wandered from one room to the next but even the small salon provided little comfort. After a few half-hearted attempts to watch television, she switched it off but the stillness was unnerving. She had never realised before how many unexplained noises could be heard in an old house. Even the hum of the fridge in the kitchen seemed unnaturally loud. On her way upstairs to her bedroom – it was better to be asleep in bed when Gregory got home she decided – she thought that she again heard footsteps upstairs in the attic. She felt a moment's panic. Supposing the killer of that Dutch tourist had broken into the house and planned to strike again? She stood on the landing her heart thudding and strained her ears but all was quiet again. It was probably only mice, she reasoned. These old places must be full of them. She must remember to mention it to Greg.

Once in bed, however, Penny could not settle to sleep. She had noticed that Gregory's shaving things were gone from the bathroom, his pyjamas no longer under his pillow. It looked as if he had cleared out his things while she had been hiding in her office. What would happen between them? What should she do about Steve? What were his real feelings? She was beginning to fear that he was only interested in having an affair and not in a permanent relationship. Was she in love with him? What did she really want? She tossed and turned restlessly while her little travel clock ticked off the minutes. She had half decided to go downstairs and make herself a nightcap when there was a soft tap at her door. She sat up and snapped on the bedside light, her heart pounding, her throat dry, hoping against hope that it was Gregory coming to make up with her.

However, it was Rod who tiptoed into the room. 'I thought I saw your light and came to see how you're doing,' he said, speaking in a mock conspiratorial whisper. 'Well sister dear, I see the gardai haven't dragged you off to prison on suspicion of murder.' Although he sounded his usual flippant self, she thought she detected a certain nervousness about him.

'Rod! You scared the living daylights out of me!' She stifled her disappointment, adding after a moment, 'I don't suppose we're of much interest – or help – to the gardai.'

'Even if I spoke to that girl on the night she was killed?' Rod sat down in the chair by the window and gently rocked back and forth, a habit she knew from childhood when he was distressed.

'You spoke to her?' She stared at him, feeling the blood leave her face.

'Yes, I spoke to her down at McDowds. She was with a group of other kids and I spoke to them all. They were having a ball.'

'Did you tell the police that?'

'Of course, why not? I have nothing to hide.' The look Rod gave his sister was defiant. 'Someone would have seen me talking to her anyway - one of those barflies at the pub who have nothing better to do than watch other people. It would have looked strange if I hadn't told them.'

'But what did they say?'

He shrugged. 'Not much. They wanted to know if she was worried or scared about anything and I told them that as far as I could recall she wasn't. I only talked to her for a minute, just the usual small talk. She was a pretty little thing.'

'Did they believe you? I mean, you spoke to her and then her body was found near here. They're bound to be suspicious.'

'Why should they be suspicious of me? Probably a lot of people spoke to her that night.'

'But how awful,' said Penny. 'It makes it that bit more personal, doesn't it? It's bad enough that her body was found just down the road but you've actually spoken to her on the night she was killed.'

'How do you think I feel about it?' Rod stood up abruptly and began pacing up and down. 'The really awful part is that I gave her a lift back here.'

Penny stared at him, her mouth dry suddenly so that her next words came out as a hoarse whisper. 'Back here? You mean you gave her a lift back here to Ballyamber House? My God, Rod! They'll think you had something to do with it!'

'No they won't.' Rod came over to her and put his hands on her shoulders, shaking her slightly. 'I didn't tell them the bit about giving her a lift and you're not to mention it either, on no account, do you hear me? Not to anyone.' He released her and resumed his pacing back and forth across the room.

'Rod.' She licked dry lips. 'You didn't – this girl – you didn't do anything to her, did you?'

'Do anything to her?' He echoed, stopping his pacing to turn and face her. 'Look at me Penny. Do you really believe I would kill someone?'

'N-no. Of course not, but you gave her a lift and –' she stared at him, her eyes huge in her white face.

'That's all I did, I swear. Look,' he went on, sounding calmer now. 'She wanted to get back to her Bed & Breakfast here in Ballyamber so I gave her a lift. She asked to be put down at the supermarket which I did and then I drove on here. Whatever happened to her, happened after that.'

'But you might be the last person to have seen her alive. Have you thought of that?'

'That's what's bothering me.' Rod stopped his pacing again and stood looking at her, his face haggard in the light from her bedside lamp. 'With my alcohol problem they probably have me marked down as a weirdo already. Just imagine the questions if they know I gave her a lift.'

Chapter Sixteen

When Rod had gone, Penny abandoned all hope of getting to sleep and sat on the side of her bed, wrapped in her dressing gown. She believed Rod when he said he had nothing to do with the killing of the Dutch girl. But if the police ever found out that he had given her a lift back to Ballyamber village they would be suspicious, especially as he had not owned up to it straight away.

She felt chilly after a while and got back into bed, snapping off the bedside lamp and trying to compose herself. But sleep did not come. As the little travel clock ticked the minutes and then the hours away, her thoughts turned again to Greg and what would become of their marriage. Were they going to go on as before pretending to the outside world that all was well and secretly hating each other? Or would they go their separate ways and try to put the fiasco behind them? Since her marriage she had seen a few couples, friends of Greg's, who appeared together in public, were always polite to each other and who each had at least one lover in the background. She did not believe that she could live that kind of life but being alone again did not appeal to her either. Not that she would be alone if she were with Steve, but the more she went over what he had said, the more she was coming to realise that he had not made any definite commitment. He had told her he was crazy about her but he had never suggested that she leave Greg. In the excitement of his admiration she had overlooked this simple fact.

Perhaps she should suggest that she and Rod return to London? That would get Rod out of the way of police investigations and give Greg time to calm his father down and consider what action he might want to take with regard to their marriage. It would also give her time to sort out her own feelings. As she lay there tossing and turning in the dark bedroom, weighing up possibilities and alternatives, it dawned upon Penny that she did not want to spend the rest of her life with Steve Donlon supposing he were to ask her. She had been flattered by his attentions and lonely because Greg neglected her whenever his father was around and she was resentful of the fact. Steve was charming, handsome, successful and she had been bowled over by his attentions but if she were honest with herself, she did not think that he had much substance behind all that glamour. Falling into bed with him had been part revenge on the Wallace's, on Greg for not having the courage to stand up to his father and on Stanley for his obvious contempt and neglect.

How to undo the damage was a separate problem. She could try and explain to Gregory how hurt and let-down she felt at his behaviour and hope that he would understand. He must still love her, she reasoned, and surely she could win him back? Her father-in-law was a different proposition. He was no doubt delighted at the prospect of their marriage breaking up. She had failed to produce an heir and her background was not up to his standards, two major reasons he wanted Gregory to part from her. Well, now she had given him grounds enough to fulfil his wish, she thought bitterly.

With thoughts like these for company she was never going to get off to sleep, she decided. Best thing to do was to sneak downstairs to the kitchen and make herself a milky drink or possibly raid the newly installed bar in the library for a glass of brandy. Stanley sometimes sat up late in the library but she could check if there was a light on there and stick to the kitchen if necessary. The hands of her travel clock told her it was nearly one thirty in the morning. With a bit of luck her father in law would have gone to bed. And if she happened to meet Greg, well so much the better, it would be an opportunity to talk to him about everything. She slipped into dressing gown and slippers and padded softly to the bedroom door, opening it as gently as she could – the lock was stiff and had a tendency to squeak. All was quiet and she padded along the corridor to the landing. She had one foot on the top step of the stairs when she heard a door open and close downstairs from the direction of the library. Someone was still up. It was probably Stanley, she thought, getting himself a nightcap from the drinks cabinet in the library. If she took the back stairs she could get to the kitchen without meeting him, provided he stayed in the library, but she was reluctant to take the risk. As she stood there, undecided, she thought she heard voices. Was Gregory still up, too? He was more than likely discussing the events of the day with his father. She would have liked to be a fly on the wall. She stood motionless, shivering suddenly in the draught of air which came up the wide stone staircase. Downstairs a door closed again and she thought she detected rapid footsteps in the passageway. Stanley or Greg coming back upstairs. Not wishing to be detected here on the landing she crept back to her room and slipped under the covers. Better forget the nightcap until she heard Stanley return to his room down the corridor. But although she waited, nerves a-stretch, for what seemed like hours, Stanley did not return. She had just managed to doze off when the creak of floorboards overhead jerked her momentarily awake. All was quiet again but just before she drifted off to sleep she thought she heard the soft thud of the back door followed by the sound of a car's engine. The noises became part of a troubled dream as she slipped deeper into slumber.

*****

    Penny woke to the sound of the rain battering against the windows, driven by the strong wind. She had never felt less like getting out of bed but it was time to face up to whatever strife the day would bring. The grey clouds and drip of rain outside mirrored her feelings. Her head throbbed and her eyes felt sore and gritty from lack of sleep. With an effort she pulled back the covers and padded into the bathroom. She stood under the shower, trying to marshal her thoughts and form some sort of plan of what she should say to Gregory today but her brain felt as if it had been injected with lead. While towelling herself down she heard the bedroom door open. For a moment she hesitated, then she reached for the dressing gown on the back of the door and stepped out of the steamy safety of the bathroom.

    Gregory was standing at the open door of the wardrobe. He turned around to face her and she was struck by the haggard look on his face.

    'Hi,' she said around the lump that suddenly formed in her throat. The sight of him this morning made her realise that she really did love him, loved him more than she had ever been aware of loving him before. There had been times in the past when she had hated him for his blind obedience to his father but on seeing the suffering etched on his face this morning, she was deeply sorry for the moment of madness with Steve and overcome with the sudden burst of her feelings for her husband.

Gregory merely inclined his head in reply to her greeting then turned back to the wardrobe. He began to take out some clothes, pulling them off their hangars and draping them over his arms. 'I didn't expect to see you here,' he said in a tight clipped voice. 'I thought you'd left with lover Steve.'

'He's not my lover. It's not like you think. Oh Greg, I'm really sorry.' Her voice was thick with repressed tears. 'I must have been crazy –'

He made no reply, merely turned to the chest of drawers where he kept his underclothes and began to pull out underpants and socks, some of which fell onto the floor. With a muttered curse he picked them up and stuffed them into the pockets of his jeans.

'I'll be sleeping in the guest room in the East Wing,' he said. 'We don't have to see each other until all this has been settled.'

He made for the bedroom door and she ran across the room to bar his way. 'Greg, please. We have to talk. You can't just ignore me as if I didn't exist!'

'What would you say if you came home and found me in bed with another woman? I was only away one single night, Penny, and you couldn't wait to be with Donlon. How do you think I feel?'

'I made a terrible mistake. I'm so sorry. I've been such a fool. Please believe me. I was unhappy and feeling left out of things. You and your father always discussed things as if I wasn't there.'

'So it's my fault now? Grow up, Penny. You fancied Donlon all along. The two of you were always sloping off to Killglash. I expect you couldn't believe your luck when I went to Dublin for that exhibition.'

Penny threw up her hands in a gesture of despair. 'I love you Greg. I didn't realise how much I loved you until now. What can I do to make you believe that, to make you believe that I'm really sorry?'

He hesitated a moment and she thought she had got through to him but then he brushed past her. 'Mrs Quinn arrived to make breakfast half an hour ago. I suggest you come downstairs and that we behave as normal as long as Mrs Quinn is in the house. We don't want the neighbours to spend all their time laughing at us.' With that he pulled open the bedroom door and left her.

Penny leaned against the door and cried in great racking sobs. But there was no one to hear her or offer comfort and after some minutes she pulled herself together and went back into the bathroom to get dressed and to apply make-up to camouflage the traces of tears.

When she entered the kitchen she found Gregory already seated at the scrubbed wooden table eating eggs and bacon with Mrs Quinn fussing in the background. The dining room next door was earmarked for complete re-decoration and would be unusable for some time to come. Most of its furniture was stacked in a corner of the large kitchen. Penny disliked having to eat there with the housekeeper privy to all that was said.

'What will you have?' Mrs Quinn asked. 'I got some lovely rashers at Gleason's supermarket if you'd like some.'

'Just tea and toast for me,' Penny said. She slid into the chair opposite Gregory who had the daily paper open beside his plate. He avoided looking at her and concentrated on reading an article on the front page. She turned to Mrs Quinn who was making the toast. 'Tell me, Mrs Quinn, why is it called Gleason's supermarket? It says "The Diamond" over the door but everyone refers to it as Gleason's.'

'Well, that was the name of the family that owned it. They had to move away, but that's a long story now,' Mrs Quinn said. 'It was sold a couple of years ago and the new people took it over. It'll never be called anything else except Gleason's.'

'How very Irish,' Gregory said drily without looking up from his newspaper.

'Is Mr Stanley going to have breakfast?' Mrs Quinn enquired as she set down a fresh pot of tea in front of Penny. 'He's usually down by this time.'

'I expect he's in the library,' Gregory said. 'Could you go and tell him that we're having breakfast, please, Mrs Quinn? He's inclined to forget the time when he gets into one of his room designer moods.'

Mrs Quinn looked from one to the other of them, her eyes sharp with curiosity. 'Of course I will. The toast is ready now.' She fished two slices out of the toaster and put them in the toast rack on the table. 'I see Mr Donlon's car is gone,' she added. 'He must have got up very early.'

'Yes, he's gone back to Dublin. He wanted an early start.' Gregory looked up from his newspaper. 'You might want to do his room out today.'

'To be sure.' Mrs Quinn said cheerfully. 'I'll go and call Mr Stanley now.'

When she had gone, Gregory looked across the table at Penny. 'Try and eat something, there's a good girl. No point in falling over from hunger. That won't help anyone.'

Penny felt the tears well up again at his remark. It was a small sign that he still cared for her, she thought. But how could she win him back again? How convince him that she hated herself for what had happened?

There was a sudden scream and the sound of running footsteps. Mrs Quinn burst in to the kitchen, her face white with shock.

'Come quick! There's blood everywhere in the library,' she panted. 'And I can see someone on the floor over by the window.'

Chapter Seventeen

Both Gregory and Penny stared at Mrs Quinn, the moment suspended in time, then Gregory took charge of the situation.

'Stay here.' He jumped to his feet, gesturing to his wife to remain seated and left the room at a run.

'Oh my God!' Penny's body started to shake all over. Her hands flew up to cover her face. 'Did you see – who?' Her voice was a barely audible whisper.

'I didn't go near enough to see who it is,' Mrs Quinn said. She pulled out one of the chairs from the table and sat down on it heavily. 'I suppose it's Mr Stanley seeing as how he's in and out of that room all the time.'

'You said there was blood everywhere. Was he – I mean – he must be badly hurt. We should call the doctor and the police, too.'

'There might be someone still in the house,' Mrs Quinn said.

'I hadn't thought of that.' Penny removed her hands from her face and stared at the housekeeper for a moment. 'I've left my mobile upstairs in the bedroom. I'll have to use the house phone in the hall.' She half rose from her chair, then sat down again as her legs gave way under her. 'Let's wait for Gregory,' she said.

Her common sense told her that the body in the library could only be her father-in-law but until she had this confirmed part of her mind raced with wild speculation. Last night she had heard Stanley go downstairs. Surely he would have shouted, called for help, if he felt himself in danger?

The thoughts buzzed in her brain like a swarm of angry bees as she tried to think back. Gregory had slept in the guest room in the East Wing. Had he heard anything sinister during the night? What about Rod? Her stomach tightened in sudden fear. Was it her brother who was lying in the library? His non-appearance at breakfast was not unusual. He often slept late and wandered into the kitchen for a cup of coffee around half past ten or so. Nevertheless, she would be glad to have confirmation that he was safe and sound in his bed. The idea of a burglary gone wrong made her sick with fear.

The two women sat facing each other in silence across the dining table, each busy with her own thoughts. Although it seemed like hours, it was in reality only a few minutes before Gregory came hurrying back into the room, his mobile phone at his ear. It was evident from his side of the conversation that he was talking to the gardai. 'No doubt about it,' he was saying. 'His body is as cold as ice. Yes, of course, I'll telephone for an ambulance but there's nothing they can do.'

As soon as he had finished the call, Penny blurted out the question which had been tormenting her. 'Your father?'

Gregory nodded. His face was as white as Mrs Quinn's. 'It's dad. He's dead. There's blood everywhere.' His voice caught then he recovered himself. 'I need a drink. What about you, Penny? A brandy?'

'Yes,' she said then added hastily 'What about Rod? We need to make sure he's all right.'

'Let Mrs Quinn do that,' Gregory said quickly, turning to the housekeeper. 'Just tell him to get dressed and come down straight away. The police will be here in the minute and they'll want to talk to us all.' He strode out of the kitchen and returned a few minutes later carrying a bottle of Courvoisier. He took two tumblers from one of the kitchen cupboards and poured generous amounts of the liquid, handing one to Penny.

'What if there's someone still in the house?' Mrs Quinn had remained seated. She looked from one to the other of them. 'I'd rather not chance it.'

Gregory hastily took out another glass and poured her a smaller brandy than the one he'd given Penny. 'I doubt if the person who did this would be hanging around the house,' he said as he handed it to her. 'They've almost certainly gone by now, now that we're all up and about.'

Mrs Quinn took a sip of the brandy and looked uncertainly from Gregory to Penny, clearly reluctant to leave the safety of the dining room.

Gregory downed his brandy in two gulps and set down the glass on the table with a slight thump. 'Tell you what, Mrs Quinn, I'll go up and wake Rod myself. You get some strong tea brewed up. I've a feeling we're going to needs lots of tea this morning.'

Penny watched him go with some misgiving. She took a sip of the brandy and felt it run through her like fire. She had a sudden urge to go into the library and take a look at the body of her father-in-law. She even got to her feet before reason kicked in. The scene of the crime must not be disturbed, everybody knew that. She sat down again and tried to calm herself.

'I'll put the kettle on.' Mrs Quinn heaved herself to her feet, leaving Penny alone at the table, her nerves quivering in expectation of what Gregory might find upstairs.

Gregory's reappearance put an end to her speculations. 'Rod is getting dressed,' he said. 'He's as shocked as we are.' He came up to Penny and pulled her gently out of her chair and into his arms. 'I just can't believe it,' he said, burying his face in her neck like a child seeking comfort from its mother. 'What on earth are we going to do?'

Penny held him tight. She had never pretended to be fond of her father-in-law and had often wished him out of their lives. But not like this, she thought. Never like this.

Mrs Quinn stuck her head around the door. 'Sergeant Murray and Garda Flynn are here,' she said.

Chapter Eighteen

Murray stood in the middle of the library and took in the scene, trying to get a feel for what had happened. Stanley Wallace lay face down near one of the windows. They would have to wait for the coroner's examination and the results of the Forensic team's work, but Murray's first impression was that Wallace had been hit several times with tremendous force on the back of the head with the heavy glass vase which lay beside him. His face had been gashed by a shard of glass which accounted for the pool of blood in which his head lay. One of the library windows was open and the room had been ransacked as if the intruder was looking for something specific.

'Someone was really mad at Stanley Wallace,' he observed in a low tone to Flynn who stood beside him. 'There's something not quite right about the way the room's been left. What do you think, Jim?'

'Unless the intruder was looking for a safe,' Flynn said.

'That's a possibility. I can't see anyone breaking in to steal the collected works of William Shakespeare.'

Murray opted to use the big dining room for the interviews. Although it was chilly and sparsely furnished, he wanted to sit behind a table with witnesses on the other side. In addition, it gave Flynn a bit of elbow room to take notes. Mrs Quinn brought them tea and homemade scones and then sat down to tell them how she had gone to the library at Gregory's request to remind Stanley Wallace that breakfast was ready. No, she said, she had not noticed anything amiss until she opened the door and walked into the library.

'Which door do you use when you come to work?' Murray asked. The library was the first room on the right of the front entrance.

Anyone walking up the steps to the front door would have noticed that one of the windows was open.

'I come in the back door.' She fidgeted with the folds of her apron. 'I park round there. They wouldn't want me parking in front of the house.'

'You didn't notice that the library window was open when you arrived?'

She shook her head. 'It was like any morning,' she said simply. 'I got here at around quarter past eight and drove round the side of the house and parked at the back, then I came into the kitchen and started making breakfast.'

Although visibly shocked both Gregory and Penny attested to the fact that they had not heard anything untoward during the night. They had slept in separate rooms following a family row and had not noticed anything wrong when they came downstairs for breakfast that morning. Greg had chatted to his father in the library before going to bed.

'That would be about eleven o'clock or so,' he told them. 'Dad was in very good form, full of plans as usual.'

'Separate bedrooms. It sounds like they weren't playing happy families last night,' Murray remarked to Flynn as they were waiting for Rod Kirwin to appear. 'We'll have to dig a bit to find out what that row was about. I'm not satisfied with Gregory saying it was just a "domestic squabble" between him and his wife.'

'I think Penny Wallace could tell us a bit more,' Flynn observed. 'She might be shocked but she seemed more nervous than bereaved, if you know what I mean.'

'That's just what I was thinking myself. As I said, there's more to this domestic squabble business than Penny Wallace overspending on her husband's credit card.'

'People like the Wallace's don't have problems overspending on their credit cards,' Flynn said, sounding almost wistful. 'They have so much money they wouldn't miss a few thousand. She probably gets more housekeeping money that my salary.'

Before Murray had time to reply Rod Kirwin entered the room. There were shadows under his eyes which might have been the result of a late night or shock at the murder which had taken place. He shook hands with both men and took the chair opposite them indicated by Flynn.

'A terrible business,' he said, sounding more subdued than when they had last interviewed him.

To Murray he was a person of interest in Stanley Wallace's murder. According to his own version of events, Rod had had a row with Stanley at the party on Saturday because he was paying Sophie Winslow too much attention. He had even thrown a punch at Stanley if he was to be believed. Had they fought again only this time Rod had picked up a heavy cut glass vase instead of using his fists?

'Your sister tells us that you were out last night,' Flynn started off the questioning. 'Can you tell us where you went and what time you got back to Ballyamber House?'

'I want to make something clear,' Rod leant forward slightly, his brows knit together in what could only be described as a scowl. 'I had nothing to do with knocking old Stanley off. Nothing whatsoever.'

'Could you just answer the question, please?' Flynn spoke in an exaggeratedly patient tone.

'I was out all day, if you must know. I went to Killarney and then for a long drive.' Rod began to jig his foot up and down. 'Penny, Greg and Stanley had a big row or at least that's what I gathered. Everyone was mad at everyone else. Not my scene. So I skipped off for the day.'

'Anyone see you in Killarney?'

Rod pursed his lips. 'I can't think. Probably.'

'What was the row about?' Flynn was still doing the questioning.

Rod scowled at him. 'Does it matter?'

'Yes, it could matter,' Murray said. Before he questioned Penny and Gregory Wallace on the subject again he wanted a bit more information. The interviews today had been perfunctory and he needed to explore their version of this family row but it might be a good idea to see what Rod's story on it was. As he observed him he reflected that Rod was overdoing the injured innocent pose. Surely he should react with a bit more sensitivity to the murder of his sister's father-in-law?

'Didn't they tell you what happened?' Rod stopped jigging his foot and sat up straight again.

'Look,' said Murray in as pleasant a tone as he could muster. 'Just tell us what you know about it. We like to be able to cross things off our little shopping list.'

Rod ran a hand through his blond mane, making it stand up in untidy spikes. 'Well, I doubt if it will help you but here's what I know. Stanley and Gregory went to Dublin to visit some exhibition or other and get some new business. Sophie went with them. Steve Donlon and my sister decided to spend the day together. Stanley and Greg came come home very early next day. They weren't expected quite so soon. I believe that my sister and Steve Donlon got a bit over-fond of each other. How over-fond I can only guess. Anyway, there was a lot of shouting, which woke me. I heard Steve barging into his bedroom which is next to mine. I'd just about had it with all the jealousies. Stanley insulting me because Sophie and I got on so well together and now Penny being accused of something or other. So I cleared off.'

'What time did you get back here?' Flynn looked up briefly from his notebook to ask the question.

Rod shrugged his shoulders. 'Must have been around half past eleven, getting on for midnight even, I'd say. I drove down to the Dingle peninsula and walked on the beach for a couple of hours. I needed to think about things, if you must know.' He looked at the two men as if debating what to tell them. 'I mean, Stanley Wallace paid for me to dry out – I already told you all about me and my little drink problem. Old Stanley gives me an allowance which keeps me going. I've wanted to break away from him for a long time.' He was silent for a minute or two before continuing. 'I intend getting a job. I've beaten the alcohol thing, I think. Time I left the fold.'

'You sound as if you don't care that much for Stanley Wallace,' Murray remarked.

'I hate him.' The words were surprising in their vehemence. 'He just likes controlling people. That was his way of controlling Penny.'

'Controlling your sister? How?' Rod Kirwin was burning with anger, Murray thought. Was it enough for him to hit Stanley Wallace over the head and kill him?

'He didn't want her to marry Greg. There was some kind of marriage settlement that if they ever got divorced she would not have a claim on Greg's fortune, she'd only get a minimum amount. In exchange for which Stanley would pay for my treatment and give me a monthly allowance. I expect no one thought I'd actually dry out and be able to keep myself.'

'I see.' Murray nodded, more to himself than to Rod. If Rod's information on the marriage settlement proved true it cast an interesting light on motive or lack of motive for murder. 'You arrived back here some time after half past eleven. How did you get in to the house?'

'How?' Rod looked puzzled for a minute. 'By the front door, of course. I parked Penny's car round the back but as it was so late I thought I'd better go in the front door as my room is at the front of the house and I wouldn't run into anyone.'

'Did you normally do that?' Murray asked.

'Sometimes I use the back door but my room is at the front of the house, over the library, in fact.'

'And you didn't hear or see anything unusual?'

Rod shook his head. 'Nothing.'

'Did you notice that one of the library windows was open?' This from Flynn.

'No, I'm afraid I didn't.'

'The light was left on in the library. Did you notice that?' Flynn continued his line of questioning.

Rod wrinkled his forehead. 'I don't know. I can't remember. I had other things on my mind.'

'But you'd have seen if there was a light on in the room?' persisted Murray. 'It would be impossible not to see a light in the library windows when you were approaching the front door.'

'Yeah,' Rod said. He ran a hand through his hair again. 'I just never took any notice. Everything seemed normal to me. I wanted to get up to my room as quickly as I could. I'm sorry I can't be of more help.'

Chapter Nineteen

Murray and Flynn stayed late at Killglash garda station going over all the statements they had taken.

'You know what's really strange about all this?' Flynn selected a piece of pizza from the cardboard box which Killglash's only Italian restaurant and takeaway had just delivered. 'A girl is found dead nearly on their doorstep and they don't seem worried. You'd think they would have installed security cameras, that sort of thing. Makes you think.'

'I can't see them having anything to do with Maike's murder,' Murray said. 'It doesn't make sense. She's a complete stranger to them. There'd be no reason to kill her. Not unless we're missing something vital. I hope we find her mobile phone soon, it might throw light on who she was in contact with before she was murdered. I have a gut feeling that the clue is there somewhere.'

'Rod Kirwin admits that he spoke to her in McDowds the night she was killed and a few witnesses have confirmed that they saw him talking to her,' Flynn objected. 'He might have made advances to her and got mad when she rejected him. Laid in wait for her in Ballyamber. Or someone else might have. We haven't finished talking to everyone who was in the pub that night.'

'She said she was meeting someone,' Murray said. 'She told the people at The Emerald B&B that and she told Rod that, too. It sort of tallies.'

'Do you think he's in the clear?' Flynn sounded doubtful.

'Mmm, no, no one's in the clear.' Murray spoke through a mouthful of pizza margherita with extra cheese. 'Rod Kirwin has a chip on his shoulder as big as the oak tree in Father Keegan's garden. But does that make him a killer?'

They were both silent for a few minutes, deep in thought.

'What's your take on the Stanley Wallace murder?' As he spoke Flynn dropped the uneaten half of his pizza back into its cardboard box and closed the lid. 'No sign of a break-in or a struggle of any sort, just a few things thrown around to make it look like a burglary. Must have been one of the family.'

'Looks like it at the moment,' Murray conceded. 'Gregory Wallace, Rod Kirwin or even Penny Wallace could easily have done it. As could Steve Donlon depending on when he left Ballyamber House. Their fingerprints will be all over the place including on that vase that was used to kill him.'

'The whole thing is going to be a huge headache,' Flynn said with relish. 'The media will be haunting us for the next week.'

'It'll be worth your while to get a new haircut before you appear on telly,' Murray said drily. 'Mind you, Percy won't want us stealing the limelight.'

As he negotiated the narrow mountain road back to Ballyamber, Murray went over all the events of the day. Flynn was right. The murder of Stanley Wallace would attract media interest, lots of it. Percy would take care of that side of things, giving statements and appealing for information. He would also draft in extra officers to help with enquiries although Murray would be in charge of the investigation. The pressure would be tremendous. Two murders within such a short space of time would have the media buzzing. Reporters would be analysing everything to see if they could find some connection however tenuous between Stanley Wallace and Maike Bloem. He could only hope that they did not dig so deep that they revived the mystery of Sheila's disappearance. Murray felt he had had all he could take on media interest in his wife's case.

Tomorrow would be a crazy day, he thought grimly, as he negotiated the last bend before the village. Here was Agnes O'Toole's house, windows dark, curtains closed. Had she really not seen or heard anything the night Maike was killed? The car's headlights picked out a dark figure emerging from behind the hedge which bordered Agnes' garden and in an instant he recognised Ginger Ford, Harold Brannigan's friend. They had checked out

Ginger and had not found anything suspicious in his past. What was he doing in Agnes' garden at this time of night? Murray wondered. He pulled up next to the man.

'Want a lift, Ginger?'

Ford bent down to look in through the car window. He wavered slightly on his feet and his voice was thick. 'Oh 'tis you Sergeant. I'm not doing any harm.'

'Where are you off to?'

'I'm going back to Harold's place.'

'You're a bit out of your way, aren't you? Were you visiting Agnes?'

'Visiting Agnes?' Ginger repeated. 'I hardly know the woman. I was down the pub and I wanted a walk before I went back to Harold's place. Can't drive when I've had a few drinks, can I? I took a leak in the garden, that's all.'

'Harold didn't come down the pub with you? Has he given up the drink?'

Ford straightened up, still swaying slightly. 'He wanted to watch sport on the telly, said he didn't have the money for a pint so I went off on me own. Not much to do here, is there?'

'And there's me thinking we're the Las Vegas of the South-East. Get in Ginger and I'll drop you down to Harold's cottage.'

Having dropped Ginger off Murray continued on his way in a still more thoughtful frame of mind. If Ginger found it so boring down here in Ballyamber why was he visiting Harold Brannigan? And another thing bothered him: Ginger might sound as if he'd had a few pints too many but there had not been much smell of alcohol from him. He would have to check with Agnes in the morning to see if anything was missing from her garden shed. It was one more thing in a very long "to do" list.

Chapter Twenty

The days following the murder of Stanley Wallace went by in a haze for Penny. Every corner of the house and grounds seemed to be invaded by white-suited figures from the Forensics team. Reporters appeared at the front door and a television crew spent a morning filming the area having been refused permission to enter the grounds. There was even a short interview with Agnes O'Toole on the evening news in which she aired the legend of Ardnabrone mountain claiming three lives a year, managing to convey the idea that anyone living within sight of Ardnabrone mountain was in danger of being cursed and this applied in particular to the residents of Ballyamber House. This slant on the story had at least the advantage of diverting media attention somewhat as did the news that Sophie Winslow had been a guest in the house. Sophie, currently staying with friends in Dublin, had said a few tearful words into the TV cameras before pleading for privacy. Another television crew was sent to film Ardnabrone and interview anyone prepared to talk about the murders of three women a few years before. Sergeant Murray – who declined to be interviewed - was cited as being the star detective who had found the killer and brought him to justice and there was inevitable mention of the fact that his wife Sheila had gone missing on the mountain several years before.

Penny should have found some comfort in the idea of having such a competent officer in charge of the case but it made her more uneasy than anything else. She had not told the gardai that Rod had come to see her on the night of the murder. Her brother's confession that he had given Maike Bloem a lift to Ballyamber weighed heavily on her and she was afraid of admitting anything which might make her give away more information than she or Rod wanted.

If she had thought her conversation with Sergeant Murray and Garda Flynn on the day Stanley Wallace's body was found had sufficed as a statement, she was soon proven wrong. She was interviewed again and at more length by two gardai from Killglash. She found it surprisingly easy to stick to her story of not having heard anything suspicious but she would have dearly loved to know what the result of all this questioning might be. She was starting to feel increasingly isolated. Gregory still kept her at a chilly distance. Although they took their meals together Gregory read the newspaper the entire time and escaped to the large salon as soon as they had eaten. Rod seemed to be avoiding her, too. He borrowed her car nearly every day and came back too late to have dinner with them.

She would gladly have taken the first flight back to London if that had been practicable but there was a lot of business to be attended to and Gregory needed her help. Thus she sat in her office on most days and typed up the letters which her husband had drafted, letters to all the shareholders in the various companies owned by her father-in-law and to anyone else connected with the business. It kept her busy but her thoughts wandered at any given moment. Who had killed Stanley Wallace and why? She remembered the look of pure hatred on Rod's face a few nights ago when Stanley had been so crushing in his remarks. Could it be possible that her brother had something to do with the murder? Was that why he was avoiding any opportunity of a tête-a-tête with her?

Alone in her bed at night, starting up at any strange sound in the house, her mind raced like a runaway train. What would become of herself and Greg? Would he keep up this cold politeness forever or would they be able to sit down and discuss it? Greg had not been brought up to discuss private feelings, to talk things out. His father had laid down the law and no one resisted him. Greg's mother had died when he was in his early teens but from remarks he had made Penny gathered that she had been more interested in a glamorous lifestyle than in objecting to any plans her husband might make. There was a price tag on being the wife of Stanley Wallace and she had been happy to pay it. Would they remain here in this village which she hated in a house where a murder had taken place? She desperately hoped that Greg would decide to put the house on the market and move back to London. They didn't belong here, they were unwelcome and they had made an enemy of that old witch Agnes O'Toole who had almost certainly put one of her special curses on them. When she got this far, Penny forced herself to calm down. She did not believe in witchcraft or evil spells, she assured herself. And yet, the sight of Agnes who still came on most days to stand in the driveway and stare up at the house as if wishing them all kinds of torment, kept intruding on her thoughts.

It was nearly a week after the murder before Steve Donlon contacted her. 'I'm sorry I haven't been in touch until now,' he said, his voice grave, 'actually I'm in Spain, in Alicante. When I got back to Dublin a friend of mine asked me to look at a few holiday homes with him. He's been badgering me about it for quite a while now. It couldn't have come at a better time after what happened so I jumped at the idea.'

'I see.' It sounded to her as if he had decided to make himself scarce and had found an excuse to do so. She could hardly blame him, she supposed. Had she had a choice she would have packed up and left too.

'This is a shocking business,' Steve went on. 'You must all be totally devastated.'

'We're all very upset, of course.' Her words sounded feeble even to her own ears. She was horrified at the murder of her father-in-law but some part of her was also relieved that she was free of his presence in her life.

'What have the gardai been doing? I take it they're asking questions. Have they mentioned me at all?'

'Well, of course they know you were here at the time it happened. They haven't said much about you, not to me anyway.'

'And you? How are you coping?'

She cringed at the intimate note in his voice. She did not know what was worse, hopping into bed with him so readily or later realising that she felt nothing for him. 'I'm being kept busy what with one thing and another,' she said. 'Greg has to deal with all sorts of queries. The funeral arrangements have to be sorted out, too, after the inquest is over. It's all very complicated.'

'I'll be coming down to Killglash soon,' Steve said, still speaking in that soft tone. 'Sergeant Murray contacted me and I've arranged to meet with him at Killglash garda station. I just need to tie up a few things here first. I'll see you at Ballyamber House.'

The last thing she wanted right now was to add the ingredient of Steve Donlon's presence to all the other undercurrents in the house. 'Are you sure that Greg will – allow that?'

'I've actually spoken to Greg last night. He wants me to complete the plans for Ballyamber House and has no objection to my staying there again.'

'What?' Penny put a hand to her head, wondering if she had heard correctly. 'You spoke to him?'

'Yes. It was only a short call. We didn't talk about anything personal. He contacted me, not the other way around. We're both professionals, after all. I suspect that he will want to sell the place but in order to get the most money for it, it needs a bit more work. Which is where I come in.'

'I see.' Having Steve around the place was a complication she did not think she could face. Had Greg really no objection to him coming back to Ballyamber House? Did it mean that Greg had found a way of coping with her infidelity, that it no longer hurt him as much as it had initially? If only he would talk to her, tell her what his thoughts were.

'We're going to have to be very discreet,' Steve was saying now. 'Neither of us want to start tongues wagging, especially not now after what happened to Stanley. We'll sort something out when I get there.' There was the sound of voices in the background and when he spoke again, it was to say in a hurried tone. 'I have to go. Bear up until I see you. Love you.'

She could not voice a reciprocal "love you" and wondered if Steve had noticed. She wasn't surprised that the gardai wanted to interview him, they had enquired about his whereabouts. Restlessly she stood up and went to the window which overlooked the approach to the house. Agnes O'Toole was standing where the drive curved, staring up at the house as usual. If I were superstitious, Penny thought with a little shiver, I'd almost believe that she did put a curse on us. Two murders in the space of a week and both of them right here. It almost seemed as if it couldn't be a coincidence.

Chapter Twenty-One

Murray took his seat at the top of the table in the incident room at Killglash garda station and faced the team which had been formed to work on the Stanley Wallace case. Although he was nominally in charge of both this case and the Maike Bloem murder investigation, Percy, who sat on his right, would keep a very close eye on both these cases which meant there would be regular meetings to report on progress. That was Percy's modus operandi although it did not suit Murray who thought that progress often came in leaps and bounds and was not necessarily guaranteed by prolonged status meetings.

He cleared his throat as a signal that he was about to start the briefing and the chatter in the room died down. 'According to the coroner, Stanley Wallace was killed by blunt force trauma to the head,' he said, referring to his notes. 'Time of death estimated at between approximately eleven o'clock when his son said goodnight to him downstairs in the library and when he was discovered at around nine o'clock this morning. He was fully clothed which might be an indicator of the timeframe of when he was killed. According to his son, he usually went to bed around midnight.' He paused a moment before continuing. 'A vase was found near the body and analysis shows it is the murder weapon. It is a heavy cut-glass affair and it would have required a bit of strength to pick it up and use it as a weapon, especially with such force. The vase was fractured and a piece of glass had cut the deceased's cheek.'

'What about fingerprints and any DNA on the vase?' Percy asked, sounding impatient. He was already feeling the pressure to solve this case as quickly as possible. 'How long before we get the lab results on that?'

Murray referred to his notes, more to hide his annoyance at being interrupted than to refresh his memory. 'Fingerprints were found on the vase. There is a partial fingerprint on the shard of glass. The forensic report says it looks as if the killer stood over the victim and moved the piece of broken glass slightly. Everyone who was in the house that night will be fingerprinted as will the workers who did the upstairs decorating some weeks ago, oh and Mrs Quinn the house keeper will have her prints taken as well.'

'That architect fellow Steve Donlon was there that night, wasn't he?'

'I've already spoken to him,' Murray said. 'He's coming in to see us as soon as he gets back from Spain. We'll get his fingerprints then for verification. We have isolated some prints in the house as most probably being his but as I say we have to confirm that for the record.' He would have been very thankful if Percy let him get on with his report without interrupting all the time.

'Good.' Percy nodded. 'So Wallace was in the library, still dressed when his son said goodnight to him. He might have been waiting for someone to call.'

Murray had already had his own thoughts on this aspect but decided not to comment at this stage. 'It would seem that Wallace was attacked from behind and beaten several times over the head with such force that the vase fractured,' he said. 'The first blow to the head must have stunned him. There are no defence marks of any kind. Either the killer sneaked up behind him or he knew his killer and wasn't expecting any threat.'

There was a murmur from the officers around the table at this information. 'This wasn't a burglary gone wrong, then?' The question came from Dan Foley.

'One of the windows was open but it hadn't been forced,' Murray said. 'The room had been trashed, chair cushions thrown around, the few books tossed onto the floor, that kind of thing. However, as far as anyone is aware, nothing is missing. Gregory Wallace told me that nothing of value was stored in the library as it hadn't been re-decorated yet. It looks as if Stanley Wallace was killed by someone in the house or someone he let in to the house, someone he knew. He seems to have been taken by surprise. What we're looking for now is motive. That should lead us to our killer.'

'Any connection with the Maike Bloem murder?' Again it was Dan Foley who asked the question.

'Not as far as we know but we're keeping an open mind on it.' Murray waited for any more questions but none came and soon afterwards the briefing was over.

As the officers filed out of the room, Percy turned to Murray. 'We need to get this sewn up as quick as we can,' he said. 'We can keep the media quiet for now by saying we're following several lines of enquiry but that won't keep them quiet for long. Not if we don't show any progress in the next week or so.'

Percy was forever stating the obvious, Murray thought wearily. 'If I were a gambling man, I'd say it was one of the family who killed Stanley Wallace,' he said. 'We'll get to the bottom of it.'

'Good.' Percy managed to make the word sound like a grunt of disapproval. 'Now what about this young Dutch girl? We're not making any progress on this, are we?'

'We need to clear up a couple of things. We haven't been able to interview everyone she spoke to on the night of her murder. She spent some time in McDowds pub. She mentioned to a few people that she was meeting someone but so far we haven't found out who that was. The barman who was on holiday has come back and he remembers seeing her but it was a busy night because there was a hen party of some kind. A lot of customers can't give a straight answer because they were pissed.'

'No clues from her parents or friends?'

Murray shook his head. 'Her mobile phone and her wallet are missing. If we could find her mobile it could tell us a lot.'

'I see what you mean,' Percy said. 'Who did she intend meeting up with? And why hasn't he – or she, I suppose it could be a she? – why don't they come forward to talk to us about it?'

'We have a long list to work through.' Murray felt in his pocket for his pack of cigarettes. Talking to his superior always made him crave a smoke.

Percy put a hand on Murray's shoulder in a rare gesture of solidarity. 'I've managed to get us a good team for this but we don't want to drag our feet. I know you'll do your best as always.' A thought occurred to him. 'Have the Dutch police located the boyfriend yet? He seems a possibility with that record of violence.'

'No luck as yet,' Murray said. 'He's what you might call The Flying Dutchman at the moment.'

Chapter Twenty-Two

'Sophie! How good of you to come back!' Greg's voice was warm with emotion as he enfolded his father's girlfriend in a tight embrace. He had come hurrying downstairs as soon as she arrived.

Penny stood to one side, watching them with a cold, sinking feeling in her stomach. It seemed to her that her husband was looking to this comparative stranger for comfort and it was no consolation to realise that it was all her own fault. Part of her wanted to run away and leave them to it, but a stubborn streak made her stand her ground. She'd play hostess to this unwelcome guest no matter what it cost, she vowed.

'Oh, Greg, I'm so shocked, so absolutely appalled! I came down as soon as I could get away.' Sophie moved back a step and flicked a tear from the corner of one eye with a red-tipped finger. 'What's been happening? How are you all? It says in the papers that no one has been arrested yet.'

'They've been doing tests, forensic stuff. We've had our fingerprints taken. It seems there is no sign that anyone broke into the house.' Greg hesitated as if he realised what that statement implied. 'They haven't told us much.'

'I hope they're not dragging their feet.' Sophie glanced briefly in Penny's direction. 'How absolutely awful for you all. Have the media been bombarding you? Stanley was such an influential figure in the business world, such a wonderful man.'

That sounded like a well-rehearsed statement to the media, Penny thought bitterly. Clearly Sophie would use her connections to the Wallace family to her own advantage. It was very possible that she sensed something amiss in Greg's marriage and had already picked him as her next partner. Judging by his behaviour, she might even be successful.

'I'll make us some tea,' she said, 'you must be tired after your journey down from Dublin.' She did her best to smile at Sophie before heading off towards the kitchen although it went against the grain not to be privy to their conversation.

Rod joined them for tea in the small salon which was where the family usually congregated. Penny presided at the small table by the window, helping everyone to tea and scones, jam and cream. She found herself relegated to the background as usual but as she had nothing to say to Sophie, this did not disturb her unduly. Most of her attention was focused on her brother who seemed completely engrossed by their guest.

'I hear you've been busy in Dublin,' Rod said, speaking in a soft tone to Sophie who sat on his right. 'Congratulations!'

'Yes, I've got a part in that new soap that's going into production in the summer.' Sophie smiled at him. 'It's all very much at the preliminary stages. They haven't even decided on a name for it as yet. Where did you hear about it?'

'Nothing's a secret these days,' Rod laughed. 'It was in the entertainment section of all the Irish papers. There's a stunning picture of you at the Cannes Film Festival last year. You starred in some French film, didn't you?'

'I had a small part in *Charlotte of Montmartre*. It's too much to say I starred in it. Anyway, it didn't win any awards.'

'Is this soap being shot in Ireland?' Gregory wanted to know.

'Yes, it will be set in Dublin. It's a joint English-Irish production. I'm playing a career woman who prefers business to men.' She gave a tinkling laugh which set Penny's teeth on edge.

'We really appreciate your coming down here,' Gregory said, determined to cut Rod out of the conversation. 'Sergeant Murray has been asking about you so I expect they'll want to have a word.'

'But I wasn't even here when – when all this happened.' Sophie turned her big blue eyes on him. 'I'm only too happy to talk to the gardai, of course, but I doubt if I can tell them anything that will help.'

'As I said, we really are grateful to you,' Gregory told her. 'I can come with you when you speak to Sergeant Murray. He's a very nice approachable man.'

'You were all here that night, weren't you?' Sophie looked round the table at them. 'You must have heard something, some disturbance, surely?'

'If we did, we'd have told the police, don't you think?' Rod said. He sounded annoyed. 'I don't think we need to play guessing games about it. The gardai are quite competent, in my opinion.'

'One of the windows in the library was open and it could be that this – person – came in that way,' Gregory said with a frown in Rod's direction. 'We'll have to beef up our security and get an alarm system and camera installed. I've been speaking to a company which does this kind of thing and they're sending someone round next week. We couldn't do much until the gardai were finished their forensic work.'

'With Agnes O'Toole playing the local witch, you'd think that Stanley would have been more careful.' Rod set his cup back in its saucer with rather more force than was necessary.

There was an awkward silence for a few moments. Penny tried to catch Rod's eye to signal her disapproval of his behaviour but he refused to look at her.

'Steve Donlon was here that night,' Gregory said suddenly with half a glance at Penny. 'He left next morning very early. He might have seen something. I'm sure the gardai will want to speak to him if they haven't done so already.'

'Speaking of witches,' Rod said. 'Does anyone think Agnes O'Toole might be responsible? After all she and Stanley were at loggerheads about selling that cottage of hers. I know she's old and feeble but she might have got someone to do it for her.'

'You don't believe in witches, do you?' Sophie gave a theatrical shiver. 'Ballyamber is a bit creepy I grant you with that big black mountain, but *witches*?'

'Of course we don't believe in witches.' Gregory reached out and put a hand on her arm. 'That's just hocus pocus. We're not afraid of that old woman. Don't you worry your head. They'll find out who did it.'

Penny sat and watched all three of them. Both Rod and Greg were completely caught in Sophie's web. They were already rivals for her attention. Not for the first time she wondered if Stanley's murder had been an act of jealousy and if so, by whom?

Chapter Twenty-Three

The mountain road from Killglash to Ballyamber had many dangerous twists and turns and required care and attention from road users but Murray's thoughts were elsewhere as he headed towards the village. He was due to meet with Jim Flynn at Ballyamber House for further questioning of the occupants but before that he wanted to check out Agnes O'Toole's cottage. She had never reported anything being stolen but that did not necessarily mean much. Agnes was not the type of person who sought help from the gardai, preferring no doubt to sort things out her own way. He wondered again what business Ginger Ford had in her garden the other night.

It took some minutes for Agnes to answer the door to him. He saw her peering through the window to see who her caller was and then the snick of a bolt being pulled back as she opened the door.

'Sergeant Murray!' She sounded anything but pleased to see him.

'Were you expecting to be invaded, Agnes?' Murray asked with a laugh. 'I've never known you to put that bolt across before, not during the daytime anyway.'

'You can't be too careful, what with all that's going on around here.' She pulled her threadbare cardigan more closely around her. 'Well, Sergeant Murray, have the gardai found out who killed that poor little girl?'

'Not yet,' said Murray. 'We're working on it, Agnes. You'll be the first to know.'

She squinted at him out of eyes set deep in her wrinkled face. 'And what about Stanley Wallace?'

'We'll get to the bottom of it,' Murray assured her. 'In the meantime, I think you're wise to keep the door bolted.'

'I keep a big stick by my bed,' she told him. 'Anyone comes in here will get his skull knocked in.'

Murray took in her skinny stooped figure and the hands gnarled with age and rheumatism. He doubted she could defend herself against anything more deadly than a wasp. She was not top of his list of suspects in Stanley Wallace's murder. It was possible, of course, that she knew someone who would do her dirty work for her. If village gossip was to be believed, she had employed people in the past to terrorise those she had a grudge against. But that was all a long time ago and he was not aware of any wrongdoing in the years since he transferred to Killglash garda station.

'Just be careful,' he said. 'You know I want you to get one of those alarms that you can press if you feel threatened at any time. There are some very good systems out there and they're not too expensive.'

'I'll think about it.'

Murray knew that this was the end of the discussion on this topic because he had been through it with her several times before. Ballyamber was a peaceful village and its crime rate was practically zero if you discounted the murders of three young women a couple of years ago. The villagers looked out for each other and although Agnes was treated with caution on account of her habit of cursing people, in general her neighbours kept an eye on her to see that she was all right. The idea of having an alarm system installed was completely foreign to her and to most of the villagers.

He decided to change the subject. 'Do you keep that garden shed locked up?'

'I keep the coal and wood in it and Ian Creedy puts stuff in there for the garden. There's a padlock on the door but I don't bother locking it. There's nothing in there that anyone would want to take.'

'Do you mind if I have a look?'

'No, go ahead.'

There was indeed a padlock on the door of the shed but as Agnes had stated, it had not been used to secure the door. The place had been searched as a matter of routine by the Forensic team when Maike's body was found but nothing out of the way had been discovered. He stood in the middle of the room, taking in the neat pile of logs in the corner and the bags of coal and garden fertilizer along one wall. An ancient table was propped against the other wall and several empty plant pots were stacked on top of it. Gardening implements were arranged neatly in boxes under the table. The floor and shelves were covered with a layer of dust. There was nothing remotely suspicious here. He was about to leave when a rustling noise attracted his attention. It seemed to come from where the coal bags were stored. Probably only a mouse, he thought, feeding off the few seeds from Agnes' flower pots. He leaned over to inspect the spot. At the back of the bags of coal and almost out of sight was a clear space as if something had stood there for a while protecting it from the dust. When he moved one of the heavy bags of coal, he saw that underneath it the floor was also free of dust. Whatever had stood here was wider than the coal bags and was more the size of a crate of some kind. The coal bags had been moved to disguise where it had stood.

Agnes had come to the door of the shed and was watching him with her shrewd eyes. 'What are you looking for, Sergeant Murray?'

'Do you know how many bags of coal you have here?'

'I've no idea. I always order a couple of bags from Creedys and I give Ian the money when he comes to do the garden for me. He takes care of that for me.'

'When did he deliver the coal last?'

'Oh that would be a couple of months ago, December or thereabouts. I always stock up for Christmas but now that I have the central heating in I don't use the open fire as much as I used to.'

Murray looked around him once more. Everything else seemed normal but that tell-tale clear space told him that Agnes' shed was used to store something other than bags of coal until recently. What was it and when had it been moved?

'Does Ian store anything else here?'

'Just the wood and the coal and the gardening stuff. He'll be doing some planting for me next week. I like to keep the garden nice.' Her eyes narrowed. 'Why do you want to know? Is something missing?'

'Nothing for you to worry about, Agnes. I'm just checking everything.' He would have another word with Ian Creedy, Murray decided. Ian had already given a statement and had an alibi for the time of Maike's murder but even if he was not involved in it, he might be able to throw some light on what had been stored in the shed.

'Does Ginger Ford ever come and visit you?'

'Ginger Ford? Brannigan's friend, is it? No, he's never called on me.'

'You're sure you've never seen him around here?'

She hesitated as if weighing up what she should say. 'I might have seen Ginger walking on the road once or twice but not to speak to, you know. I expect he doesn't know what to do with himself during the day when Brannigan is working.'

Murray remembered a quotation – he wasn't sure from where – which said something about "the lady doth protest too much". There was more than a grain of truth in it, as he had often observed. Agnes was not telling the truth, not the whole truth anyway. And why was she suddenly so security-conscious? He did not believe that Maike Bloem's murder or if it came to that Stanley Wallace's murder would account for her behaviour. The consensus of opinion in the village was that both victims were killed by someone known to them who had nothing to do with Ballyamber. The increased garda activities in the area served to reassure them further. Agnes bolting her door during the day was out of character. Did she feel threatened or was she actually being threatened and if so, who was doing the threatening and why? Ginger? Brannigan? Or someone else?

Murray stood looking down at the wizened old woman and thought how he would like to shake the truth out of her. What had Ginger Ford been doing up here the other night? Was he involved in some illegal activity in the area unbeknownst to the gardai? Did Agnes know about it or think she knew? Was she even involved in it? That expensive furniture he had seen in her little cottage could be the result of someone paying her to use her shed and keep her mouth shut. Would the old woman really agree to something like that? Or was his imagination working overtime?

'If you see Ginger around here again let me know, will you?'

'Ginger is yer man, is he? Suspect Number One as they say on them crime stories on the telly.' Agnes gave that cackling laugh again but somehow it did not ring true to Murray's ears.

'Take care of yourself, Agnes,' he said as he took leave of her and even though the words sounded trite he really meant it.

He drove up the avenue to Ballyamber House in a thoughtful frame of mind. Agnes was a character with a reputation for putting curses on people who crossed her and while most of the villagers did not believe she had any magical powers, they found it better not to get in her bad books and left her to her own devices. She enjoyed her reputation and managed to look as mysterious as possible whenever she went into the village to do her shopping or collect her pension. If she were involved in anything illegal she might well have bitten off more than she could chew. Criminals would be several steps ahead of her no matter how clever she thought herself.

Jim Flynn was waiting for him at Ballyamber House and greeted him with: 'Has Agnes been mixing a potion for you?'

'One of Agnes' concoctions might be better than all the forensics in CSI,' Murray said. 'Now, who are we interviewing first today?'

'The lovely Sophie Winslow. I saw on the papers that she's got a part in an Irish soap.'

'Glamour comes to Ballyamber. Another beauty for you to fall in love with, Jim. I'd be wary of these show business damsels. They'd be after your body and your payroll.'

Flynn rolled his eyes but made no answer and as the door was opened to them by Gregory Wallace both men immediately returned to the business at hand.

Chapter Twenty-Four

Sophie Winslow had the self-assured air of someone who was well used to being the centre of attention. Murray had the feeling that she was sizing himself and Flynn up just as much as they her.

'It's very good of you to talk to us,' he said when they were seated and the usual expressions of regret at Stanley Wallace's passing had been made and Sophie had pronounced herself "deeply saddened and shocked".

'Anything I can do to help.' She dabbed at the corner of one eye with a wisp of lace. 'What can I tell you, Sergeant?'

'There was a birthday party for you here in Ballyamber House and I believe that there was some kind of altercation between Stanley Wallace and Rod Kirwin that night. Could you tell us what happened?'

'Altercation! How serious you make it sound! Rod danced with me a few times and Stanley was a teeny bit jealous.' She crossed one slim ankle over the other. 'Men can be so – possessive, can't they?'

'Can you tell us more about this – altercation?'

Sophie hesitated for a moment. 'As I said, Rod and I danced together a few times. Rod is very charming, I have to admit, but of course I was not going to take him seriously. Stanley didn't like all this attention which Rod was paying me and so he took us both to one side and asked Rod to leave me alone. That was all.'

'Rod didn't protest or object in any way?' Murray recalled that in his conversation with Rod, he had claimed to have taken a swing at Stanley although he didn't actually hit him and that Sophie had been crying and begged them to stop.

'We're civilized people, Sergeant Murray. Rod apologised and that was that.'

'Did Rod remain at the party?'

She seemed puzzled by the question. The faintest of frowns appeared between her well manicured eyebrows. 'I imagine he did. To be honest I don't remember seeing him afterwards. We avoided each other for the rest of the evening – obviously.'

'What happened next morning when the party was over? Was everyone back to normal with each other?'

'Why yes, of course. We all had a late breakfast with our guests. Stanley and Rod drove some people to the airport. Everyone was a little bit tired, the party went on quite late and I suppose there were a few hangovers.' She smiled at both men, as if sharing a secret, then added with a more serious expression. 'Stanley and Rod were on good terms again, or seemed to be.'

'Have you any idea why someone would want to kill Stanley Wallace?' It was Flynn who asked the question.

'I have absolutely no idea. He was such a kind generous man.' Here she was stopped by a sob and she put a hand to her mouth before continuing after a moment. 'As far as enemies are concerned, I'm afraid I never knew anything about that side of his life.'

When she had left the room to fetch Rod, Murray turned to Flynn. 'Well Jim, that's a woman to make you kick a hole in our lovely garda station window.'

Flynn rolled his eyes. 'Don't let Percy hear you say that.'

'I think she invented herself,' Murray said slowly, 'she thinks she's starring in the Ballyamber House soap of the year.'

'She doesn't seem too put out about what happened to Stanley Wallace,' Flynn remarked. 'It's a bit surprising that she came down here again. We could have arranged an interview with her in Dublin.'

'Percy let you off to the fleshpots of Dublin?' Murray gave a short laugh. 'That's not even worth half a thought. But I agree with you about Sophie not seeming too heartbroken. A few tears wiped away with a lace handkerchief. Is she trying to protect Rod or just imagining that things were all right between himself and Stanley again? There's bound to have been a bit of antagonism there after what happened. I think Rod was telling us the truth when he said he took a swing at Stanley. It's interesting that she didn't tell us that.'

'She probably doesn't want to be mixed up in any scandal,' Flynn said. 'You can imagine what the media would make of it all. The question is, was Rod sufficiently angry and jealous to want to get Stanley out of the way? And if he was, did he hit him over the head with that vase?'

'Rod is certainly a person of interest,' Murray mused. 'He came home late the night Stanley was murdered. Claims he doesn't know if there was a light on in the library. At any rate, as far as we can piece it together, Stanley said goodnight to Gregory and stayed on in the library instead of going to bed. Just why he did that, we don't know. He might have been waiting up for someone. At some time during the night he met his attacker. Did he let him in himself? Or was it someone already in the house?'

'It's not likely Rod Kirwin would kill two people within a short space of time. Unless of course he is responsible for Maike's murder and Stanley knew something to incriminate him and confronted him with it. Only it's hard to imagine what that might be.'

'I think we're going to have to concentrate on Penny Wallace in order to get a handle on this case,' Murray said thoughtfully. 'She's the weakest link in their little chain of perfection.'

Chapter Twenty-Five

As soon as Penny heard the door of the small salon open and voices in the corridor she hurried to where Rod was in the process of showing out Alan Murray and Jim Flynn. Gregory had told her he was taking Sophie into Killglash so she knew she would be alone with her brother. It was an opportunity too good to miss.

'Let's go and have a coffee in the kitchen,' she said when the two officers had taken leave. 'I need to talk to you.'

Rod followed her slowly. 'What's the matter, Penny?'

She closed the kitchen door behind them and put on the kettle. 'What did the police have to say to you this time?' She kept her back to him as she took down two mugs from the tall cupboard above the cooker and spooned coffee into them.

'The usual.' He pulled out a chair from the table and sat down. 'What did you think? That they suspect me of killing Stanley?'

'Well, do they? I expect you told them that you were out that night. Perhaps they thought you did it when you got home.' She carefully poured boiling water then stood at the table clutching the mugs for a moment before putting them down. Her hands were shaking.

'Sister dear,' Rod leaned back in his chair and studied her expression, a smile on his face. 'Why on earth would I want to do something like that?'

'You had an argument with him over Sophie Winslow at the party on Saturday. You could have started fighting with him again.' Her words came out in a rush, two spots of colour burned on her cheeks. 'And then there's the young Dutch girl. You spoke to her in McDowd's pub.' Her voice trailed away as she looked at him.

'You reckon I might be accused of killing two people, now?' Rod gave her another of his mocking smiles. 'What a dangerous person, eh? You must be really proud of me.'

'I know you would never harm anybody but the police don't know that.' A tear inched its way from the corner of her eye and she brushed it away impatiently. She sat down abruptly in the chair opposite him.

Rod reached across and covered both her cold hands in his. 'Bear up, Penny. I didn't kill anyone.' He took his hands away again and concentrated on putting three spoons of sugar in his coffee, stirring the dark liquid vigorously. 'The question is what happens now,' he went on. 'Are you and Greg going to remain here in Ballyamber House or are you going back to civilisation where you belong?'

'I don't know,' Penny admitted. 'Oh Rod, ever since I made that stupid mistake with Steve Donlon, Greg hasn't spoken more than two words to me. He's taken off to Killglash with Sophie this afternoon rather than stay here in the house.' She was crying in earnest now, the tears trickling down her face. 'I don't know what to do for the best.'

'He'll get over it,' Rod spoke confidently. 'He's obviously in shock over his father's death. You mustn't forget that.'

Penny fished a tissue out of the pocket of her jeans and blew her nose. 'I hate it here,' she said. 'I want to go back to London. Now that Stanley's dead, there's nothing to keep us here as far as I can see.'

'I imagine that's why Greg is asking Donlon to come down and finish off the designing he was doing for Stanley. You surely don't need to hang around when the workmen come back and start doing their thing.'

She took a sip of coffee. 'But we can't leave until Stanley's murder is solved. I'm sure the gardai would object to that.'

'Quite right. But I assure you that I had nothing to do with it. Yes, we had a bit of a tiff over beautiful Sophie but really I was only paying attention to her because the party was just too boring otherwise.' He smiled again, as if at some secret pleasant memory.

Penny turned troubled eyes on him. 'But Rod, if it wasn't a burglary gone wrong, then it must be – ' she broke off, staring at him with a look of sheer terror on her face. 'I mean, if it wasn't,' she tried again to formulate the words but had to swallow hard before she could finish the sentence. 'If it wasn't you and it wasn't a burglar, that means it could only be Greg or Steve or me, I suppose, except it wasn't me.'

'Which is what the gardai think, no doubt.'

'But could it be true? I don't think Greg would ever do anything to harm his father, not in a million years.'

'You mean, you think Steve Donlon did it?'

'I don't know.' She put her hands up to her face in a defensive gesture. 'It's impossible to believe that anyone we know did it. Of course I don't believe that Steve was involved. He'd left the house long before it happened.' Again she remembered those footsteps and the muffled voices downstairs. And what had sounded like the creak of floorboards in the room above her bedroom. 'Rod, have you ever heard or seen anyone in the attic?'

He looked startled. 'In the attic? No, I can't say I have. I know that old Stanley wanted to do something with the space up there. He and Donlon have been up there a few times. Why do you ask?'

'It's just that I thought I heard footsteps the other night after you left, and come to think of it, I've heard floorboards creaking a few times. I could swear the noise was coming from up there.'

'I expect it was mice or rats or something. Wood creaks a lot, you know, especially in these old houses. Are you scared here now?' He sounded concerned.

'N-no, not really scared.' She gave a little shrug. 'Yes, I am scared if I think about it. There was no sign of a break-in and nothing was taken. Stanley must have been killed by someone with a grudge against him or against all of us, if it comes to that.'

'Stanley had a lot of enemies,' Rod said with feeling. 'Maybe one of them snuck down here to Ballyamber, hid in the shrubbery and did him in when we were all in bed.'

Penny picked up her coffee mug, avoiding Rod's amused gaze. 'I don't know how you can make so light of it.'

'Because I never liked the old bastard. Yes, I'm sorry he got knocked off but I'm not going to be hypocritical and pretend to cry over it.'

'Why did we ever come here? There's been nothing but trouble from day one.' She let out her breath in a gusty sigh. 'Oh god, how I wish it were all sorted out and finished with and we were back in

London again. I would give anything to be able to walk out of this place and never set eyes on it again.'

'Do your best to make up to Greg,' Rod said gently. 'He's the one with the money, sweetheart. And I think he cares about you. After all he married you despite old man Stanley having a fit.'

The mention of money caused a sudden stir of anger in Penny. Rod had always been a problem even when they were children. She had covered up for him, defending him against every criticism and bailing him out when his misdemeanours threatened to get him into serious trouble. Upon her parents' death she had felt herself doubly obliged to look out for him, to lend him money she knew she would never get back. Greg had not been so understanding of her brother's behaviour but she had managed to convince him that Rod needed treatment for his alcoholism. Greg had spoken to his father about the matter and Stanley had come up with the idea of a special agreement in which he paid for Rod's treatment in a renowned clinic and afterwards, provided he cooperated fully with the rehabilitation measures, he was to receive a small monthly allowance until he returned to work. In the meantime, he was allowed to stay at Ballyamber House until he found suitable employment. She had to admit that it was a very generous arrangement, one that surprised her. Stanley had never made any secret of his contempt for Rod. She wondered, not for the first time, if her brother was actively looking for a job. Somehow she doubted it. He might complain about the dullness of country life and his comparative penury but his current idleness appeared to suit him.

'I daresay you'll be glad to return to London,' she said now, trying not to sound waspish. He was her only ally after all and it would do no good to fall out with him. 'It should be easier to get a job there.'

'I would have said yes, yes, yes, to that remark up to maybe a week ago.' Rod grinned at her. 'Haven't you noticed? I've fallen in love.'

Chapter Twenty-Six

It was dark and the rain was coming down in torrents as Murray pulled up outside the cottage where he lived and switched off the engine. He sat for a moment without moving and as was his wont, went over all the events of the day, ticking things off in his head in the vague hope this might help him get a better night's sleep than the last few nights. The two murder cases and their lack of progress bothered him more than he cared to admit. Investigations were slow and methodical – that was the way he liked to work – but sometimes he hoped for a breakthrough like the ones seen on television. Sitting in his car like this he could admit his frustrations to himself. At Killglash garda station he had to keep up the appearance of having everything under control.

As he got out of the car the door to the cottage next door opened and Nicola appeared, her body silhouetted against the light which streamed out onto the path.

'Alan, could you come in a minute? If you have time, that is.'

'Sure. No problem.' When did he ever say no?

He followed her into the little living room which he knew so well from the days when Elena had lived here. Elena had done a lot with the place. She had turned the kitchen into a cosy living cum dining area, banishing the kitchen to a small built-on at the back of the premises. And she had been his anchor, his soul mate, he could now acknowledge to himself.

'I'm sorry to bother you,' Nicola said in that apologetic tone she so often used. 'Please sit down.' She gestured towards the armchairs on either side of the fireplace.

'What's the problem?' Murray was bone tired and would have liked a shot of whiskey and a cigarette although he knew he was not in line for either of those two things. Which reminded him of Elena again. How many nights had he sat here drinking a hot toddy while she cooked them dinner? He pushed the thought away and concentrated his attention on Nicola.

'It's about Vanessa,' she said, perching on the armrest of the other chair. 'I just don't know how to handle her at the moment. She isn't home yet and its after ten o'clock.'

'You mean you don't know where she is?'

'She told me that she was going to the cinema with her friend Eileen and she'd be back by ten o'clock and it's gone that now. It's possible that the show isn't over yet.' Nicola began to play with the colourful bangles she wore on her left arm. 'Eileen's mother is supposed to collect them but when I met her she gave me the impression of being a bit unreliable, if you know what I mean? I think Eileen is allowed do what she likes. I don't want Vanessa hanging around Killglash.' She looked at him anxiously. 'Or do you think I'm being too fussy?'

'Where does Eileen live? Here in Ballyamber?' He suspected that this was all just a pretext to talk to him. He was at a loss as to how he should react. If she really needed help, he liked to think that he was there for her but he did not want to encourage any other feelings she might harbour.

'Her parents are farmers, they live a couple of miles from Ballyamber.'

Murray thought it over but couldn't see the problem. Then again, he reminded himself, he had no children of his own and therefore no experience in teenage matters.

'Why not arrange with Eileen's mother next time that you'll pick the girls up and drive them home?

'You're right.' She sighed loudly. 'I'm being a nuisance, I know. It's just that with all the things going on around here, I get worried if she's not home on time.' She looked at him anxiously. 'Are the gardai making progress on finding out who killed that poor Dutch girl? The very thought of anything like that —'

'We're working on it.'

'I know, I'm sorry. I expect everyone asks you the same stupid question.' She smiled uncertainly at him. 'The newspapers have been saying how you solved the murders of those three girls here in the village. You're quite a hero.'

Murray waved a hand in dismissal. 'To get back to Vanessa,' he said. 'I don't know about these things but I would have thought she was an intelligent girl with a mind of her own. I'm sure she's well able to look after herself but I don't advocate anyone, young or old, male or female, taking silly risks. As long as there are arrangements in place on how she gets home, I shouldn't think you need worry.'

'This friendship with Eileen is fairly new,' Nicola said. 'I've only seen her once when she and her mother called here to pick up Vanessa. Do you know the family at all? Quirke I think is the name.'

'Yes, I know the Quirke family. They've been here since Noah beached the Ark. They're a good solid family. Eileen is the middle child.'

The smile she gave him was whole-hearted now. 'Then I suppose I have nothing to worry about. I'm glad she's making friends. I don't get out much myself.'

'It takes time to settle in a new place,' Murray said, aware that this could be dangerous ground. He stood up. 'I'd better be getting home. It's been a long day. Take care of yourself.' He was gone before she could do more than wish him goodnight.

No use encouraging her, he told himself as he hung up his jacket in his cottage. Sure, it would be nice to have female company but hardly fair to let her think he was interested in forming any kind of relationship. He surveyed the pile of ashes in the hearth and debated whether it was worth his while to get the fire going. He liked the comfort of it but he felt too bone tired to go to all the bother of cleaning out the grate. The central heating was on a low setting and the room was chilly. A hot whiskey was the best answer he decided and proceeded to make himself one. There was a tap at the door just as he was carrying the glass with the steaming liquid over to the armchair by the fireplace. He put the glass down on the table and went to open the door.

Nicola was standing on the doorstep.

'Sorry to bother you, again.'

She sounded a little out of breath. 'I forgot to mention that I read in the papers today that this Dutch tourist's mobile phone was missing. Vanessa's phone has been missing since round about the same time. I thought I should tell you, just in case it has any bearing on the case.'

Chapter Twenty-Seven

'I'm going to pop into Killglash to do some shopping, we're out of butter and tea, of all things,' Penny said as she, Gregory and Rod were having breakfast. Sophie Winslow had returned to Dublin the previous evening following a call from her agent, leaving the three of them to their own devices. Penny might not like Sophie but she found that at mealtimes she would have been glad of her never-ending supply of small talk (mainly centred around Sophie) even if it meant Gregory hanging on her every word.

'Like to come with me, Rod?'

She turned to her brother who was moodily spreading marmalade on his toast. He wasn't usually up so early but she was glad of his company at the table. Gregory was still ignoring her for the most part while being extremely polite at the same time. It was like being a guest in her own home, she sometimes thought.

Rod pulled a face. 'I'd hoped to be able to use your car today.'

'I'm sorry but I need it to do the shopping.' She cast a quick glance in Gregory's direction, hoping he might offer to drive her to Killglash.

'Steve Donlon should be here soon,' Gregory said without looking at her. He helped himself to one of Mrs Quinn's floury scones. 'There's a lot of work to be done so I'll be tied up with him most of the day. I'll need my car as we're planning to drive to Tralee to talk to a builder who might do some work on the house for us.'

Penny's heart gave a quick bump. She hadn't realised that Steve was coming today. When they had spoken on the phone he had not mentioned a time. She would have to find an opportunity of speaking to him and confessing that she did not care for him and their affair was over. The sooner she cleared the air between them the better, she told herself, however distressing it was likely to be.

'Can't you use Donlon's car?' Rod sounded sulky.

Gregory gave him a withering look. 'I prefer not to. He charges the earth as it is.' He spread a thick layer of jam over the buttered scone then put it down on his plate. 'Look, Rod. I think you need to start looking for a job in earnest. You won't find anything around here, will you? I suggest you think about going back to London and making an effort to find suitable work.'

'I'm not sure the gardai would approve if I took off at this stage. Don't worry, I won't trespass on your hospitality longer than need be.'

Penny looked from one to the other of the two men. Here we go again, she thought. Gregory had taken over where Stanley had left off. She was intrigued by Rod's evident reluctance to leave Ballyamber. It seemed that he had spoken the truth the other night when he had laughingly told her he was in love. He'd refused to say who the girl was, only that she was from the area. 'I'm deadly serious,' he'd said. 'It's the most wonderful thing that's ever happened to me. You'll get to meet her, don't you worry, but give me a bit of time to pave the way.' Not for the first time she wondered who it could be and also why he felt the need to keep it a secret. Perhaps she was a married woman. It would be just like Rod to get himself involved in a complicated messy relationship. One thing was for sure, she acknowledged to herself, she was more than glad that Sophie Winslow was not the girl of his dreams. Or was she?

'I shouldn't need more than an hour or so to do the shopping,' she said now. 'You can have the car after that.'

'Thanks. Appreciate it.' The smile her brother gave her was a little strained.

'I thought we might go out to dinner tonight with Donlon,' Gregory said slowly as if the idea had just occurred to him. 'There's that restaurant in Killarney that we've been to before. Sweeney's Pavilion I think it's called.' He turned to Penny. 'What do you think? It's Saturday night, should we book a table?'

Penny was both surprised and pleased that he asked her opinion even if Steve's presence would be awkward. But perhaps she'd be able to talk to him beforehand and let him know her feelings. If he was going to be around for a while, the sooner they both knew where they stood the better.

'I believe it's a popular place,' she said in answer to her husband's question. 'I've heard Mrs Quinn mention it once or twice. It's probably wise to make a reservation. What time do you suggest?'

'Half past seven a good time?' Gregory turned to Rod. 'Are you going to join us?'

'Thank you, but I have other plans for the evening.'

Gregory inclined his head. 'Don't forget what I said about looking for a job.'

Killglash was a busy little town on a Saturday morning. Even though it was still fairly early, there was an endless procession of cars down the main street. Everyone seemed to be determined to get their weekend shopping out of the way. Afterwards they would descend on the various little cafes and pubs and treat themselves to lunch or tea and scones before heading home. It was a Saturday ritual.

Penny was still not used to the way the locals drove with so little regard for the rules of the road. The car in front of her was a case in point. The driver, who had been chugging along, was obviously looking for a parking space and seeing one at the last minute slammed on his brakes, causing her to do the same. She stifled the urge to blow the horn and wave her fist. Instead she managed to negotiate past him and a few minutes later reached the supermarket where she slipped into a vacant space without any further mishaps. She could have made most of her purchases in Gleason's in Ballyamber, it was very well stocked and not noticeably more expensive than the supermarket in Killglash, but she needed a break from Ballyamber House. Both Greg and Rod were getting on her nerves. When she had finished her shopping, she decided she would imitate the locals and treat herself to a coffee at one of the little cafes in the town square.

She had not been seated there long when a familiar figure entered the café and upon catching sight of her made his way over to her table.

'Mind if I join you?' Alan Murray pulled out a chair as he spoke and sat down opposite her, dropping the newspaper he was carrying onto the table.

Penny's heart plummeted. 'Of course not.' She forced a smile at him then looked at her watch. 'I have to be going in a few minutes, though.'

'Don't let me frighten you off.' Murray ordered a cappuccino from the waitress then leaned back in his chair as if prepared for a long chat. 'They make great coffee here.'

'Yes,' she said. For the life of her she couldn't think of anything else to say.

'So how have you been keeping? This must all be a terrible strain on you.'

'It has all not - been easy.' She hesitated before continuing. 'I'm sure that you will find the person responsible. Until then, of course, we are all very', she searched for a word 'traumatised.'

'We're working flat out, believe me,' Murray said. He tapped the newspaper which was folded to reveal a column headed *Killglash gardai searching for victim's mobile*. 'The media are doing their best to help us. I hope they haven't been hounding you all too much at Ballyamber House?'

'Things have died down,' she told him. 'At the moment there isn't much for them to report on. Especially not now that Sophie has left us.'

'We all have a love-hate relationship with reporters,' Murray said. 'But they do a good job in cases like this.'

'Have you any hope of finding who killed Stanley?' She toyed with her coffee cup. 'Or the Dutch girl? The murders aren't linked are they?'

'Oh, we'll find the killer or killers.' He paused while the waitress set down his cappuccino on the table, moving the newspaper to accommodate her. When she had gone, he turned his attention back to Penny. 'How is your brother doing? He comes to Killglash a lot. I expect it's a bit quiet for him around here.'

Penny did not know why this remark should frighten her. Was Rod really a suspect in the murder of that Dutch girl? 'Rod is an alcoholic,' she said, deciding to be open and frank about it. 'He's stayed dry for several months now and I'm hoping that he's turned his life around. It was most unfortunate that he spoke to that poor girl on the night she was murdered. Rod is the last person to want to hurt anybody.'

'Did he talk to you about that night?'

'Yes, he assured me he did not harm her.' She took a last sip of coffee and set down her cup, annoyed to find that her hands were shaking. 'I expect you've spoken to him about all that yourself,' she added.

'Mrs Wallace,' Murray said, his tone gentle, 'if you want to talk to me or to anyone else at Killglash garda station at any time, if something occurs to you which you think we should know or if something is bothering you and you just need to talk it over, please do not hesitate to get in touch with us. You can call on me at home if you wish. As you probably know, I live just down the road from Ballyamber House at the end of the village.'

'Thank you, Sergeant. I'll remember that.' It would be such a tremendous relief to do just that, sit down with Murray and confide in him all the worries that were tormenting her: Rod's admission that he'd given that girl a lift to Ballyamber and the footsteps she had heard on the stairs the night of Stanley's murder. But she had given Rod her word and as for those footsteps, she was not sure whose they were and even if they mattered.

Murray's phone pinged, putting an end to their conversation. He excused himself and got up from the table to take the call. Penny felt the beads of perspiration on her forehead as she left the café and headed back to where she had parked her car. The sun had just come out from behind dark clouds and it looked like the day might clear up. It would be nice to take a drive over the mountains to one of the little beaches and get some sea air, she thought suddenly. The prospect of returning to the tensions at Ballyamber House was not inviting, especially as by now Steve Donlon would have arrived. Part of her wished suddenly to prolong her morning of freedom. She stood for a moment, car keys in hand and then decided against it. Rod was waiting for her to get back with the car. Perhaps he was meeting this girl he had fallen in love with. As she still half hesitated, her attention was caught by the glint of sun on some object which was poking out from underneath the backseat of the car. It was a mobile phone.

Chapter Twenty-Eight

'Two things,' said Jim Flynn when Murray returned to the incident room at Killglash garda station following his meeting with Penny Wallace. 'Maike Bloem's abusive boyfriend has been located. He was camping in the South of France in the mountains with a group of friends and says he wasn't getting a signal on his mobile. It seems he's in to this survival stuff or something of that sort. He's now back in Zandervoort and has given a statement to the police. His friends have vouched for him, they say he was with them the entire time.'

'I never really bought him as our man,' Murray said thoughtfully. 'He'd hardly show up in a small community like Killglash to kill her, a place where he'd stick out like a daffodil in a bunch of tulips.'

Flynn nodded agreement. 'We've finished interviewing everyone who was at McDowds pub the night of her murder. A fellow by the name of Patrick O'Sullivan says he is pretty sure that he saw Rod Kirwin and two girls getting into a car that night. He wasn't in the pub, he says, he was visiting his sister and her family and he left his car in the car park at the back of the pub. Rod and the two girls walked to a car and he only took note of them because they were laughing and giving the impression of being a bit drunk. According to Patrick, Rod had his arm around one of the girls.'

'Rod Kirwin and two girls.' Murray leaned back in his chair and looked at Flynn. 'I take it that Patrick was shown a photo of Maike?'

'Oh yes, and he thinks she could be one of the girls. It was dark and he only got a glimpse but one of the girls had long blonde hair like Maike's. Rod had his arm around the other girl. She was a stranger to Patrick. He's not a local.'

'Well, well, our dear friend Rod Kirwin. He told us he only chatted to Maike very briefly and that she was with a group of other hikers. Now it turns out he was with two girls, one with long blonde hair, on the night of Maike's murder. So he has something to hide. But what? What motive could he possibly have? And who was this girl in the circle of his arm?'

'The circle of his arm.' Flynn gave the ghost of a smile. 'Very romantic, Alan. But we both know that the nice young man, the boy next door who wouldn't harm a fly, is sometimes our man.'

'The nice guy who goes out killing people is usually a character with a couple of dark problems who nobody notices,' Murray said slowly. 'There's something odd about this killing. I'd say it was done in a hurry and her body dumped as quickly as possible. Whoever did it must know she'd be discovered fairly easily. It looks to me as if he wanted to make a quick getaway, so he was not intending to kill or he'd have thought of a better way to hide his tracks. Rod doesn't really fit. He's a recovering alcoholic as the clever specialists call it and he has a sister who probably dotes on him. In other words, family who've been keeping an eye on him. He has a bit of a chip on his shoulder, I'll grant you that, but we haven't been able to turn up one single thing about him which would raise a red flag. Why would he kill a Dutch tourist who he was seen talking to in McDowd's pub on the night she was murdered? Doesn't really add up unless I'm missing a few lines from the plot.'

Flynn consulted his notes. 'Patrick O'Sullivan is pretty sure it was Rod that he saw with two girls,' he said. 'The lighting isn't great in the car park and he only got a glimpse as he drove past them. They were just getting into the car.'

Murray sat in silence for some minutes going over this new information. The team working on the two murders had put in countless hours and interviewed numerous individuals. Sooner or later someone or something would provide the key to unlock the mystery of the young girl's death. A German colleague he had met many years ago had called it *Inspector Zufall,* Inspector Coincidence.

'I don't think I know Patrick O'Sullivan,' he said. 'Have you spoken to him yourself?'

'Yes, I went to see him this morning. He lives in Killarney. He has a bakery shop. Seems a reliable witness.'

'How can he be so sure it was Rod Kirwin if he's not a local man?'

'Rod has bought sandwiches in his shop now and again when he's been out and about doing the sights. Patrick says he's a very nice chatty fellow. He told him about staying at Ballyamber House and that he was at a bit of a loose end down here.'

'OK, that sounds fair enough. Anything new on Stanley Wallace?'

Flynn shook his head. 'Fingerprints all over the place, including the murder weapon but they all belong to the people who were staying at Ballyamber House. We don't have a motive here, either, and that's the crux of the matter. Who wanted to kill him? It could be our friend Rod Kirwin, they did have a row on the night of Sophie Winslow's birthday party.'

'Or Steve Donlon, our star architect. He was in Spain doing some work on a holiday home of some well-heeled businessman or other when I spoke to him. He acted very surprised and concerned about Stanley Wallace's murder. He contacted me yesterday to say that he's coming down to Ballyamber House to finish off some work he was commissioned to do. I've arranged an interview with him tomorrow morning and I'd like you to sit in on it. He and Penny Wallace have a thing for each other, as Rod told us. We'll have to get to the bottom of that.'

'It would have made more sense if Gregory Wallace was the victim and not his father if they were playing around,' Flynn observed. 'Penny Wallace herself might even have done it, if you think about it. Or someone from Stanley Wallace's past might have wanted to avenge a grudge. He's bound to have made a few enemies over the years. We haven't finished our enquiries on that yet.'

'Hmm.' Murray lapsed into silence again while Flynn moodily looked over his notes. The next briefing on the two murders would be held tomorrow morning. Both men were acutely aware that they needed more information in order to move the investigation in the right direction.

'There's another question mark in this whole thing,' Murray said after another minute or two of silence between them. 'Agnes O'Toole seems to have plenty of money. I think something was stored in her garden shed until recently. Putting two and two together I'd say she either got money for letting whoever it was store contraband there or she caught them red-handed and blackmailed them. I wouldn't put either theory past her. So far so good. The last time I spoke to her, though, she seemed a bit nervous. I've never known her to bolt her door, certainly not during the day. What's worrying her, I wonder?'

'And does it have any bearing on our two murder cases?' Flynn added. 'You said you saw Ginger Ford at her place late the other night. Himself and Brannigan might be into some kind of mischief and using that shed.'

'And there's the fellow who told us he saw lights in the woods up near Ballyamber House. The lads should be finished searching up there by this evening. I wonder if they'll find anything of interest.'

'Probably a dead sheep – fleeced,' Flynn said. He did not have much faith in anonymous tip-offs. 'If anyone was storing stuff in Agnes' shed it would be very strange not to say inconvenient for them to start hauling it through the woods up there.'

'I was in the middle of a very interesting conversation with Penny Wallace when you rang me,' Murray said, thoughtfully. 'I still think she's the weak link. I must try and have another tête-a-tête with her. I have a feeling she only needs to build up a bit more trust in me to tell me all. I wonder if she knows who this second girl is that her brother was seen with.'

'I'll be in McDowds this evening and I'll most likely hear what the grapevine has to say on the murders. We might even pick up a lead that way.' Flynn stood up and stretched his arms above his head. 'There's a new girl working behind the bar there,' he added, almost too casually. 'She's been very cooperative the last few times I was in.' He looked at Murray and there was a hint of pink in his cheeks.

'Has she now,' Murray grinned at him. 'Keep me posted, Jim – on any progress you might be making.'

Chapter Twenty-Nine

Penny opened the rear door of the car and, using only finger and thumb, picked up the mobile lying on the floor and slipped it into her shoulder bag. Her heart was beating so fast that she found herself gasping for air as she seated herself behind the wheel. Images of the headline on the newspaper which Murray had put down on the table in the café shimmered before her eyes. She had not paid much heed to the media buzz about the murder, eclipsed as it was by Stanley Wallace's murder and her own marital problems with Gregory. Her main concern had been that Rod had spoken to the girl and given her a lift to Ballyamber. She had accepted his version of events and had avoided any further information on the murder. She remembered now that Mrs Quinn had been going on about the girl's missing mobile and wallet and expressing her opinion that this pointed to a robbery gone wrong. But Mrs Quinn invariably repeated all the latest gossip as soon as she could get anyone's attention and the information had not really registered with Penny.

Now, it was all too real. She stared at her shoulder bag where it lay on the passenger seat beside her. Did this mobile belong to the girl? It must have been in the car all this time and when she had had to brake so sharply this morning it had been flung out of its hiding place under the seat. Rod was the only person apart from herself who had been driving the vehicle. On the night of the murder he had spoken to this girl and given her a lift to Ballyamber village.

What should she do? Alan Murray had seemed so approachable this morning, she thought. And yet the idea of going to the police with the mobile seemed like a betrayal of her brother. With an effort, she forced herself to sit up and concentrate. She would have to tackle

Rod immediately and let him know what she had found. After that, depending on his reaction, she would inform the gardai.

Later Penny could recall nothing about her drive home over the mountain road. All too soon, it seemed, she pulled up at Ballyamber House. Hastily she unloaded her shopping and dumped it onto the counter in the kitchen, expecting Rod to appear at any minute. She hurried into the small salon where he was sometimes to be found. The room was empty. Surely he had heard her return and would come looking for the car keys?

'Rod? Where are you?' she called, crossing the hall to the dining room. This proved also to be empty. She was about to mount the stairs when Gregory and Steve Donlon appeared from the direction of the library.

'Penny, good to see you.' Steve came forward and took her gently by the shoulders, giving her a peck on each cheek. This was his usual way of greeting her and it was evident that he wanted to appear as normal as possible.

Penny stiffened at his touch, pulling away from him as quickly as possible. 'Hi, Steve.' She was very conscious of Gregory standing in the background watching them. She stole a glance at his face but could not determine what he was thinking from his expression.

'Greg and I have been going over the final plans for the library,' Steve said, sounding very matter-of-fact. 'There's still quite a bit to be decided on so I'm afraid you'll have to put up with me for at least a week. We have to figure out what to do about the glass house and kitchen garden that Stanley was so keen on. I still think it would be worthwhile to see this through. And of course there is the question of whether it's worthwhile to upgrade the attics.'

'I see.' Penny forced a smile at the two men. 'You're very welcome, as I'm sure Greg has already told you,' she added, trying to sound as if she meant it.

The news that Donlon was going to stay so long was anything but welcome. She dreaded the inevitable heart-to-heart with him and having to admit that it had all been a ghastly error on her part. Every time she thought of that night her whole body burned with shame. As far as she was concerned, the sooner Steve Donlon disappeared out of her life the better.

'Thank you.' Donlon gave a slight bow. 'I'll try not to be a nuisance.'

'We were actually on our way up to the attics,' Gregory said, 'so if you'll excuse us.' He moved past without looking at her, Donlon at his heels.

'I thought I heard someone walking round up there a few nights ago,' she said as the two men mounted the stairs.

Donlon turned around quickly. 'Footsteps? In the attic? I doubt that very much. We don't even have mice up there as far as I know. When did you hear footsteps?'

'Well.' She hesitated, feeling foolish. 'It was one night I couldn't sleep.' This with a glance at Gregory who was standing on the stairs looking down at her. 'Two nights in fact,' she amended. 'I haven't heard anything the last couple of nights.'

'Did you tell Sergeant Murray?' Donlon asked. 'I know that the whole house was searched after – what happened.'

'I didn't mention it to the gardai,' she said. 'Perhaps I should have?'

'It's understandable that we're all a bit jittery,' Gregory put in. 'We'll have a look around now while we're up there and if we notice anything out of the way we'll report it.'

'There's really nothing up there except storage boxes,' Donlon added. 'I expect you heard the wooden floors expanding. There's always creaking and thumping in these old buildings.' He turned back to Gregory. 'We'd better get started. There's still a lot to be decided on.'

Penny waited until they were out of sight then she, too, started up the stairs. She had to find Rod and confront him with the mobile. Was it the dead girl's as she too much feared? Until she knew the answer to that question everything else was a blur.

Rod was just coming out of his bedroom when she reached the first floor. 'There you are,' he said, sounding cheerful. 'I thought I heard the car.'

'Rod, I need to talk to you.' The words came out in a breathless rush. 'Let's go back in your room for a minute.'

Rod raised his eyebrows but obediently opened the door for her. 'Steve Donlon is here,' he said in a mock whisper. 'Himself and Greg are giving the place a once over.'

'Yes, I know.' She dismissed the subject with a distracted wave of her hand. She stood with her back to the door and opened her shoulder bag, taking out the mobile and showing it to him. 'I found this in the car. I know it's not yours.'

Rod moved to take it from her but she forestalled him. 'No, don't touch it. It'll have your fingerprints on it.'

Rod took a step backwards and stared in surprise at his sister. 'Penny, what's going on? What's this about fingerprints, for goodness sake?'

Penny's whole body started to tremble. She stumbled towards the bed and sank down on it, still clutching the mobile. 'Whose phone is this? Is it that girl's, the one who was murdered? You gave her a lift, didn't you? Tell me, Rod.'

'You found it in the car, you say?' He had folded his arms across his chest and was standing in front of her now. 'That's impossible.'

'I tell you that's where I found it.' She stared up at him, her face as white as the pristine bedcovers. 'I saw Sergeant Murray today. He had a newspaper with him. It said that they're looking for the dead girl's mobile. Oh, Rod, please – just tell me. Did you have anything to do with her murder?'

Rod turned away and walked to the window, his back to her. 'Of course I didn't murder her. Do I look like -?' He broke off. 'That can't be her phone.'

'Then whose is it?' Penny's voice rose an octave or two. She was on the verge of screaming at him as she had in the bad days when he came home uncontrollably drunk and could not account for his movements.

He turned around abruptly, alerted by the tone of her voice, and came up to her putting his hands on her shoulders. 'Trust me, Penny.' His face was close to hers now. 'I did not harm that girl. Yes, I gave her a lift, like I told you, but that's all.' He gave her a little shake. 'Tell me you believe me?'

'I don't know what to believe,' Penny said in a barely audible whisper.

'All right. I'll come clean. The mobile most likely belongs to somebody else.' He released his grip on her shoulders and stood looking down at her. 'I can't say who that person is until I've checked with them. OK?'

'Why can't you say who it is? Don't play games with me, Rod.'

He hesitated then appeared to make up his mind. 'It could cause problems, let's say. Especially if the police knew about it.'

She ran her hands through her hair in a gesture of desperation. 'Why would it cause problems if it has nothing to do with the murder? Rod, you're not making sense.'

He began to pace up and down the room, his head bent. 'I know you think it's strange and maybe it's silly of me to be so careful. The best thing is for you to give me the mobile and I'll return it to the person who owns it. I'll tell you all the details when I've restored it to its rightful owner.'

Penny hesitated, unsure what to do. She wanted to believe him when he said he had nothing to do with the murder but it seemed like too much of a coincidence. 'If you'd told the gardai in the first place that you'd given the girl a lift to Ballyamber, there wouldn't be this problem now,' she said.

'Just let me have the phone and I'll sort it out.'

Penny made up her mind suddenly. She slipped the mobile back into her shoulder bag and got to her feet. 'No, Rod. I think the best thing I can do is to let Sergeant Murray have a look at it. If you have nothing to hide, then there shouldn't be a problem.'

'Penny, don't be so melodramatic.' He reached for her shoulder bag but she evaded him and before he could prevent her she was out of his room and running down the stairs.

Chapter Thirty

Murray drove down to Killarney to interview Patrick O'Sullivan. He wanted to be very sure of what this witness actually saw on the night in question. People sometimes backtracked or gave a different version to their previous one or decided they were mistaken. Rod Kirwin was supremely self-assured, on the surface at least, but that might change if he were confronted with a few facts.

In the meantime, Flynn had promised to get as much information from the regulars at McDowds pub in Killglash as he could. It was also an ideal opportunity to see the new barmaid. Her name was Kay, he told Murray, and she planned on studying for a degree in software development at the Institute of Technology in Tralee but needed to earn some money first.

'Very sensible,' was Murray's comment. 'Sounds like the ideal girl, Jim.'

Flynn had rolled his eyes and muttered something about "just friends".

The morning was bright and sunny. Ardnabrone, which according to local superstition claimed three lives a year, looked serene with the white clouds scudding past its summit. Murray felt some of the tension ease out of his shoulders as he drove. This was one of the most beautiful areas in Ireland, he reflected. No wonder that tourists came every year to climb or hill walk here.

He found Patrick O'Sullivan's little shop with no trouble. It was in a good location on the main street of Killarney. It was busy at this time of day with office workers intent on buying a sandwich for lunch and Murray had to wait until the stream of customers lessened.

He ordered a coffee and sandwich and ate at one of the little tables located outside the shop, enjoying the warmth of the sun on his shoulders. Finally, O'Sullivan was able to hand over to his assistant, who he introduced as his wife. He took Murray into a room off the kitchen at the rear of the premises.

'You're absolutely sure that the man you saw in the car park that night was Rod Kirwin?' Murray asked when they had gone over O'Sullivan's story again in detail.

'I'm pretty sure.' O'Sullivan hesitated. 'In my business, Sergeant Murray, you learn to recognise customers on the street and you kind of develop an eye for people. Whenever Rod stopped off here he was always very chatty, asking about what sights to see, things like that. I got the impression that he was bored up there in Killglash and maybe lonely, too. After all he used to work in London, he told me.'

'And the girls that were with him that night? You said one of them might have been Maike Bloem? Have another look.' He held out the photo of the dead girl.

O'Sullivan studied the photo before returning it to Murray. He scratched the bald patch on his head. 'One of the girls had long blonde hair like Maike has in the photo. I caught a glimpse of her under the lamplight in the park as they got to the car. I might be mistaken, of course. There are lots of girls with long blonde hair. The other girl I didn't get a proper look at.'

That was the best they could do, Murray thought gloomily as he drove back to Killglash. The bottom line was it could have been Rod with two girls in the car park that night or it could have been someone who looked like him. The girl might have been Maike Bloem or it might have been a girl with long blonde hair. It was all pretty vague.

Garda Dan Foley was seated at the front desk when Murray arrived back at Killglash garda station. 'Penny Wallace is waiting to see you,' he told Murray. 'I've put her in the little room at the back. She seems a bit upset.'

'Thanks, Dan.' Murray shelved the thought of enjoying a quiet cigarette in the backyard of the station and went through to the only spare interview room they had left – their two main rooms were now being used solely as incident rooms for the murder cases.

Penny Wallace was standing by the window which looked out onto the tiny backyard with its few potted plants (courtesy of Dan Foley) and rickety table complete with ashtray for Murray's use which stood next to the garden shed. She wheeled round as he opened the door. 'Sergeant Murray! I hope I'm not disturbing you.'

'Not at all. Sit down, please.' Murray pulled out a chair for her and seated himself on the other side of the desk. This little room was where they usually ate their lunch or had a quick tea break and would not normally have been used to interview anyone but these were not normal times. Like Killglash garda station itself, it needed re-decorating and some new furniture would not have gone amiss either. Right now, the shabby sideboard held their supply of tea and sugar and mugs. An ancient fridge purred in the corner, keeping their milk and Flynn's supply of organic Greek yoghurt cool.

Penny rummaged in her shoulder bag, her hands were shaking so much that she barely got the fastener to work. She pulled out a mobile phone and laid it on the desk. 'I found this in my car,' she said, her voice husky.

'In your car?' Murray's eyebrows rose in surprise. Whatever he had expected her to say it was not this. 'It's not yours then I take it?'

'It – I mean – Rod,' she hesitated then took the plunge, her words tumbling over each other. 'I saw in that newspaper article that the murdered girl's mobile was missing and I asked Rod and he said he thought he knew whose it was but he swears he never touched the girl, never harmed her in any way, it's just that he wouldn't say whose phone it is so I got worried. I thought I should come here and tell you. Clear his name. Rod had nothing to do with – with that girl's murder. He wouldn't harm a fly, I swear.'

Murray leaned back in his chair and digested her words in silence for a minute or two, trying to make sense of what she was telling him.

'Rod has been driving your car?' It was more a statement than a question.

'Yes.' Penny flashed worried brown eyes at him. 'He swears –'

Murray held up his hand. 'Let's take this one step at a time. Rod has been driving your car and you found a mobile in the vehicle. Right?'

'Yes.'

'So you spoke to him about it and he says he knows whose phone this is but didn't want to tell you.'

'Yes,' Penny said again. 'He says he has to check with the person first.'

'Why would he want to do that?'

'I don't know,' she said. She began to pick at an imaginary piece of thread on the sleeve of her sweater. 'He wouldn't tell me anything. Just said he needed to speak to the owner because it was an awkward situation or something like that. I'm not sure of his exact words.'

'Let me get this straight. You asked Rod about the phone because you knew that the murdered girl's mobile is missing. He says he knows whose phone it is but needs to check with them before he tells you. You, on the other hand, think we need to find out who owns this phone in order to avoid Rod coming under suspicion of killing the girl. Have I got it right?'

'Yes, that's exactly it. I know it has nothing to do with Rod even if he did give her a lift that night –' She broke off and put a hand to her mouth.

'Rod gave her a lift on the night she was murdered?' Murray kept his voice quiet and conversational with an effort. 'He never told us that.'

'He was afraid you'd suspect him – I promised I wouldn't mention it.' She put her hands over her face and gave a stifled sob. 'Please Sergeant Murray, you mustn't think he would ever harm anyone. I know him. Believe me, he's so gentle, such a good person.' Her voice trailed away and another sob escaped her.

'Mrs Wallace,' Murray said in as kind a tone as he could muster. 'We'll find out who owns this phone and that will solve that mystery. What I would now like you to do is to persuade your brother to come and talk to us. He is a very valuable witness.'

'I'll try.'

'I'd like to see him right away,' Murray looked ostentatiously at his watch. 'Say in around forty-five minutes? Can I rely on you to drive him here?'

After she had gone he sat and stared at the opposite wall without seeing it. Was Rod Kirwin their man? He'd half suspected him from the beginning but there had been nothing to go on. Certainly there was nothing in Rod's past that raised any flags. Even during his drinking years he had never come to police attention, never molested any females or been involved in brawls of any kind.

He picked up the mobile and carried it through to the incident room dealing with Maike Bloem's murder. Flynn was just finishing a phone call. The room was otherwise empty.

'We need to have a look at this,' he said, placing the mobile on the desk in front of Flynn. 'Penny Wallace found it in her car and we urgently need to find out who owns it.'

Before Flynn could do more than give a whistle of surprise, Dan Foley stuck his head around the door.

'Alan, visitors for you again. You're proving very popular. Two ladies this time.'

Chapter Thirty-One

When Penny arrived back at Ballyamber House she discovered that Rod had gone out. Steve Donlon had loaned him his car as Donlon himself informed her when they met in the small salon.

'He said he had an appointment,' he explained. 'I don't need the vehicle at the moment. Gregory and myself have a lot to do here. We've postponed our trip to Tralee until later this week.'

'Did he say where he was going?' How was she going to explain that to Sergeant Murray? she wondered in desperation. Really, Rod was his own worst enemy. Unless of course he had gone to meet the owner of the mobile. She refused to believe that he could have harmed the murdered girl. He was probably having an affair with a married woman and his sense of chivalry made him decide to speak to her about the mobile before he told anyone. Something about this line of reasoning did not ring true but she brushed it aside as she had brushed aside so many other matters relating to her brother's behaviour.

'What's the matter, darling?' Donlon sounded concerned. He put a hand on her arm and drew her closer to him. 'You're as white as a sheet.'

'Please,' she pulled away from him. 'Greg will see us.'

'Greg is actually gone into the village to get some paracetamol for his headache, so we're on our own, at least for ten minutes or so.'

'Oh.' The last thing she needed right now was a heart-to-heart with him.

'What's going on, Penny? Has Gregory been talking to you?'

'No, he hasn't. Has he spoken to you about – us?'

Donlon shook his head. 'Is there any way we can be alone? Can you slip out later on this afternoon?' He reached out for her again. 'We have to talk, Penny. We need to make plans.'

Penny moved a step away from him. She resisted the desire to put her hands over her face and scream out loud. 'I'm sorry, Steve,' she said, keeping her voice steady with an effort. 'I made a mistake. I thought I was in love with you. It was foolish of me. I suppose I was feeling down and – oh well the reasons don't matter I expect.' She looked up into his face. 'The best thing for both of us is to forget that anything ever happened.'

'What do you mean? Are you afraid of Gregory?'

'It's not that.' She swallowed hard, fighting the sudden lump in her throat. 'It's just that when I thought about it, I realised that I still love Greg. I can't leave him.'

'I wasn't asking you to leave him.' There was an edge to his voice she had never heard before. 'We could still get together now and then and have a good time, no questions asked.' He smiled at her suddenly. 'We're sensational together, or have you forgotten the other night?'

Penny was too stunned to think of a reply. Her pallor gave way to a flush of humiliation as she realised that she had been reading far too much into the relationship. At least when she had gone to bed with him she had believed herself half in love even if she had come to her senses shortly afterwards. It seemed that for him she was just "a bit on the side", wasn't that what men called it?

When she didn't say anything, Donlon raised an eyebrow at her. 'What if he wants to leave you? Have you thought of that? You might be glad of a bit of comfort.'

'Even if he does, it won't change the fact that I do love him and that I can't start a relationship with you or anyone else.' Penny held out her hands to him in an imploring gesture. 'I feel so guilty about what we did. I don't know what came over me. I'm sorry, Steve. Sorry and ashamed.'

She searched his face for some sign of understanding but his expression had hardened. It was he who now moved away from her.

'A lot of women would love to fall into bed with me, my dear. Believe me I could have my pick any day but I was looking for a bit of class. I thought I'd found that in you, that you were different, Penny.' He gave a bitter little smile. 'You were just easy meat, after all, weren't you? Just out for kicks. Gregory is welcome to you. I hope you'll both be unhappy together.'

He turned on his heel and stalked out of the room, slamming the door behind him. Penny sank down onto the nearest chair and putting her hands up to her face began to cry in deep racking sobs. Steve's words echoed in her ears coupled with Stanley's remarks on discovering them in bed the other morning. "I might have known you'd be up to no good" he'd said. And it was true, she thought wretchedly. She had betrayed her husband in a moment of madness, of selfishness and stupidity - she did not know what name was strong enough to describe it. As for Steve, she had totally misjudged him as she was beginning to realise. The charming, kind man she had believed in had shown just how skin deep these characteristics really were. He had not said one word about regretting that their brief affair was over before it had properly begun. His pride had been hurt and that was all. More than likely he did not feel anything for her, she thought bitterly. In which case, she did not need to feel sorry for not being able to return his feelings. Why oh why had she jeopardized her marriage like that?

The sound of the back-door slamming caused her to sit up and search for a tissue. No doubt she looked a mess and Gregory would wonder what was going on. Or perhaps it was Rod returning. All her anxieties came flooding back. She walked briskly to the door and checked the passageway. Gregory was in the process of hanging up his jacket in the hall beside the door to the kitchen. He turned around and looked at her in surprise.

'What's the matter? You look upset. Has something happened?'

The concern in his voice triggered another burst of tears and before she knew what was happening her husband had come and enveloped her in his arms, holding her tight against him. He didn't say anything and they stood like that for some minutes until she managed to control the sobs and finally stop crying.

Gregory released his hold very gently and took her face in his hands. 'What is it, darling?'

She almost dissolved in tears again but finally managed to speak even if what she said was not very coherent. 'It's – I told Steve we – I was – we're finished and that I love you and only you. Oh Greg, how can I ever make up for what I did?'

'I don't know,' Gregory said, still holding her face in his hands. There were tears in his eyes as he looked at her. 'You broke my heart, Penny.'

Chapter Thirty-Two

When Alan Murray entered the small interview room he had no idea who had come to see him at Killglash garda station. He was not prepared for the sight of his neighbour Nicola and her daughter, Vanessa. They were sitting on the edge of their chairs, both of them looking like startled deer ready to take flight at any moment.

'Well, well,' he said, giving them what he hoped was an encouraging smile. 'It's nice to see you, ladies. What can I do for you?' He sat down opposite them, wondering what was coming.

Nicola glanced at her daughter who was hunched in her chair, her hair falling over her face so that it was almost impossible to see her expression. 'I'm not sure where to begin,' she said after what seemed like an eternity. 'It's about Vanessa's mobile phone. If you remember, I told you she'd lost it somewhere?'

'I remember.' It had actually slipped his mind.

'Well,' Nicola paused again. Her hands started to play with the handle of the woven carrier bag on her lap. 'It seems that Vanessa has been seeing someone and she left her mobile in his car.' She looked up then and met Murray's gaze. 'I didn't know anything about this but the young man in question came to the house this morning. It's all a bit complicated, I'm afraid.'

Murray merely nodded encouragingly but he was already putting two and two together. 'Did this young man return the mobile this morning?' He turned his gaze to Vanessa who had not shown any sign of interest in the conversation. It was obvious that she was here under protest. She did not raise her head to answer his look.

'No, he couldn't return it because he didn't have it in his possession.' Nicola paused, a fine line appearing between her eyebrows. She was clearly surprised by Murray's calm reaction.

So that was it, he thought. His interview with Penny Wallace was fresh in his mind, in particular Rod Kirwin's reluctance to say whose mobile phone it was that his sister had discovered in her car. Was that the whole story? The witness who had seen Rod on the night of the murder had spoken of seeing him with two girls.

'It just so happens that we have an unidentified mobile here at the garda station. Do you mind having a look at it? If it can be identified as Vanessa's we can go on from there.' He stood up. 'Excuse me one minute while I get it.'

He was back in a few minutes and from the frosty atmosphere in the room he guessed that the two women had had some kind of brief confrontation. He held out the mobile in its evidence bag so that Vanessa could see it, showing her front and back. 'Is this yours?'

She leaned forward to get a good view of it. 'Yes, it looks like mine. There's the scratch on the back.' She sounded sulky.

'And you left it in Rod Kirwin's car?' He had been sure that the little scratch mark would identify the phone in a world where so many of them looked alike.

She still refused to look at him, her lips had puckered into a pout. 'I'm not sure,' she said after a long pause. 'I must have done.'

He heard Nicola's sharp intake of breath. The last thing he wanted was for her to make a comment right now and put an end to any cooperation with Vanessa. In fact, it would have been better if he could have talked to the girl without her mother being present. But that wasn't an option, at least not at the moment.

'Like to tell me when you left it in Rod's car?' He made his voice as encouraging as he could.

'I'm not sure.' This time she flashed him a nervous glance. 'He picked me up from Mitchell's. It was that Saturday night that I was babysitting, the night that girl was killed.'

Murray was silent, thinking. On the night Maike Bloem was murdered Rod had said he'd met her in McDowds pub. A few patrons of the pub had stated that they had seen him speaking to her but on being pressed had admitted that they were not sure, she had been in a group and it was hard to tell. Therefore, to date there were no reliable witnesses to corroborate his story. Everyone who had been in the pub that night remembered the group of climbers but no one could recall with any certainty who had spoken to Maike. Had Rod been telling the truth? Or was it Vanessa he'd met and not Maike? Their witness Patrick O'Sullivan claimed he saw Rod with two girls in the car park. And yet there seemed no plausible reason for Rod to claim he had spoken to Maike if in fact he had not done so. Why would he even mention her? Unless of course he dropped Vanessa off and ran into Maike on his way back to Ballyamber House.

'What time did he pick you up?' He noted that Nicola was sitting bolt upright in her chair, her face expressionless. He had the feeling that this was all new to her. Up until now she had firmly believed that Vanessa was doing what she said she was doing. She would have a long list of questions to ask her daughter. In the meantime, he was relieved that she no longer appeared to want to get in on the conversation.

'I was babysitting for Mitchells. They went out to dinner in Tralee. Must have been nearly half past eleven when they came home.'

'Did Rod pick you up from the Mitchell's house?'

Again she flashed him that look through heavily mascara'ed eyelashes. 'N-no. I told Mr Mitchell that my friend's mother was picking me and she'd be waiting for me just down the street.'

'And he believed that?'

'Yes.' She bent her head again and studied the backs of her hands.

He decided not to pursue it. 'So tell me what happened exactly. Rod picked you up and then? Did he drive you straight home?'

She hesitated then said almost too quickly. 'He picked me up and drove me home. It was late and I knew mum would be waiting up. He didn't - we didn't do anything. Only kiss, you know.' This with a furtive glance in her mother's direction.

Her body language told him that she was not speaking the truth. What was she hiding and why? he wondered. He had deliberately played down the underage aspect so as not to scare her into thinking she would get Rod into trouble. It was possible that Rod thought she was older than she really was. 'Did you see anybody on your way home?'

She shook her head. 'I can't remember. I wasn't paying attention. I don't think so.'

Murray leant back in his chair and went over the conversation in his head. Vanessa had been babysitting for the Mitchells who lived in an upmarket housing estate. They had children of their own so it seemed unlikely they would allow her to walk out of the house to a waiting car late at night without checking that all was as it should be. Killglash was a sleepy little town, it was true, but with all the things that were happening all over the country, surely they would accompany her even if it was only a few steps away? And didn't they think it strange that her friend's mother did not call at the house for her?

He had not spoken to the Mitchells regarding that Saturday night, he reminded himself. It had slipped his memory. It was fairly safe to assume, though, that John Mitchell would have come forward long ago if he seen anything untoward on the night in question. The gardai had made several appeals to the public through the local media.

'You're telling me that the Mitchells, who were responsible for your safety that night, and who normally dropped you home, let you walk out of the house late at night and down the street to a parked car without seeing the driver or making sure the person in that car was your friend's mother? Do you honestly expect me to believe that?' His voice hardened a little. It was nearly time to take off the silk gloves.

'It's better to tell the truth, Vanessa,' Nicola said suddenly. 'The gardai can check this all out, you know.'

Vanessa raised her head and sat up straight. She brushed the hair out of her face and looked from one to the other of them, her expression still mulish.

'Rod was waiting outside Mitchell's for me. I sent him a text that he could come and collect me. The Mitchell's couldn't see the car because he parked it behind that big tree in the street. They could only see his headlights.'

Murray merely grunted and scribbled a few notes on the pad in front of him. He did not believe a word of it but now was not the time to follow up. He would check with John Mitchell first and get his version of events.

'Can I have my mobile back now?'

'I'm afraid we need to do a few checks on it. If you can let us have the password to get into it, it'll make our lives easier. We'll let you have it as soon as we're finished.' He stood up to indicate that the interview was at an end.

Vanessa stared at him, her face as white as a sheet. 'What do you need it for?'

'We need to do some forensic tests on it.'

'Forensic tests!' She stared at him, her mouth a round "O" of what could only be described as terror. 'Then you'll – you'll be able to see all the calls on it, is that right?'

'That's the idea.' Murray sat down again.

Vanessa gave a long shuddering sigh, tears started to inch their way down her face. 'Rod will kill me,' she whispered. 'I promised I wouldn't say anything to anyone.' She buried her face in her hands, her sobs getting louder.

Nicola produced a tissue from her shoulder bag and handed it to her daughter. She reached out and put an arm around the girl's shoulders. 'Whatever it is, I'm here for you, darling,' she said quietly. 'Alan will help you, too, you know that.'

Vanessa blew her nose and brushed at her cheeks which were streaked with mascara. She suddenly looked what she was, a fifteen-year old schoolgirl who was both frightened and confused.

'That girl that was murdered, she used my mobile to call someone, her phone needed charging she said.' Her voice was thick with tears. 'She asked Rod to let her out at Gleason's supermarket. She said her B&B was only around the corner from there. She wanted to have a cigarette first, she said, and there was no smoking allowed in the house.'

She looked from her mother to Murray and back again, then continued, sounding a bit more confident. 'Rod gave her a lift to Ballyamber because the guy she was supposed to meet in McDowds hadn't shown up. She got out of the car at the supermarket. She was a bit upset with whoever she talked to on the phone – I couldn't understand what she said but it sounded as if she was mad at whoever it was. I didn't think to get my phone back from her. She must have let it fall or something and didn't notice. She wasn't wearing a seatbelt and Rod was driving kind of fast, so maybe that's what happened. That's all I know, I swear.'

Chapter Thirty-Three

'You know, Jim, I've always been trying to meet this "Inspector Coincidence" fellow that a German colleague told me about and he seems to have turned up finally.' The smile Murray directed at his subordinate was completely without humour. The two men were sitting in Murray's office. Nicola and Vanessa had gone with a promise of returning tomorrow for another chat, as Murray had put it. Now the two gardai were awaiting the arrival of Rod Kirwin and his sister. Penny had just contacted them to say she had finally located her brother and they would both be at Killglash garda station within the hour.

'Inspector *Zufall*,' Flynn, who had heard the story before, nodded in agreement. 'There are a lot of gaps to be filled in, mind you.'

'But we do have the phone number of the person that Maike contacted,' Murray said with satisfaction. 'It depends on what your friend in Zandervoort finds out from him.'

'Do you think he could be our man?'

Murray shrugged. 'Time will tell.'

Patience was not a virtue with which he had been blessed and his first instinct had been to call the number which Maike had used. Flynn had objected on the grounds that the fellow might not speak English or might not be sufficiently fluent to give them any satisfactory answers. Reluctantly Murray had seen the sense in waiting for the Dutch police to do the talking.

'It looks as if Rod Kirwin wanted to hide the fact that he was dating an underage girl,' Flynn said, as he checked through the notes he had made when Murray had updated him on the interview with Vanessa and Nicola. 'A pity he didn't tell us the truth straight away, it would have saved us a bit of time. If he's innocent, we could cross him off our list. Assuming the fellow that Maike phoned really is our man.'

'Maike did tell a few people that she was meeting someone. It might not be the person she phoned, of course. In which case, we're not much forwarder than we are now,' Murray said slowly. 'Vanessa said they spoke in Dutch and Maike didn't elaborate on who he was or anything. As far as she could tell, his name wasn't mentioned but we can't be certain. The way the Dutch pronounce words would make it hard to identify anything as a name. If you think about it, Jim, whoever he is, he must know that she's been murdered. He must be someone close to her. And if he hasn't come forward it makes him one of our top suspects.'

Flynn added a few words to his notes before replying. 'You don't sound convinced that he's the killer,' he observed.

'It sounds just a bit implausible. Vanessa's mobile should be able to tell us more at any rate. If the call Maike made was to Holland then the person on the phone can't have been involved. The phone call may not have anything to do with the murder.' Murray paused for a moment before adding, 'we're missing a link here somewhere. And we'd better find it and make a chain out of it before Percy has our hides tanned and hung up on the front door of Killglash garda station.'

Murray and Flynn were a good team and enjoyed throwing ideas at each other. A few years before they had brought a serial killer to justice. They were well aware that routine, painstaking detective work was the key to success but they needed to show they were getting somewhere in both Maike's murder and also that of Stanley Wallace. In Wallace's case, as he was a rich, successful businessman, the pressure was enormous. Although the media had found other stories in the meantime, there was still plenty of interest in the Wallace case. Sophie Winslow had just been given the leading role in a new soap which was the subject of a lot of publicity. Her connection to the murdered Stanley Wallace added to the interest and there was an article in some glossy magazine or a comment in a newspaper nearly every day which made some reference to the failure of Killglash gardai to find the killer. Maike's story had faded into the background and was only mentioned in passing. Percy, their boss, was doing his best to field questions and criticisms and had managed to get extra manpower to help in the investigation. 'We need to clean this up as quickly as we can,' was a favourite expression of his which was starting to grate on everybody's nerves.

Murray was just debating if he had time to slip out and have a cigarette in the backyard when the arrival of Penny and Rod was announced.

'Thanks for coming in to see us,' Murray said insincerely as they all seated themselves in the small interview room.

Rod held Murray's gaze for a few moments before clearing his throat. 'Obviously I know what this is all about,' he said. 'Penny has told me that she handed in the mobile phone to you that she found in her car. It belongs to a local girl, Vanessa Ryan. Sorry. I should have told you about Vanessa.'

'And why didn't you tell us?' Murray asked in a mild tone. It was clear that Rod was trying to carry this whole thing off with a show of bravado. Or maybe he thinks we're all as thick as two planks, he thought.

Rod had the grace to look slightly embarrassed as he answered. 'Vanessa is under age so I didn't want to get into trouble. I'm not sure what the law is over here on dating young girls. I thought she was older - at least seventeen - when I met her and by the time I'd discovered that she's only fifteen, well it was too late, I was smitten I have to confess.'

'The law in Ireland makes it a criminal offence to engage or attempt to engage in a sexual act with a child under seventeen years, even if it is consensual,' Murray said quietly. He did not let his anger show but inside he was seething. Here they were in the middle of a murder investigation and this fellow was only interested in not getting into hot water for having a relationship with a minor. 'It carries a maximum sentence of five years,' he added.

'I see. If it's any help, we didn't have sex,' Rod said. 'I'm not the kind of guy who sleeps with every girl I date.'

Murray let that comment stand for now. He did not trust Rod's attitude to the truth but at the moment there were other things which needed clearing up. 'You gave Maike Bloem a lift from Killglash to Ballyamber. Why didn't you tell us that when we spoke to you about her?'

'Who told you that? Have you been talking to Vanessa?' Rod stared at Murray. He leaned forward in his seat as if to emphasise his next words. 'Look, Sergeant Murray, I did not harm Maike. I want to make that clear.'

'Just answer the question,' Flynn said. He had been silent up to now, merely making the odd note on the pad in front of him.

Rod looked at him in surprise as if he had forgotten that he was there. 'Sorry,' he muttered with a faint shrug of his shoulders. 'I didn't tell you about giving Maike a lift because I'd have had to say that Vanessa was in the car and, as I said, I knew she was underage and we probably shouldn't have been dating.' He looked from Murray to Flynn as if trying to gauge their reaction. 'I couldn't name Vanessa as my witness that Maike got out of my car at Gleason's supermarket and that I then drove Vanessa home.'

'She approached you in the pub and asked you for a lift, is that correct?'

'Yes. She'd been enquiring about a lift back to Ballyamber and I offered to take her.'

'Maike made a phone call in your car,' Murray prompted. 'What can you tell us about that?'

Again Rod shrugged. 'Not much. Her phone needed charging she said and she needed to contact someone. That's all I can tell you.'

'She made this call and presumably arranged to meet this person at Gleason's supermarket. You drove her there. Now, I want you to think about this very carefully. Did you see anyone when you dropped her off there?'

Rod gave a gusty sigh and ran a hand through his thick blonde hair. Exactly ninety seconds ticked by according to Murray's watch before he answered. 'No. I can't recall seeing anyone.'

'Maike got out of the car,' Murray prompted again. 'What did she say?'

'She just thanked me for the lift. Wished us good night.'

'That was all?'

'I'm trying to think.' Rod attacked his hair again, rumpling it so that it stood up in spikes. 'Yeah, that's all she said. She didn't say much on the drive back to Ballyamber. She seemed tired. We said good night, have a good time, whatever. Then I drove away.'

This more or less corroborated what Vanessa had told them earlier, Murray thought. Rod and Vanessa appeared to have had very little conversation with the girl. Rod's impression that Maike was tired was a reasonable assumption considering she had been hill walking for much of the day. On the other hand, this did not tie in with the notion that she was meeting a boyfriend. And why would a boyfriend arrange to meet her late at night at a village supermarket? He could only hope that the Dutch police would be able to throw some light on this. There were still too many gaps for his liking.

Flynn's thoughts had also been on this track as his question revealed. 'Let's say Maike expected someone to be at the supermarket to meet her. Did you get the impression that she was surprised there was no one there when you dropped her off?'

'I didn't think about it. I stopped the car and asked her if this is where she wanted to be dropped and she said yes. She got out and I drove Vanessa home. We stopped a couple of hundred yards from the cottage and kissed and cuddled a bit and then I drove back to Ballyamber House.' He turned to his sister. 'I needed to get back to the party. I thought it would look odd if I didn't put in an appearance, though heaven knows it was a pretty boring affair.'

Penny had been sitting slightly in the background, her face white and set, only her eyes moved, darting back and forth between Rod and Murray as the questions and answers were made. Now she roused herself. 'I can confirm that Rod had supper with us.' Her voice was hushed, like someone speaking in church. 'And I do believe all that he's said. It's just – unfortunate – that you didn't say all this from the very beginning, Rod.'

The phone on the desk buzzed and Flynn picked it up. He spoke briefly then got up from his chair. 'Ilse de Jong is on the line,' he said, addressing Murray. 'I'll take it in the other office.' He picked up his notebook and left the room.

Chapter Thirty-Four

'Where on earth have you and Rod been?' Gregory demanded as brother and sister walked through the back door of Ballyamber House. Outside it was getting dark and the rain had started again accompanied by a cold north-west wind. Spring seemed to have upped stakes and left for the time being.

'We were at the police station in Killglash,' Penny said. 'Rod had some information for them.'

'Information? What kind of information?' The question came from Steve Donlon who had come out of the small salon in time to hear their conversation.

'Nothing to get excited about, Steve,' Rod said with an attempt at bravado.

Penny took a deep breath to steady herself. She still felt raw inside from having witnessed the interview with Alan Murray and Jim Flynn at Killglash garda station. Rod really was impossible! He did not appear to be overly sorry that he had not spoken the truth at the various interviews he had had with the police. Nor did it appear to worry him what the consequences of his actions might be. On the way home he had told Penny that he was in love with Vanessa and his priority in the whole business was to keep her name out of the spotlight. Based on what Sergeant Murray had said, Rod's relationship with Vanessa would now be under investigation. It was possible that her brother would be prosecuted, even sent to prison, for having a relationship with a minor. And he had deliberately withheld information which was almost certainly punishable by law. Rod himself seemed totally oblivious of the seriousness of the situation.

'It's so unfair that Vanessa's mobile should have ended up in your car,' he'd said on the drive back to Ballyamber House. 'I just hope that her mother doesn't decide to lock her away and not let me see her.'

Penny was at a loss to know what to say to him. He had always been the spoilt younger brother, she supposed. His alcohol problem had ensured that she made excuses for his behaviour. Up until now she had not realised the extent of his thoughtlessness. Selfishness was perhaps a better description of his behaviour, she thought. It did not occur to him that she was desperately worried by the implications of his meeting with the murdered girl. As far as Rod was concerned he had dropped her off at Gleason's supermarket and that was the last he saw of her. What he didn't seem to realise was that he was the last person to have seen her alive. And Penny doubted very much if Sergeant Alan Murray believed all that Rod had said. But Rod appeared to think everyone was satisfied and he now only needed his sister's intervention to solve the romantic side of the affair.

'I have to talk to Vanessa's mother,' he'd said. 'Maybe you could come with me and vouch for me? I've never been so crazy about any girl as I am about Vanessa.'

Penny had not made any reply. The idea of calling on Nicola Ryan and pleading for her brother was not something she was prepared to think about.

'Penny?' Gregory's voice roused her from her thoughts. 'Can we change the venue for the dinner reservation for tonight and eat in Killglash? I have to take a call from New York later on so we should make it earlier – around seven if that suits you?'

'Whatever you think best,' she said. She realised that she had lost track of the conversation. Who cares where we go to dinner? she thought. She would not be able to eat a bite. Having Steve Donlon dine with them was an added source of unease. He was clearly resentful of her breaking off their relationship but seemed to be just as clearly determined to complete whatever assignment Gregory had given him. Why couldn't he just take himself off back to Dublin? She murmured some excuse and hurried upstairs to her room. Once there she sank down on the side of the bed only to get up after a few minutes and begin pacing the room. The scene with Steve Donlon, Greg's palpable unhappiness and Rod's involvement with the murdered girl all raced around in her head, each one succeeding the other, until her temples ached.

There was a gentle tap at the door and she heard Greg's voice. 'Penny? Are you ready? We'll be leaving in fifteen minutes.'

'I won't be a minute,' she called back. The fact that he did not stick his head round the door seemed to emphasise the gulf that was now between them. With a little sigh of pure sadness, she went to her wardrobe and selected a simple silver grey dress for the evening. Mechanically she re-applied her make-up, brushed her hair and added a touch of lipstick. In the mirror her face looked pale and drawn.

On her way downstairs she paused on the landing for a moment. Some impulse made her walk to the window which overlooked the front of the building. Dark clouds obscured the top of Ardnabrone, the band of trees halfway up the mountain which looked black in the fading light, added to its sinister appearance. On the road below a car drove past, its headlights cutting a swathe of yellow through the dusk. Her eyes followed it for a moment before a movement caught her attention. Was there or was there not a figure standing in the curve of the avenue staring up at the house? Agnes O'Toole, the local witch as she sometimes thought of her, was still haunting them and casting her evil spells on the house. A shiver ran through her body. When she thought of all the things that had happened since they came to Ballyamber House she was forced to admit that Agnes had triumphed.

Chapter Thirty-Five

Ilse de Jong did not have much information to impart as Flynn explained to Murray later on that day. 'When she checked out the phone number on Vanessa's mobile it was answered by a male who said his name was Sem Hannen. He said he's from Amsterdam and that he got to know Maike on a dating website but never actually met up with her. He said, yes, she phoned him on the night of her murder. Well, he didn't actually know she was murdered that night until Ilse told him but that was when he spoke to her, quite late, after midnight he said.'

'After midnight? Oh, that's Dutch time, they're an hour ahead.'

'He'll be coming in to talk to Ilse on Friday afternoon when he's finished work.'

'Met her on a website?' Murray raised his eyebrows. 'And then decided that their first date should be in the middle of an Irish village? Pass the salt.'

'A lot of people meet on dating websites nowadays, it's a common thing,' Flynn said. 'It seems he told Maike that he was going to be in Ireland and claimed he knew where Ballyamber was, that he'd been there before. He admitted to Ilse that that was a lie. She'll know more when she interviews him.'

'What's the name of this dating site? Sounds like the perfect way not to meet someone.'

'It has an English name: FindMe. I looked it up.'

'So where are you meeting your dream girl? Outside a chipper in old Amsterdam?'

Flynn rolled his eyes to show that he was not amused. 'The site is pretty much the same as all the other online dating sites. You have to register and there's a long list of information you have to give about yourself, including a picture.'

'We'd better wait until your friend Ilse has talked to this guy. He sounds weird to put it mildly.'

'Are we buying Rod Kirwin's explanation about Maike?'

'You know, Jim, my gut feeling tells me that he's not our man. We've always wondered who Maike was supposed to meet that night and now we know – more or less. I won't rush to judgement on it, but I can't see what motive Rod had for killing her. He claims he's in love with Vanessa Ryan and he might be for all I know. It's unlikely he'd have designs on Maike who he'd only just met. I may be wrong but he doesn't strike me as the kind of guy who drives around a country road, picks up a strange girl and strangles her.'

'Put like that, I suppose you're right. Ilse will ring me as soon as she's taken a statement from Sem Hannen. That should tell us more. And they'll be checking out his profile on the website and his online presence in general.' He glanced at Murray with half a smile on his face. 'Rush to judgement. That sounds very psychological, Alan.'

'Our next briefing is tomorrow morning at nine sharp,' Murray said, changing the subject quickly. He recognised the phrase as one which Nicola had used a few times and was disconcerted that he had picked it up so easily. He could hear her now speaking in that pleasant musical voice of hers 'Vanessa's chemistry teacher seems a bit unsuitable but I won't rush to judgement', or again 'Gleason's supermarket really is the limit, I'm sure they charge twice as much as any other shop, but there again I won't rush to judgement on it.' She was just a pleasant neighbour after all, damn it, he thought in sudden irritation.

'I hope the team has come up with something on the Stanley Wallace case.' He continued now, aware that Flynn was looking at him curiously. 'In the meantime, I'm going to drive up to Gleason's supermarket and have a nose around there. I know all that area was searched already but something might have been overlooked.'

Half an hour later Murray was standing in front of the supermarket in Ballyamber village. It was a quiet time of day with most people having supper in their homes. He surveyed the road which snaked down from Killglash and through the village. From here he could see Agnes O'Toole's cottage and nearby the sweep gates which marked the entrance to Ballyamber House. Maike would have stood here having a cigarette if what Vanessa Ryan said was true. Had she seen something that made her curious? But what could that be? No one had reported anything unusual that night. No strange car, no screams for help. Everyone was at home watching television or had gone to bed for the night. And yet, something had happened, something so swift that Maike had no time to call out.

Murray walked slowly back and forth, his eyes probing the ground. The place had been searched in the hope of finding Maike's mobile or wallet but without success. At that point in time the searchers had not known that Rod Kirwin had dropped Maike off here. It might be an idea to do another sweep of the area, he mused. This decision made, he turned to walk back to where he had parked his car. As he was about to get into the driving seat, his foot slipped on a piece of sodden brown paper which must have been blown about by the wind. He bent down to detach it from his shoe and saw the cigarette butt lying nearby. Some instinct made him pick it up. It had been smoked halfway. He could read the brand name. It was a Muratti.

'Another visitor for you, Alan,' Flynn told him when he arrived back at Killglash garda station. 'You have more audiences than the pope today.'

This time the visitor turned out to be the local vet, John Mitchell. He was looking very agitated, pacing up and down in the little interview room.

'I had a call from Nicola Ryan today,' he said before he was even seated. 'She told me that Vanessa has been saying that she was baby-sitting for us on the night that tourist was murdered. That's not so.'

Murray raised his eyebrows. 'Are you telling me she wasn't at your house that night?'

'That's exactly what I'm saying.' Mitchell said, sounding angry. 'She does some babysitting for us now and again but that night we were at home. I just wanted to make that clear. I don't want anyone to think we'd not look after her properly.'

'No one is accusing you of that,' Murray said. 'It looks like Vanessa made a mistake.'

'A mistake!' Mitchell snorted. 'I wonder why she'd say something like that? She must have been up to mischief and is telling lies. I won't have her helping out in my surgery again, let me tell you. I have my reputation to think of.'

Later Murray updated Flynn on what he had learned. 'We'll have to find out what Vanessa was doing that night,' he said wearily. 'She can't have been with Rod Kirwin all that time because he was at the party in Ballyamber House.'

'Just imagine how much faster we'd be clearing up this case if everyone told us the truth,' Flynn said in exasperation. 'I'm seeing Kay tonight when she's finished at McDowds,' he added almost shyly. 'She might be able to tell me something. She knows nearly everyone around here.'

Murray decided not to comment although he was pleased that his subordinate appeared to have a found a girlfriend. 'We'll have a word with Ginger and Harold as soon as we have the Muratti cigarette checked for DNA.'

'It might not mean anything. Ginger could have chucked it there at any time,' Flynn remarked, relieved no doubt that this time Murray was not teasing him about any budding romance.

'I think we'll just pay him and Harold a flying visit and then check Agnes out.' Murray decided. 'We might have a bit more to report tomorrow morning to keep old Percy off our backs.'

On their way back to Ballyamber Murray changed plans. 'Let's call on Agnes first,' he said. 'Something was stored in her garden shed until recently and unless I'm mistaken it won't be a supply of prayer books. Supposing Maike Bloem saw something she shouldn't have? Or Stanley Wallace found out something? He was known to have called on Agnes a few times. Seems to me that she's got the wind up. Last time I called the place was barricaded like she was expecting the siege of Limerick.'

'I suppose all the people she put the evil eye on are looking for retribution.'

'You know something, Jim? You're developing into a comedian.'

Agnes answered their knock promptly, which made Murray think she had been watching them out of her cottage window. She insisted on making a pot of tea and bustled about placing cups on the table while keeping up a monologue on the weather, her aches and pains and the general state of the country, all of which she claimed were in a bad state. Finally, she deemed the tea had brewed long enough and poured it out.

'I didn't do any baking today,' she said, offering round a plate of biscuits. 'I haven't been down to the shops so I've only got gingernuts.'

'I'm glad you're keeping well despite the old rheumatism,' Murray said, declining the offer of the biscuits. He hated gingernuts.

'I did get a bit of a turn the other day,' Agnes admitted. 'Dr O'Reilly sent me into the hospital for a check up but they couldn't find anything wrong with me.'

'So you're as fit as a fiddle?'

'I am indeed.'

Although she spoke with emphasis, Murray noted the way her fingers knotted and unknotted in her lap. It might be his imagination but he thought that her face looked more drawn than usual. Something had upset Agnes in a big way. 'Have you seen Ginger Ford around recently?' He kept his voice casual as if he were asking after the health of a common acquaintance.

'Ginger Ford?' Agnes stopped twisting her hands in her lap. She looked at him sharply. 'I can't say I've seen him but a lot of people pass my door, you know.'

'Does he store things in your garden shed?'

'Ginger Ford? Store things in my shed?' Her face expressed only injured innocence. 'What makes you think that?'

'Because I've seen Ginger in your garden late one night. And something has been stored there for a while.'

Agnes picked up the teaspoon on the table next to her mug of tea and began playing with it. She appeared to be thinking hard. The measured tick of the clock on the mantelpiece was loud in the silence. After a full minute she seemed to make up her mind.

'I might have let him store a cardboard box there a while ago but that's all. There's no harm in that, is there?'

'Did he pay you for storing this cardboard box?'

'Just a few bob.'

'And you only did this the once?'

'That's all.' She sounded more cheerful now, no doubt feeling she was on safe ground.

'When was this, Agnes? You said a while ago.'

'That would be last month around end of January or maybe it was the beginning of February. About a month, anyways. Ginger called one day and said he was moving stuff for a friend and could he use my garden shed to store a few cartons. We agreed on the price – 'twasn't much I can tell you - and he came one evening with that friend of his Brannigan. That was all.'

'So he didn't pay you enough money to buy fancy furniture or anything like that?' As he spoke Murray cast his eyes around the kitchen, letting his gaze rest on the obviously expensive armchairs by the fireplace and the enormous state-of-the art television set which had pride of place in the room.

'What would I need a lot of money for?' Agnes shifted in her chair. 'I just wanted to do the man a favour.'

'And you don't know what he stored in the shed? You were never the least bit curious about that?'

Her eyes darted from Murray to Flynn and back again. 'I know nothing about what he stored there. He gave me some money and I let him use the shed. That's all I know.'

'You say he asked you to store stuff about a month ago. That's when all this started?'

'Yes. He knocked on my door one evening. He was very polite. Said he was visiting Harold Brannigan. He just needed to store some stuff for a couple of weeks. It was for someone down here who couldn't take it before that.'

'You didn't think that was strange? I mean, why wouldn't he store the stuff at Brannigan's if they were friends?'

'I don't know.'

'Come on Agnes. You might as well tell us the truth.'

'That is the truth. I swear it.'

'Was Ginger on his own when he moved stuff from your shed? Think carefully, Agnes.'

She went quiet again. It seemed as if she was sizing up her options and the advisability of telling the whole truth or only a suitably edited part of it.

'I don't know. I never saw him moving it. I used to hear a car stopping but it was the middle of the night and I couldn't see anything in the dark anyway.' She hesitated then added, 'If I thought Ginger had anything to do with killing this poor young girl I'd be the first to tell you.'

'What makes you think we suspect Ginger of being involved?'

'God only knows what the gardai think.' The shrewd eyes looked at Murray from under wispy eyebrows. 'All this questioning about what he stored in the shed. No one can say that Agnes O'Toole had anything to do with anything like that. I have me faults but I'd never hide a murderer.'

'Don't make me cry, Agnes,' Murray said. 'We'll check all this out and we'll get to the truth of the matter, believe me.' He nodded to Flynn who had long ago abandoned any attempt to drink the strong tea put in front of him and who had remained stoically silent throughout the interview. 'We'll be off for now, but we'll be back to see you, don't you worry.'

'We'll have to dig a bit deeper on Ginger,' Murray said in an undertone as the two men walked down the garden path to their car. 'And we'll have to have another look at that garden shed of hers. She's up to her neck in something and now she's trying to backpedal.'

Chapter Thirty-Six

'Are you going to continue seeing Vanessa Ryan?' Penny looked anxiously at her brother. It was the day after their visit to Killglash garda station and they were having breakfast together. They were alone. Gregory and Steve Donlon had both breakfasted already and were upstairs in the West Wing which was shortly to be redecorated.

Rod spread some marmalade on his toast before he answered. 'My relationship with Vanessa is completely above board so I don't see the need for me to do or not do anything.' He smiled at his sister. 'Cheer up, Penny. If I understood Gregory correctly last night, he's thinking of upping stakes and moving back home to London. After all, he's inherited a pretty fortune as the only son and heir to Stanley Wallace.'

'What do you mean, he's upping stakes?' Penny decided not to take him up on the remark about the Wallace fortune. She had been too distressed to even think about the implications of what the inheritance would mean to Gregory. Her husband had gone alone to London for his father's funeral and to hear the reading of the will and had not given her any details of what had transpired.

Rod took a bite of toast and washed it down with a sip of tea before he answered.

'I overheard him talking to Steve last night. From what he said I gather that Greg wants to sell this place as quickly as possible. Steve was advising him to do a bit more to it. He offered to move in and supervise the work. He said he'd stay on if Greg wanted to leave before a buyer could be found. Apparently that was the original idea anyway, that Steve would be manager of the place. Old Stanley never intended staying here all the time. He probably knew himself that he'd have got tired of it after twelve months and gone back to London.'

'Did Greg actually say he was planning to move back to London?' Penny thought of the flat in Kensington and of all the things she missed about the city. They could be happy there together, she told herself. In time, Greg would forgive her and they could go on as before – or even better than before because the spectre of Stanley Wallace was gone.

'He didn't say in so many words but let's face it, there's nothing to keep him here apart from the blunder his old man made by buying this place.' Rod looked thoughtfully at his sister. 'I must say that I would be sorry to have to leave Ballyamber and give up seeing Vanessa. I'm going to have to get a local job as far as I can see and that won't be easy. Or maybe Greg can help me out for the time being.'

'But Rod, this girl, it's just an infatuation, surely? She's much too young and immature. She doesn't fit in your world.'

'That's what good old Stanley always said about you, sister dear.' Although the words were lightly spoken, Rod's eyes flashed with sudden anger. 'I'd have kind of expected you to stick up for Vanessa. Forgetting your roots, are you?'

'It's not that.' Penny flushed. 'You hardly know the girl, after all. If we do move back to London, I'll expect you to move with us. The idea of Greg supporting you here in Ballyamber is laughable.'

'Forget I mentioned it.' He sounded sullen, reminding her of their childhood days when he had been crossed in some outrageous plan and made toe the line.

Chapter Thirty-Seven

'That's it, then,' Murray said, summing up what he had told his team at the briefing on the Maike Bloem case. There had been a few murmurs of surprise when he revealed that Rod Kirwin had dropped Maike off at Gleason's supermarket and had a witness in Vanessa Ryan to prove it. He waited until they had all quieted down again before continuing. He glanced at Flynn. 'Jim, can you just say a few words about Sem Hannen, the fellow that Maike phoned on the night she was killed?'

'Sem Hannen was interviewed by Ilse de Jong of the Dutch Police,' Flynn told the assembled officers. 'He met her via an online dating site called FindMe and after a bit of back and forth, she told him she was going to Ireland to do some hill walking. They never actually met up, it was all via the site. When she mentioned her trip to Ireland he says he wanted to impress her and said he was planning a trip to Ireland, too, and that he knew the area well having been there before a few times. They arranged to book a double room at The Emerald B&B, cheaper than two single rooms, he says. He told her he'd sleep on the floor and she was happy with that – or so he claims. They agreed to meet in McDowd's pub in Killglash. He had no intention of going, of course. Ilse de Jong says the picture he put up on FindMe is a phoney, in reality he's a skinny middle-aged man who's been out of work for a couple of years. He says that Maike phoned him the night she was killed and he told her he couldn't make it to Ireland. He had no idea she'd been murdered, he says, or he would have contacted the police immediately.'

'Are we buying his story?' Percy interrupted with a glance at Murray.

'Yes,' Murray said concealing his annoyance at the question. 'I mean, you couldn't make it up, could you? Emails between himself and Maike confirm what he said about planning to meet in Ireland. She seems to have fallen for him in a big way. The bottom line is that Sem Hannen has a few mental health issues, let's say, but he does have a cast iron alibi for the time in question.'

Percy nodded to Flynn, 'go on but make it short.'

Flynn, who liked the limelight and disliked cutting corners on a report he had meticulously prepared, glanced at his notes before continuing. 'Hannen says Maike was annoyed at him when he said he couldn't make the trip and he thought she was getting suspicious, so he got cold feet and closed his account with FindMe. That's about all we have on that.'

'So we're back to square one on this. Rod Kirwin is still our only suspect.' Percy jiggled some loose change in the pocket of his trousers. His tone managed somehow to suggest that they were all slacking. 'I take it we're still waiting on the DNA on that cigarette butt you found at Gleason's supermarket, Alan?'

'That's right.' Murray nodded. 'We know that both Ginger Ford and Harold Brannigan were smoking Muratti cigarettes so one of them could have thrown it away at any time over the past couple of weeks. What I did find interesting is that Maike told Rod Kirwin she wanted to smoke a cigarette before going back to the B&B. If she stood there in front of the supermarket she had a clear view of Agnes O'Toole's cottage and the entrance to the drive leading up to Ballyamber House. And of course anyone driving down that road would have seen her. According to Rod Kirwin's statement she was no longer there when he came back from dropping off Vanessa Ryan.'

'What's the story on Harold Brannigan and his sidekick Ginger Ford?' Percy asked. 'Their alibis are cast iron, are they?'

'More or less,' Murray said. 'We've spoken to them a few times and they corroborate each other's story. We checked on Ginger and he seems above board. His neighbours told our Dublin colleagues that he often works as a driver for transport companies and is away a good bit. He has the reputation of being a nice quiet man.'

'So Ginger doesn't have a criminal record of any sort,' Percy mused. 'And Brannigan has kept his nose clean for a good few years now. Still, you never know what he might be capable of if he saw a young girl standing around on her own in the middle of the night. No one ever found out his motive for killing that girl in Dublin.' He turned abruptly to Murray. 'Let's look at the Stanley Wallace case. Are we getting anywhere on that?'

Later that evening Murray sat at his desk and went over all the notes on both murder cases. Percy had been his usual critical self regarding their handling of the Stanley Wallace murder and Murray had to grudgingly admit that his boss was right. They were overlooking some glaring fact, that was for sure. Once you reached a dead end the standard practice was to start from scratch and go over all the statements and reports. Had someone said something that they should have picked up on? They had learned that Stanley Wallace had a number of enemies including at least two disgruntled employees. However, their British colleagues had established that the two employees had reliable alibis and although some of Stanley's associates were not very complimentary about his business practices, their grudges did not appear to be of the kind that would make him a target. That left the common motives of greed and jealousy.

Next on his list was Steve Donlon who he had not yet interviewed with regard to Stanley Wallace's murder. When he had spoken to him on the phone, Donlon said that he left Ballyamber House around half past ten or eleven on the night Stanley was killed. Penny Wallace stated that she was in her bedroom and had heard his car driving off but could not verify the time. Gregory Wallace claimed that he said goodnight to his father in the library at around eleven o'clock and had gone to bed. He was using the guest bedroom in the East Wing which faced the front of the house. Rod Kirwin was out, presumably with his girlfriend Vanessa Ryan. Rod had had an altercation with Stanley. Was that a motive for killing him? Somehow it did not tie in with Rod's infatuation for Vanessa Ryan. Murray doubted that Rod had the resolution to carry out a murder.

Gregory had perhaps the most obvious motive in that he was sole heir to the Wallace fortune. He might have had a disagreement with his father regarding Penny's affair with Steve Donlon. Stanley had ordered herself and Donlon out of the house. But even before this affair, there had been trouble between his father and his wife. Friends of the family had revealed that Stanley Wallace considered his daughter-in-law as an outsider and treated her with contempt.

They had several stories to tell on that subject, either what they had observed themselves or what was being gossiped about in their various circles.

Gregory might have had another motive. He lived in his father's shadow. 'No comparison with his father' had been a favourite remark by all their acquaintance. Some years before Gregory had briefly managed a small publishing company which his father had acquired on a whim but it had been wound up within two years. There were many who claimed this was because of Gregory's incompetence but the police officer in London who had conducted the enquiries had made a note to the effect that the publishing company could not have been saved without a further investment by Stanley Wallace which he was not prepared to make. Gregory had then been given a non-executive role in a mining company in South Africa with a suitably handsome salary and was not required to have anything to do with running the business itself. Had Gregory's resentment at this treatment been festering and finally come to a head? Gregory's shock and grief over his father's murder had appeared genuine both to Murray and to the two officers who had taken a lengthy statement from him. It was generally agreed among their joint acquaintance that Stanley and his son were very close. But who knew what went on in Gregory's head?

Murray studied the sketch he had made of the layout of Ballyamber House. The Wallaces were in the habit of parking their cars round the back and entering the house by the rear door. However, on the night of the murder Rod had entered by the front door. He claimed that he had not noticed that one of the windows in the library was open nor that the light was on in the room. Was that possible? Or had the window been closed when he came home? The coroner had put the time of the murder between approximately eleven when Gregory had said goodnight to his father and four or five the next morning. What time did Rod come home? Why had Mrs Quinn not noticed if the light was on in the library and the window open when she arrived for work?

Murray resisted the craving for a cigarette and sat in thought for a few minutes before turning back to the information they had compiled on Steve Donlon as part of their routine enquiries. He was a colourful character who had spent several years in Beverly Hills working with the rich and famous on designs for their homes, according to what he told acquaintances. His name was not well known, however, as the police officer who was helping them in their enquiries was able to tell them. A little more digging revealed that Donlon was the live-in lover of Maybelle Charles, a Hollywood actress no longer in the first flush of youth who had minor roles in several films and TV shows. She had many friends in the area and Donlon received commissions from them mainly as a favour to her. Most of his work appeared to be in the area of garden maintenance but he had twice worked with an eminent interior decorator and had glowing references from his days in Beverly Hills. When he split up with Maybelle he returned to Ireland where he started a small company specialising in the improvement and design of houses and apartments. A check on his finances revealed that, if not making a fortune, he seemed to be doing all right, much of his work being on holiday apartments around the Costa Blanca area in Spain. No one knew exactly how he came to Stanley Wallace's attention but his involvement in the improvements to Ballyamber House, property of business tycoon Stanley Wallace, had certainly done him no harm.

    What motive could he have had for killing Wallace? Rod had hinted that his sister and Steve Donlon were getting very friendly and there had certainly been a lot of tension in the house when Murray and Flynn had called there. Enough motive to kill Stanley Wallace? It was believed that Wallace still owed Steve Donlon a sizeable sum of money for the work he had carried out so far and there was still a lot to be done. Would he kill the goose that laid the golden eggs? Donlon had the reputation for being hot-tempered but it was a big step from there to killing someone. Opportunity he certainly had, Murray mused. There was only his and Penny Wallace's word for the time of his leaving the house. Donlon was due to come in for an interview the next morning and Flynn had prepared a list of questions in their file on him. Murray read these through slowly and added one or two of his own.

    He finally gave up the struggle and pulled his cigarette packet out of his pocket. He made for the rear of the building but stopped just as he got to the back door as a thought struck him. Ginger Ford and Steve Donlon had something in common. They both travelled regularly to the continent.

Chapter Thirty-Eight

Steve Donlon arrived punctually at Killglash garda station for his interview with Murray and Flynn. He had acquired an attractive suntan during his time in Spain, a fact emphasised by his open-necked white shirt.

'As you can imagine this whole business has absolutely devastated me,' he said. 'It's the last thing anyone could expect to happen. Stanley was a businessman, a very successful one, but I don't know of a single person who would have wanted to harm him.'

Murray watched him from the other side of the desk. Donlon appeared supremely self-assured with no hint of nervousness evident about his interview with the gardai. He looked like a man with nothing to hide which did not exactly suit Murray. 'I appreciate your taking the time to come and see us,' he said. 'There are just a few things that we'd like to discuss with you. You didn't know Stanley Wallace that well, did you? When did you first meet him?'

Outside the sun made a sudden appearance through the clouds and glistened on Killglash's still-wet streets. Somewhere in the building a door slammed and there was the sound of muffled voices which meant, as Murray knew, that Garda Ger Buckley was sneaking out for a smoke in the backyard. Ger might be a pessimist by nature but he firmly believed – and frequently said – that smoking was not necessarily an unhealthy thing to do. There were times when Murray would have liked to believe him.

Donlon shrugged slightly. 'We met at a party in London, actually, some time last year. Stanley had just purchased Ballyamber House and was full of talk about turning it into some kind of Irish castle.'

'Who introduced you?' This from Flynn.

'The party was thrown by a men's fashion boutique owner who I happened to know from my time in Beverly Hills. Jon Smythe-Jones. He'd just opened a store in Kensington High Street, the party was to launch that. Stanley and Greg both shopped at his stores. Jon knew I was into interior designing so he introduced us to see if I could help Stanley in any way.'

It sounded reasonable, Murray thought, and was easy to verify if it became necessary. Time to move on to the next point on the list of questions. 'I understand there was some unpleasantness between Stanley Wallace and yourself. Could you tell us about that, please?'

Donlon looked embarrassed for a moment then he recovered himself. 'I had started an affair with Penny Wallace and we were discovered in bed when Stanley and Greg came back unexpectedly from their trip to Dublin. Stanley read me the riot act and said he wanted me out of the house.' He looked from Flynn to Murray as if to see how they took this piece of information. 'I knew he'd calm down given time but I thought it best to quit the house as soon as I reasonably could.'

'What time were you and Mrs Wallace discovered?' Murray remembered the tension in the house when he and Flynn had called there.

'Around half past ten or so.'

'But you didn't leave the house until much later. Why was that?'

'I wanted to speak to Stanley Wallace and to Greg, of course. Stanley is a man of the world and I reckoned that when he had calmed down he'd realise that he still needed me. And I was pretty sure that he'd be able to persuade Gregory to think as he did.' Again Donlon glanced from one man to the other. 'Penny Wallace is an attractive woman but obviously the whole affair was just that – a passing fling, if you will. We'd only just started, the whole thing never really got off the ground.'

There was a minute or two of silence while all three of them contemplated his words.

'And did you get to see Stanley Wallace?' The question came from Flynn who sat next to Murray with his notebook open in front of him.

'I saw Stanley very briefly,' Donlon said, speaking slowly as if choosing his words. 'He didn't want to discuss the situation with me. I reminded him that he owed me a lot of money on the work I had done and then I packed my stuff. I looked all over the place for Greg but couldn't find him. And of course I wanted to take all my plans and designs with me. I was half afraid Stanley might tear them up or something.'

'What time did you see Stanley Wallace?' Flynn asked the question.

'I'm not sure of the exact time,' Donlon said. 'The whole day is a kind of blur. Let's face it, it was one hell of a shock having Greg walk in to the bedroom and catch us in bed. I went for a very long walk just to get out of everyone's way and give them time to calm down. It would have been some time in the afternoon when I ran Stanley to earth. He was in the small salon having tea, so I guess it was around four o'clock.'

'And when you'd spoken to him, what did you do next?'

Donlon wrinkled his forehead. 'I went looking for Penny but she wasn't anywhere to be found downstairs. Neither was Greg. I half hoped they'd got together and made their peace with each other.'

'But that wasn't the case?' Murray's expression remained neutral, masking his thoughts. It appeared that Donlon was a ladies' man, quite used to having affairs be they long or short. His opinion that everything could be smoothed over was almost naïve but what angered Murray was the man's total indifference to any hurt he might have caused to Penny Wallace's husband. It showed a remarkable callousness in regard to other people's feelings.

'I finally found Penny in the kitchen having some supper at around six o'clock or so. I gathered from her that she hadn't spoken to either Greg or Stanley. After that I went upstairs to finish off my packing. I remembered that I'd left some drawings in the attic and I went to fetch them but couldn't find them at first, they'd been stuffed into one of those cardboard boxes up there and moved to another part of the room. All in all, by the time I was ready to leave the house it must have been half past nine or ten o'clock. I didn't check the time to be honest but I did get home to Dublin at just after 2 a.m.'

'No one saw you leaving the house?' This again from Flynn.

'No one saw me leaving the house. After all that had happened you could hardly expect one of the Wallace family to stand on the doorstep and wave me off, now could you?'

'Did you stop anywhere on the way? Fill the car up, for example?' Murray asked.

'No. I filled the car up in Killglash that morning and I didn't need to stop anywhere.'

Murray and Flynn exchanged a quick glance. 'You drove into Killglash before you left? You didn't mention that before.'

Donlon stared at them for a moment. 'Sorry, I forgot about that, like I said, everything about that day is a bit of a blur. I'd ordered a book through that little newsagents near the supermarket and I wanted to pick it up. It's on local history and hard to come by. I like to read up on stuff like that when I'm working in an area. And I filled up the car while I was there. That would have been in the early afternoon.'

'Do you have receipts from the newsagents or from the filling station?'

'Yes, I can let you have those. They'll be in my office in Dublin. I give everything of that nature to my accountant. But they'll probably remember me at the newsagents.'

'Do you know Ginger Ford?' Murray sprung the question and had the satisfaction of seeing Donlon at a loss for an answer but only for a moment.

'Ginger Ford? Who's that? I never heard the name before.'

'You do business on the continent,' Murray said smoothly. 'Ginger is a long-distance lorry driver. He was down here not long ago. I just wondered if there was any connection. You've never used his services?'

'A connection? No, I've never heard of him until now. Do you suspect him of having anything to do with Stanley's murder?'

'You know us, we ask all sorts of things,' Murray said conversationally. 'You went to Spain the next day after you left Ballyamber. When did you get back?'

'A friend of mine had asked me if I would I come to Alicante with him to look at some houses and I rang him to say I would. He told me he was leaving that very day, the day after my arrival back in Dublin and he got me a plane ticket. I stayed a week with him and only got news of Stanley's murder through friends in Dublin and of course when you contacted me there.'

When Donlon had left them, Murray turned with raised eyebrows to Flynn. 'Beverly Hills comes to Ballyamber. What do you reckon, Jim?'

'Let's see if Donlon's car was picked up on a camera anywhere between here and Dublin on the night in question.' As he spoke Flynn got to his feet and stretched himself. 'I'll get on to that now. I'm meeting Kay for lunch at the hotel so, as it's next door, I can check up on the newsagent where he says he picked up the book.'

Murray felt a momentary pang. He and Flynn invariably had lunch together, either a quick takeaway eaten at the station or a more leisurely meal in one of Killglash's many eateries. It looked as if that was slowly coming to an end. Not that he didn't wish his young subordinate all the luck in the world in his affairs of the heart but he would miss the companionship.

'I'll see if I can have lunch with Nicola Ryan and young Vanessa,' he said. 'We have to find out where she was before Rod Kirwin picked her up on the night she was supposed to be babysitting for the Mitchells.'

At the door of the interview room Flynn paused. 'Are we really getting anywhere on these two cases, Alan? Sometimes I think we keep turning down a blind alley.'

'A blind alley? Very romantic. You've been reading Raymond Chandler again, me lad. This is real-life Killglash. Every road has a silver turning.'

Chapter Thirty-Nine

Nicola agreed to meet Murray in Killglash's only Italian restaurant, the San Marco, which was located in the little shopping mall.

She was already seated at the coveted window table when Murray arrived. A smile lit up her face at the sight of him, causing him a momentary feeling of guilt at her obvious pleasure that they were to have lunch together. He had not yet figured out a way to signal that he was not interested in forming a relationship with her or indeed any one else. It might mean that he was lonely but at least his life was not complicated. There was a lot to be said for being heart-whole, he sometimes told himself.

'Vanessa will be along in the minute, she finishes classes at one o'clock today,' Nicola told him when he had sat down opposite her. 'I haven't been here before,' she added, with an approving look around the cheerful room. The place was only half full at this time of day, making it an ideal location for a private chat.

'The food's good,' Murray assured her. 'You have to book a table in the evening but lunch time is pretty slack for some unknown reason.' He and Flynn often ate here or ordered a pizza take-away if they were very busy.

Vanessa joined them while they were still studying the menu. She looked younger today in her school uniform with her face free of make-up.

Alessandro, the proprietor came to serve them and he and Murray exchanged a bit of chit chat about the weather before moving onto choosing what they wanted to eat. In the end they all plumped for spaghetti a la San Marco which was the house specialty.

'I think you enjoyed this last time,' Alessandro said with a smile at Vanessa. 'Your young man certainly enjoyed, but love makes all things sweet.'

Vanessa coloured up to the roots of her hair and her mouth formed a sulky pout. She looked from her mother to Murray. 'I suppose you got me here on purpose,' she said.

'Of course not,' Nicola reached out a hand to her daughter and patted her on the arm.

'No, not on purpose,' Murray said almost at the same time. 'But seeing as how we've got into deep water so fast, I might as well come clean. We do need some straight answers from you, Vanessa, and I'd prefer to get them off-line so to speak. I'm going to ask you something and I want the truth from you.'

He had their full attention now and as far as he could tell, Vanessa was bracing herself for his next question. 'What did you do on the night the Dutch tourist was killed? John Mitchell swears you were not babysitting for him that night. You could not have been with Rod Kirwin because he was at a party in Ballyamber House. So where were you, Vanessa, from five o'clock to let's say around eleven o'clock on that night?'

He thought she was going to cry but she checked herself and after a swift glance at her mother, she answered him in a steady voice. 'I visited a classmate. We've only just become friends. I told her I was meeting Rod but that he wouldn't be able to get away until late because of this party for Sophie Hampshire. We stayed in at her place. Her mum and dad were out at some do or another. Rod picked me up there. We went to McDowds pub but he couldn't stay too long because he had to get back to the party. We met Maike in the pub and Rod offered her a lift when she said she needed to get back to Ballyamber.'

Murray cast a warning glance at Nicola who had drawn in her breath in an audible gasp. 'This is the whole truth, is it?' he asked.

Vanessa nodded. 'Yes.'

'Can you tell me the name and address of this classmate?' He pulled out his notebook. 'It's important we speak to her, as you can understand.'

'Her name is Orla McKenzie and she lives here in Killglash. She won't get into trouble, will she?'

'I can't think why she should,' Murray said. 'But we do need to verify your story, especially the timeframe.'

'OK. Can I call her first so she doesn't get a fright? You won't tell her mum and dad?'

'You can certainly call her but when we talk to her we'd like one parent to be present.'

Vanessa digested this in silence then nodded. 'Thanks,' she said and sounded as if she meant it.

They were interrupted by the arrival of Alessandro with their order. When he had satisfied himself that they had everything they needed, Nicola turned to her daughter.

'You've been here with Rod? When was that?'

'A few times. I might have told you I was helping out at Mitchells.' Vanessa's voice was subdued.

'I see.' Nicola was obviously keeping her wrath in check. 'I take it that Rod made no objection to your telling me a pack of lies?'

Vanessa flushed and the sulky look came down over her face again. 'He didn't know. He didn't really ask me about things like that and I didn't tell him.'

Murray helped himself to extra parmesan cheese and took a sip from his glass of mineral water, wondering how to ease the tension. At least they had gotten to the bottom of the mystery of where Vanessa had spent the evening while she waited for Rod. They could tick another item on their list even if it did not get them very far in solving the mystery of why Maike was murdered.

The meal progressed in a stony silence. Nicola pushed the food around on her plate, obviously too upset to eat, and Vanessa concentrated rather fiercely on her meal. Although Murray cleared his plate with every appearance of enjoyment, his thoughts were in fact elsewhere. It looked as if Rod Kirwin was in the clear, at least as far as Maike's murder was concerned and his gut feeling told him that Rod had nothing to do with Stanley Wallace's death either. Which while narrowing the field of suspects, left far too many questions unanswered. They desperately needed a motive and then proof.

It was a relief when Alessandro came to collect their plates. They all declined dessert and ordered coffee, a latte for Murray and Nicola and a cappuccino for Vanessa. It was while they were savouring their coffees that Vanessa dropped her little bombshell. She had been shifting about in her chair and toying with her cup and now she wiped some of the froth from her upper lip with the back of her hand and addressed Murray

'You remember you asked me if I saw anything on our way home to Ballyamber that night, the night the Dutch girl was killed? I've been thinking about that. I did see something but I don't know if it means anything.' She hesitated a moment before continuing. 'A white van stopped down the road from the supermarket. It was just when we were dropping Maike off in the village.'

'A van came along as Maike was getting out of the car?'

Vanessa nodded. 'Yeh. I turned around to wave back at her and I just saw the white van pulling in down the road a bit. I didn't think anything of it.'

'Rod Kirwin didn't see it?'

'No, I don't think so, he was looking ahead through the windscreen, you know. He was driving.' She pulled the sleeves of her school jumper down over her hands and studied the result.

'A white van? You're sure of that?'

'Yes, pretty sure.'

'You saw it pulling in, you said. Pulling in where, exactly?'

She appeared to think about this for a minute or two. 'I'm not sure. I know it stopped but I'm not sure where. It was further down the road at any rate. A bit away from the supermarket where Maike was standing.'

'Did you see someone getting out of the van?'

'No. I only looked back quickly as we were driving off. I didn't see anyone.'

'Would you recognise the van if you saw it again?' Ginger Ford drove a white van, he was thinking. Was Ginger their man in all this?

Vanessa shook her head slowly. 'It was a white van, like the ones that plumbers and electricians drive,' she said. 'That's all I can remember.'

Murray signalled to Alessandro for the bill. 'Do you have time to come down to the station with me and have a look at pictures of different kinds of vans? This could be very important.'

Chapter Forty

'That's all we have.' Murray finished his report on what Vanessa had told him. He and Flynn were on their way to Harold Brannigan's cottage. 'It'll be interesting to see if that van was Ginger's, given that he told us he was sleeping like a baby that night.'

'If he was storing stuff in Agnes O'Toole's shed I'd expect people would have seen that white van of his around the village,' Flynn remarked. 'You can't sneeze in Ballyamber village without someone noticing it.'

'There are a fair few vans driving around the countryside these days with all that online ordering and delivery services. People don't take much notice any more. Now that we know about a white van in the village on the crucial night we might jog a few memories. The word will be out on local radio tomorrow and Percy is being interviewed as well.'

'I expect he'd prefer if we showed more progress on the Stanley Wallace case.' Flynn slowed down to negotiate the car round a sheep which was standing in the middle of the road. 'Which reminds me,' he added, 'just before you came back Dan Foley reported on the search of the woods up at Ballyamber House. It looked as if someone has been using that old right of way recently but with all the rain it was kind of hard to say how many people or how often. There were a few cigarette butts lying around but not your Muratti brand. They'll be analysed, of course, but it's doubtful if they'll tell us much.'

'Interesting. Could be a poacher or one of our sheep rustlers. We haven't had any complaints about missing sheep in recent months, though, have we?'

Flynn gave a short laugh. 'Considering that Agnes O'Toole has been fighting Stanley Wallace about that right of way, it might even be Agnes who's skulking around there casting spells or trying to frighten them in some way.'

They were now approaching Ballyamber village and Flynn slowed the car to walking pace as both men tried to visualise the night of Maike Bloem's murder.

'It would be easy to see anyone standing by the supermarket,' Flynn observed. 'But just here there are no street lights so Vanessa couldn't have seen too clearly. The white van would stand out, of course.'

'What was Ginger doing just there, though?' Murray spoke his thoughts aloud. 'The turnoff for Brannigan's cottage is further back. He could only be stopping at Agnes' cottage. We'll have a word with her before we approach Ginger.'

'If Ginger stopped at her place it was probably something to do with the stuff stored in her shed,' Flynn said as he halted the car in front of Agnes' cottage. 'The question is of course why he would do that in the middle of the night.'

When they knocked on Agnes' door, however, there was no answer. 'She's probably having a nap,' Flynn said. 'We can try again on our way back.'

'I hope she's all right,' Murray said. 'Agnes could be playing with fire without knowing it. The last thing we need is for her to get hit over the head.'

They drove back down the road and took the turn off for Harold Brannigan's cottage.

'I don't see Ginger's van,' Murray remarked as they waited for a response to their knock on the door. 'I expect Harold isn't back from work yet so no one's home to us by the looks of it.'

They were about to retrace their steps when Harold Brannigan pulled open the door and stood blocking the entrance with his bulk. A frown of displeasure appeared between his bushy eyebrows.

'What do ye want?'

'We'd like a word with you and Ginger,' Flynn said. 'We won't keep you long.'

Brannigan folded his arms across his massive chest and leant against the door frame. 'Ginger's not here. He went home last night.'

'Home to Dublin, is it?' Flynn was the one asking the questions.

Brannigan hesitated then apparently decided that he would impart that information. 'Yeh. Dublin.'

Murray stifled his irritation. 'Can we come in? There's no need to get out the champagne for us.'

'What do ye want?'

'Just a chat,' Flynn said, taking over again.

Brannigan unfolded his arms and moved out of the way to let them enter the kitchen. As usual the daily newspaper was on the table open at the page giving the runners for today's racing fixtures. Murray and Flynn sat down on the only two chairs without being asked and Flynn moved the overflowing ashtray to the furthest corner of the table.

Brannigan leaned against the ancient aga cooker and looked at them from under his thick eyebrows. 'Well?'

Murray decided to come straight to the point. 'What do you know about Ginger's dealings with Agnes O'Toole?'

Brannigan's eyes flickered for a moment then he recovered himself. 'Ginger and Agnes? I know nothing.'

'I think you do,' Murray said. 'It'll be better for you to tell us straight out, Harold. At the moment, we just want to know what's going on there.'

'Why don't you ask Agnes?'

'Well now, we'd never have thought of that all on our lonesomes.' Murray gave a loud sigh to indicate he was running out of patience. 'You must know if Ginger was up to something. Was he out late at night? Did anyone call to the cottage here looking for him?'

'I told you, I know nothing.' Brannigan straightened up and reached for a pack of cigarettes on the shelf above the Aga – Murray noted that they were the Marlboro brand and not Muratti. 'Ginger came down to visit me and I helped him move a box of stuff to Agnes O'Toole's shed. He was to deliver it to some friend of his who couldn't store it straight away. That's all I know about that. Now he's gone back home. I was working most of the time he was here so I've no idea what he got up to.'

'We'll be talking to Agnes,' Murray said. 'If she says different then you're in trouble, Harold.'

'I've told ye the truth. If that's all ye want from me we're finished, so ye can feck off out of my house. I'll get my solicitor on to ye.'

'I wouldn't let Father Keegan hear you using bad language, Harold,' Murray said, as he and Flynn both got to their feet. 'We'll be back don't you worry. Get your solicitor by all means if you think you need him to protect you from us dangerous types.'

As they walked to the car they heard Brannigan slamming the door behind them. Murray looked at Flynn as they drove off. 'Agnes will be just as hard a nut to crack as our friend Harold. Let's see if she's back at her cottage by now. I think Brannigan knows something.'

'Agnes claims Ginger stored some stuff in her shed when he came down to visit Brannigan.' Flynn said. 'She might be telling the truth. Why would he come down here and get mixed up in something with the local witch? Do you really think that makes any sense of anything? It can't be tied to the murders, surely.'

'Unless Ginger broke into Ballyamber House and Stanley Wallace discovered him.'

'No unidentified fingerprints were found at the scene of the crime or anywhere else in the house,' Flynn reminded him. 'It'll be hard to prove anything against Ginger without some kind of evidence. What would he have been looking for in the library?'

'He might have thought there was money lying around or other valuables,' Murray said. 'I don't really believe the theory myself but it won't do any harm to check on Ginger again. We'll talk to Agnes and see where that gets us. I'm beginning to think that our friend Ginger was down here for a specific purpose.'

Chapter Forty-One

'You wanted to see me, Sergeant Murray?' Penny Wallace sounded breathless as if she had been running.

Murray had been standing by the window of the small salon at Ballyamber House as he waited for her. He was alone, judging it would be easier to gain her confidence than if he had Flynn scribbling in his notebook in the background.

'There are a few things I'd like to clear up.' He hoped she would relax a bit, right now she looked as if she might faint at any moment.

'Please sit down.' Penny gestured towards the fireplace where two armchairs were placed on opposite sides of the empty grate.

The room was chilly although the central heating was on. It would be expensive to keep the place warm in winter, Murray reflected. The high ceilings and large windows would let in a lot of cold from the icy winds that swept down Ardnabrone mountain.

'What would you like to ask me?' Penny seated herself in the chair opposite Murray.

Murray took stock of her face, noting her pallor, the shadows under her eyes and the restless way she played with the bracelet of her watch. Penny Wallace was under severe strain and it was his job to find out what that strain was and if it had any bearing on what had happened in Ballyamber House. Rod Kirwin had remarked that Penny and Steve Donlon were getting "a bit over-fond of each other" and that there had been a row. Steve Donlon had played it down, although admitting they had been discovered in bed together. That was perhaps the best place to start.

'Were you and Steve Donlon having an affair?'

Penny gave a visible start at the directness of the question. She stared at him, her brown eyes wide with surprise then she looked away, fixing her gaze on the empty grate in the fireplace so that he could no longer see the expression in her eyes. After what seemed an age she nodded. 'We didn't really have what you'd call an affair, nothing so permanent as that implies. It was – it all sounds so sordid and cheap.' Her voice trailed away then she recovered herself. 'I'm sure you'll think me a terrible person. Steve and I had a one-night stand - I suppose that's what you'd call it. It was all a mistake, it should never have happened. It's over now.'

'I'm not here to judge you,' Murray said quietly. 'Now, let's get the facts straight. You and Donlon ended up in bed together. When was this?'

'Gregory and Stanley had gone to Dublin with Sophie Winslow for a business meeting. It was the day before Stanley was murdered. I suppose I was feeling lonely - neglected.' She flashed an almost defiant glance at him before continuing. 'I was flattered that Steve should be interested in me. We had a pleasant day's outing and then that evening we – it happened. Greg and Stanley came home early next morning from Dublin, I'm not sure why exactly and we were discovered.'

Murray waited for her to go on. It was all pretty much as he had imagined it: Donlon was attractive to women, there was no doubt of that. Penny Wallace was a beautiful woman at a loose end, feeling neglected by her own admission. Or maybe she just wanted to have fun. Women's logic often surprised Murray. Even his wife Sheila's way of reasoning had occasionally remained a mystery to him. And as for Elena. But here he stopped himself. Sheila had been missing now for more years than he cared to remember and he himself had screwed up on his relationship with Elena. No one could accuse him of understanding how to deal with women.

Penny evidently found his silence encouraging because she started speaking again. 'Stanley was furious and wanted to throw myself and Steve out of the house but Greg managed to calm him down. Steve came to see me, to say goodbye and that he would be in touch when he got to Dublin.'

'What time was that?' Murray knew the answer because he had checked it before coming here. In her previous conversations with

Flynn and himself she had told them that Donlon had left Ballyamber House at around 11 p.m.

'I'm not exactly sure,' she said slowly, her forehead furrowed in concentration. 'I was having something to eat in the kitchen. That would have been around half past six or seven o'clock. He came to say goodbye, that he'd be off as soon as he'd finished packing. Later on I heard a car driving off so I assumed it was Steve but that was much later.' She stopped and looked at Murray. 'Of course that might have been Rod's car. When he got back he came up to my bedroom for a chat.'

'So you don't know if it was Donlon's car you heard or if it was your brother's car when he came home? Is that what you're saying?'

Penny clasped and unclasped her hands, her blonde hair fell over her face as she bent her head in concentration.

'Well?' said Murray when the silence had stretched beyond his patience.

'Oh, I don't know, Sergeant. I'm not sure of anything any more. The last I saw of Steve was when he came to say goodbye while I was having supper in the kitchen. I couldn't really tell you what time he left the house. I thought it was his car I heard but maybe I was mistaken. I was so upset anyway that I might have imagined it.'

'You never mentioned that your brother came to see you that night. What time was that?

'That was the night he told me he had given the Dutch girl a lift back to Ballyamber.' She closed her eyes briefly as if trying to shut out the memory. 'I couldn't say what time that was exactly but I know I went upstairs to bed at around ten o'clock. I couldn't sleep and had the light on. Rod popped in for a chat around half past eleven or quarter to twelve, I should think. Yes, that's right. I remember looking at my travel clock before that. He left after ten or fifteen minutes. I still couldn't sleep and I was thinking of making myself a hot drink in the kitchen but then I heard footsteps and thought it might be Stanley going downstairs. I didn't want to run into him so I stayed in my bedroom.'

'This was somewhere around midnight?' Murray hid his surprise. According to the coroner's report, Stanley Wallace had been killed some time between 11 p.m. and 9 a.m. If what she said was true, they could pinpoint the time of the murder more accurately.

'It must have been around one o'clock or possibly later.'

'How did you know it was Stanley Wallace? It could have been your husband, could it not?'

'Greg had moved into the East wing. He was using the guest room next to Rod's. I wouldn't have heard him from my bedroom. The only person in my corridor was Stanley Wallace. I'm sure I heard his bedroom door open. There were voices downstairs, I thought it might have been Rod he was talking to.'

Chapter Forty-Two

Following his interview with Penny, Murray returned to Killglash garda station to find his boss Percy pacing up and down.

'I'm getting so much stick over the Stanley Wallace case,' he said. 'Are we progressing on this? It shouldn't be too difficult. The evidence suggests that there was no forced entry and that leaves us with Gregory Wallace, Rod Kirwin and Steve Donlon as suspects, or even Penny Wallace come to that.'

Murray filled him in on his conversation with Penny, pointing out that they still had to verify the exact time that Donlon had left Ballyamber House.

'And motive?' Percy lowered his voice only a fraction. 'What motive could Donlon have had for killing Stanley Wallace? A motive for killing Penny Wallace's husband, yes, I'd buy that. He might have wanted to get him out of the way. Killing the man who's paying him tens of thousands for his services doesn't make sense.'

'Stanley did kick him out of the house according to Penny.' Murray knew that when Percy got into one of these moods it was next to impossible to calm him down.

'Hmm.' Percy looked about him as if checking that he could not be overheard then said in an almost normal tone. 'Alan, I know you were successful in getting the killer when those poor girls were murdered a few years back but we have to get Wallace's murder sorted fairly quickly. Some smart reporter is going to come down here in a month's time and say we're dragging our heels. We have to nail whoever did this as quick as we can. Not to mention clearing up Maike Bloem's murder.'

When Percy had gone, Murray updated the file on the Stanley Wallace case in readiness for the next briefing. Flynn had already left, he noted, again feeling a small stab of loneliness. Not so long ago they would both have stayed on throwing up ideas and theories on the murders.

On the drive home Murray went over his conversation with Percy and conceded that his boss was right. The murder of a wealthy businessman and lack of police progress was still getting media attention albeit not so much as at first. Maike Bloem's murder had slipped out of the news as other headlines claimed attention but Ballyamber House itself, the supposed curse of Ardnabrone claiming three lives a year and the Wallace family fortunes were all rich pickings for any journalist who was at a loss what to write about in his Sunday newspaper column.

He had just taken off his overcoat when there was a soft tap on the door.

'Alan, I've been waiting up to see if I could catch you.' Nicola Ryan's voice was agitated as she stood in the doorway.

Murray was tired and his head was starting to ache. It had been a long day. He had been looking forward to slumping down in his shabby armchair beside the fire and switching off his brain for the night. Instead it looked as if Nicola had problems of some kind which she needed to discuss with him.

'Come in.' He held the door open for her. 'What can I do for you?'

She came and sat down on one of the kitchen chairs. 'I might just be getting over-anxious about this,' she said. The room was chilly and she drew her coat more closely around her. 'I hope I'm not wasting your time but I thought I should tell you.'

'No problem. Let me light the fire first before we both get frostbite.' Murray took a box of matches from the mantelpiece. He had set the fire this morning before going to work – in the days when Elena lived next door she would have come in during the day and done this for him – and now held a match to it. As the flames licked around the kindling, he seated himself at the other side of the kitchen table and looked encouragingly at Nicola. 'What's worrying you? Everything all right with Vanessa?'

She pulled a face at the mention of her daughter. 'Vanessa is being her usual mulish self. She's at that difficult rebellious age. What she really needs I suppose is a father.'

'Is she still seeing Rod Kirwin?'

'I've told her he can come and visit her at home here with me but she mustn't go out alone on dates with him. The Mitchells have told her they don't need her any more so she's feeling pretty low at the moment.'

'You've spoken to Rod?'

'Yes, I have. My first impression is that he's a brooding sort of young man, not someone you can get to know easily, I should think. But there, I won't rush to judgement on it. He says he loves her and is quite happy to do the right thing.' She looked earnestly at Murray. 'Is he going to get into trouble?'

Murray shrugged. 'We'll refer it to the child welfare people. They'll give you advice on how to handle the matter and decide if any action needs to be taken.'

'But maybe you could talk to her and to him, just to drive the point home? I really would prefer if Vanessa concentrated on school. She likes you, so perhaps your words will have more weight than mine.'

'I can try,' Murray said. He was surprised to learn that Vanessa should like him. That could only be Nicola's influence, he reflected, and was irritated at the feeling of guilt which this thought produced. Damn it all, he had never given her the slightest encouragement. 'Was that what you wanted to see me about?'

'No, it was something else.' She chewed her lower lip for a moment before continuing. 'I was in the post office this morning to send off a parcel to my niece in Canada. She's just had a baby. That old woman Agnes O'Toole, who everybody says is a witch, was in front of me at the counter. She was having a great gossip with Mrs Scanlon and I couldn't help but hear some of it.'

The post office in Ballyamber was really a newsagent's which sold knickknacks of every sort and had a small section at the back devoted to post office business. It always surprised Murray that the place survived considering its proximity to the supermarket but Scanlon's shop had its share of loyal customers who spent part of their pension there every Friday.

'What did Agnes have to say for herself?' Murray asked. 'Who did she put a curse on this week?'

'Mrs Scanlon was talking about Ballyamber House. She was wondering if the Wallace family would sell it now and go back to live in England. And then she mentioned how the gardai weren't getting anywhere on finding who killed Stanley Wallace.' Nicola coloured slightly. 'You probably know that the village is forever moaning about something,' she said apologetically.

Murray gave a short laugh which was totally devoid of humour. 'The good people of Ballyamber watch too much television,' he said. 'They think we can look at a piece of thread or a footprint, nod our heads and arrest the right person in-between the washing powder commercials, all within a few hours of the crime.'

'You know I don't think that,' Nicola said hastily. 'I can appreciate how difficult it might be for you all.'

'What did Agnes have to say to it?'

'She said that she had a pretty good idea who the murderer was. Then she started to whisper so I didn't catch more than a few words. She said something like "but I saw the car driving away so it has to be him."'

Chapter Forty-Three

'She saw the car driving away,' Murray repeated to Jim Flynn as the two of them sat in his office the next morning. 'We have three suspects for Stanley Wallace's murder: his son Gregory, Rod Kirwin and Steve Donlon. The only one of those three who would be driving away from Ballyamber House late at night is Steve Donlon.'

'We'll have to see if his car shows up on CCTV somewhere that night,' Flynn said. 'It's still hard to figure out what his motive would be, though.'

'He'd started an affair with Penny Wallace and Stanley was furious about that and wanted to throw him out. Maybe they got into an argument. It looked like Stanley was not expecting to be attacked. On the other hand, Stanley owed him a lot of money, or so he claims.'

'Agnes had better watch herself,' Flynn observed. 'She's playing a dangerous game. Did anyone else overhear her in Scanlon's shop?'

'Nicola said she was the only other customer. Not that that means much. Mrs Scanlon is as big a gossip as Mrs Quinn.'

They were interrupted by the persistent ringing of the phone. Flynn answered it and as he listened to whoever was on the other end, his body became taut with tension. He pulled his notebook in front of him and opened it at a new page.

'Torrevieja? Where's that? The Costa Blanca? Yes, sure, can you spell all that for me, please? Yes, we'll get back to you on that as soon as we can.'

He scribbled hastily for some minutes then finally signed off and put the phone back in its cradle. 'That was the police in Spain, the *Policia Municipal*' he said, consulting his notes. 'It appears that

Ginger Ford has turned up in a place called Torrevieja. That's on the Costa Blanca. He was interviewed by the local police about his involvement in a forgery racket. He's asked to speak to you, Alan.'

'What with the *Politie* in Holland and the *Policia Municipal* in Spain, we're getting to be very international down here in Ballyamber,' Murray observed to Flynn as the two of them waited to board a flight which was to take them to Alicante. 'We'll have to watch it or Percy will be sending us to language classes.'

'Might not be a bad idea,' Flynn laughed. 'Maybe we should call to Zandervoort on our way back from Torrevieja. Have you been to Spain, Alan?'

'No, I've never been further than Co. Mayo on my holidays,' Murray said, which was not strictly true. 'What about you?'

'I've been to Ibiza a few years ago,' Flynn admitted. 'I enjoyed it, I must say. Went with a few of the lads and got a bit of a suntan.'

'Sun, sea, sand and sin.' Murray grinned at his companion. 'You didn't fall for a pretty senorita, I take it?'

'There were a lot of pretty girls there,' Flynn said reminiscently. 'We had a great time.'

'There's our flight being called,' Murray said. 'Spare me the romantic details until I have a few tequilas inside me.'

'Tequila is Mexican not Spanish, Alan.'

'Which proves what a man of the world you are, Jim.'

Murray's first impression of Torrevieja was of blue sky, warm sunshine even at this time of year, and dazzlingly white buildings. The taxi put them down at an unprepossessing yellow washed building which housed the local police station on the *Calle de la Pedrera*. A smart young officer with limited English showed them into a waiting room only to collect them again minutes later and escort them to a small office at the end of the corridor. Murray began to worry that they should have brought an interpreter with them.

'Welcome to Torrevieja,' Comisario Felipe Herrera, the police officer Flynn had spoken to, put down the copy of the *Costa Blanca News*, one of the English language newspapers in the area, which he had been studying and came to shake hands with them. He ordered coffee for them all and when it had been served he got down to business. His English was fluent and almost without accent.

'We raided an apartment in the *Calle Leandro* yesterday which we believe was the centre of a smuggling operation and Mr Ginger Ford was found to be sleeping there. He has refused to cooperate with us, claiming that he knows nothing about the two men who were also in the apartment. He says he was delivering furniture to a villa near the *Playa del Cura* and was told he could get a bed in that apartment.' Hererra shrugged his shoulders and spread his hands. 'We will have to let him go if we cannot find anything to charge him with. His vehicle has been searched and it is clean. He told us you would vouch for him.'

'We certainly know him and as far as we have been able to establish, he doesn't have a criminal record,' Murray said, speaking slowly. 'What about the two men arrested with him? Have they said anything?'

Herrera shook his head. 'No, but we have enough evidence from other sources to hold them. They are on our wanted list. With Mr Ford it is different. They also say they do not know him. Perhaps he will come clean with you. We really have nothing to hold him on. We also have no criminal record of him here. He has never come to our attention.'

'We'll give it a whirl.' Murray drained his coffee cup, wiping his mouth surreptitiously on the back of his hand. This elegant young Comisario with his fluent English was starting to make him feel like a slightly out of touch cop.

'When you have finished, may I invite you to dinner tonight? My wife will be very pleased to meet you. You are staying in town, I believe?'

'That's very kind of you,' Murray told him. 'We're staying at the *Luz del sol*.' He shot a triumphant glance at Flynn that he had managed to remember the name.

'Ah yes.' Herrera nodded. 'This is owned by an Englishman. Torrevieja is very popular with the English and the Irish,' he added hastily. 'The apartment we raided is owned by an English lady, I believe she is an actress, Sophie Winslow. Perhaps you have heard of her?'

Ginger Ford perched on the edge of his chair, his hands clasped between his knees and kept his eyes firmly fixed on the toes of his scuffed trainers until Herrera had left the room. When the door closed, he breathed an audible sigh of relief and straightened up in his chair.

'I had nothing to do with those men,' he said. 'I was delivering a table and chairs to a villa near the *Playa del Cura* and a key was left for me to use the apartment where the police found me.'

'Who left the key for you?' Flynn asked.

Ginger blinked rapidly at the question. 'The customer I delivered the furniture to arranged it. The police took all my documents but it's on there, there's a note that I could sleep in that apartment in *Calle Leandro.*'

'The customer is a Mr Geraldo Butler del Rosario,' Flynn said, reading from the notes he had made at the meeting with Comisario Herrera. 'Did he contact you directly to deliver the furniture?'

'His sister-in-law in Dublin rang me and arranged it. The table and the two chairs were stored with her. They're supposed to be valuable but I wouldn't know.' Ginger sounded sure of himself. 'You can check my mobile phone and you'll get her number.'

That part of his story probably added up, Murray thought. Comisario Herrera had checked on Geraldo Butler del Rosario and discovered that he was out of the country on a visit to Argentina leaving a caretaker in charge of his villa. The caretaker had confirmed Ginger's story saying that the key to the apartment in the *Calle Leandro* had been left in an envelope in the mailbox. No, he had not opened the envelope but it had felt like there was a key inside it. No, he could not say who had put the envelope in the mailbox. 'We've strayed into Alice in Wonderland territory,' had been Murray's remark on hearing this and Flynn had been hard put to translate for the Comisario.

'You'll be able to get me out of here?' Ginger looked at them with something like panic in his eyes. 'I've told that Comisario fella all I know. They've nothing on me.'

'We'll have to see,' Murray said. He leaned forward, resting his hands on the hard wooden table in front of him. 'Tell me now, how do you know Sophie Winslow?'

Ginger's reaction was everything he could have hoped for. The colour drained out of his face and he stared at Murray as if seeing a ghost. He shifted in his chair and swallowed hard. 'Sophie Winslow? I've heard of her. She's an actress, isn't she?'

'She owns the apartment in the *Calle Leandro* that you were sleeping in,' Murray said. 'She's been staying at Ballyamber House on and off for the past few weeks. Now, isn't it the most wonderful of coincidences that you should happen to get a key to her apartment, especially as this key seems to have materialised under very mysterious circumstances? What do you say, Ginger? What should we make of this?'

Ginger licked his lips, his eyes darting from Flynn to Murray and back again. 'I'd no idea the place belonged to her. How could I? I'm just the delivery boy.'

'Ginger's version of injured innocence is a joy to behold,' Murray remarked as they were having breakfast next morning. 'Are you going to eat that?' He nodded at Flynn's plate.

'It's delicious,' Flynn said. 'You should try some. It's called *churro*.' He took a hearty bite of the doughnut-like roll.

'I'll stick to what I know.' Murray smeared jam onto his toast. 'Mind you, the coffee is tasty. I wonder how they make it.'

'*Café con leche*.' Flynn was clearly in his element. 'It's latte really. We have time to stop off at the local supermarket before we go to the airport if you want to get some.'

'Probably wouldn't taste the same,' Murray said. 'Not in all that rain that comes down in Ballyamber.' He leaned back in his chair and gave a sigh of satisfaction. 'I could get used to working over here.'

'I expect Felipe doesn't notice the scenery,' Flynn remarked. 'Just like we don't notice the mountains around Killglash.'

Murray's phone pinged before he could answer. It was Felipe Herrera.

'Something interesting for you, Alan. Can you come down to the office before you leave Torrevieja?'

They paid their bill at the hotel, collected their overnight bags and caught a taxi to the police station. By Flynn's reckoning they had an hour at the most before they needed to make the journey to Alicante airport.

Herrera was waiting for them.

'I am sorry to have put you to the trouble of coming back,' he said. 'I have only just found this out. We took all Mr Ford's belongings, you understand, and we gave them back to him when he was released yesterday evening after your visit.' He gestured towards some items in a plastic bag on the side table in his office. 'Unfortunately, there was a – how do you say it? - a mix-up and we did not return everything to him. I thought you would like to see what we forgot.'

He produced a box of forensic gloves. 'I think you will want to wear these before you examine the items.'

They obediently pulled on the gloves before inspecting the contents of the plastic bag. Murray extracted a wallet. He knew even before he opened it and found the student identity card with her name and photo on it that it had belonged to Maike Bloem.

'I wonder how our good friend Ginger is going to explain this.' He turned quickly to Herrera. 'You released him last night, I think you said?'

Herrera shrugged. 'We could not hold him. There was nothing to charge him with and he wished to return to Ireland. I think he will be on the way to France to the ferry by now.'

Murray swore under his breath. 'We can still pull him in. Anything else in that bag, Jim?'

Flynn carefully removed the other two items: a comb and a pair of sunglasses. 'These could be Ginger's,' he said, 'looks like a man's sunglasses at any rate and I think girls are more likely to use a brush for their hair. It's not on the list of items missing from Maike's body. Should be easy to check.'

'If Ginger uses those sunglasses for driving, he'll have discovered that he left them here,' Murray observed. 'It won't take him long to work out that Maike's wallet has been found. I wonder if he had her mobile on him.' He turned to Herrera. 'Was there a list of items taken from Ginger when he was arrested? I know you had his driving licence and passport. Was there a second mobile phone among the things you took?'

Herrera went to his desk and glanced through a sheet of paper. 'We returned Mr Ford's mobile to him but there was only one mobile phone.' He paused before adding, 'Mr Ford signed for everything. He did not mention the wallet.'

Flynn checked his watch. 'We'd better start for the airport, Alan, or we'll miss our flight. We don't want to stay another night here.'

'I think if we did, even Percy's heart would melt when he knows the circumstances.'

Chapter Forty-Four

'Guess what? I've been offered a job in New York with Allyinson & Lyle.' Rod Kirwin came and hugged his sister where she stood at the kitchen worktop peeling potatoes for that evening's roast. 'They want me as account manager for a couple of clients in the IT business and they're offering a fantastic salary!'

'A job? In New York? Oh, Rod, I can't believe it!' Penny returned his embrace and gazed at him in amazement. 'Is it really true? How did this happen?'

'You remember Arabella Bond? I dated her for a bit way back when I started university?'

Penny shook her head. 'I can't recall. Did I meet her?' She put down the peeling knife she had been using and turned to face him, leaning back against the kitchen worktop for support. She had been brooding over how to get Gregory to agree that they should return to London while the workmen were implementing Steve Donlon's improvement plans. He had not spoken to her about it and she took this as an indication that he was undecided. How best to convince him that this was the right thing to do? Once on home ground she felt that she had a better chance of repairing her marriage. With a bit of luck, she reasoned, a suitable buyer would be found for Ballyamber House and the nightmare would be over. The only stumbling block was Rod's insistence that he wanted to stay here because of his infatuation for Vanessa Ryan. She felt he could not be entirely trusted if he were left to his own devices.

'You might not have met Arabella. We only went out for a few weeks.' His face lit up. 'We've kept in touch, not regularly or anything. She moved to New York last year to start work for Allyinson & Lyle and when they were looking for someone with a background in IT marketing she mentioned me and they were interested. I sent them my C.V. ages ago and didn't expect to hear anything but then I had two telephone interviews with them last week and I got an email this morning asking me to come to New York to sign a contract. I didn't want to tell you until I was sure.'

Penny had never seen him so excited. She would have liked to share his enthusiasm but knowing Rod and his schemes she needed something more concrete to justify his belief that he had actually landed a job. She looked at him earnestly. 'I'm delighted for you but – forgive me for asking – why choose you out of x-amount of American candidates? They must know about your drinking problem, too.'

'Sister dear, don't rain on my parade.' Rod put both hands on his sister's shoulders and gave her a gentle shake. 'It just so happens that I'll be working for Arabella and she specifically requested me for the job. It's not so extraordinary as you think. She's Zachary Lyle's niece, he's one of the owners of the agency, and he's looking for new ideas. He's seen some of my work she says and he was impressed. As well as that, Arabella is getting a bit homesick and he thought someone from the old country might be a help. You don't sound very pleased,' he added, letting go of his hold on her and moving away a pace or two.

'Of course I'm pleased, delighted for you!' She came and planted a kiss on his cheek. 'I'm just so flabbergasted. It's the last thing I expected.'

'They want me out there as soon as possible. The long-term plan is to establish an office in London. You'll have to come out and visit.' His eyes sparkled. 'Get old Greg to come as well.'

'What about me?' Gregory's voice asked from the doorway.

'Rod's got a job in New York,' Penny said. 'He was just saying we should come and visit him when he gets settled in.'

For a moment there was silence then Gregory nodded in Rod's direction. 'Congratulations,' he said, his tone brusque.

'Thank you.' Rod glanced uncertainly from his sister to his brother-in-law. 'Will you excuse me for dinner tonight? I need to talk to Vanessa.'

He was gone before Penny could say anything and to her dismay, Gregory followed him from the room without a backward glance.

Penny would have been glad of Rod's company at dinner time. Although Donlon and Gregory were perfectly polite to her, they spoke almost exclusively to each other about their plans for decorating the remaining rooms and which contractor should do what work. Their relationship was emphatically business-like, there was no hint of friendship in their discourse. More importantly for Penny, they did not mention the possibility of the Wallace's returning to London while Donlon remained at Ballyamber House to supervise the work. Perhaps Rod had got it wrong, she thought dejectedly, and Greg really had no immediate plans to leave.

As she no longer had the slightest interest in anything to do with the refurbishment of Ballyamber House, she soon allowed her mind to wander. Rod's unexpected offer of a job in New York was a cause for joy. He seemed to be starting to turn his life around. And if it meant he would give up his infatuation for this girl Vanessa, so much the better for everyone. Mingled with the joy however was the knowledge that she would miss him badly. He might be exasperating, might have caused her many a sleepless night in his drinking days but he loved her unconditionally and she felt less alone when he was in the background. The prospect of losing Gregory, too, should he decide to end their marriage put Penny into a complete tailspin.

She was roused from her thoughts by a remark of Greg's. 'I hear that Agnes O'Toole claims she knows who killed my father,' he said. 'She claims she saw a car driving away that night. I'd almost given up hope of the gardai ever getting off their backsides and finding the killer.'

'Is she to be believed? From what I've heard she's always telling tales.' Donlon gave the ghost of a laugh.

'I have no idea how seriously the police are likely to take her,' Gregory said. 'I just hope they solve the case so that my poor father can rest in peace and we can all start to move on however difficult that will be.' He cast a swift glance in Penny's direction as he spoke.

Halfway through the meal Donlon received a call on his mobile and excused himself, leaving the room at almost a run.

Gregory turned to Penny. 'Is it really true that Rod has got a job?'

'Oh yes, I'm so thrilled for him.' She related the details of how her brother had been offered the position.

Gregory listened in silence. 'He's a lucky fellow,' he said. 'And I have to say he's done well, better than I would have thought, all in all.'

This was praise indeed. Without his father's influence Gregory's prejudice against her brother was already subsiding, Penny felt. Perhaps, given time, he would be able to forgive her for her foolish affair with Steve Donlon.

'I can give him some money to set himself up with an apartment in New York,' Gregory went on as if he had been thinking this over. 'He won't have very much spare cash on hand I'm sure.

'Oh Greg, that's so good of you!' Penny stretched out a hand across the table towards him but before he could respond, Steve Donlon came back into the room.

'I'm sorry about the interruption,' he said, sitting down again.

Gregory turned immediately to him to take up a point they had been discussing and they were soon talking shop again. Penny could have cried. She was sure that Gregory would have taken her outstretched hand and if she was not deceiving herself, there might have been a reconciliation, however tentative. The fact that he had thought about helping Rod seemed to suggest that his feelings were softening. Donlon's return could not have been more ill-timed.

The meal seemed to last for ever. Donlon appeared flustered, Penny thought, observing him with interest as he struggled to answer Gregory's questions on the best way of tackling the proposed work. Normally he was a smooth talker who could argue his point or make a recommendation without effort. Now he seemed to lose track of what he was saying while attempting to explain a minor point Gregory raised about the planned work.

When they had finished their coffee, Gregory excused himself muttering something about contacting a business friend who was interested to hear what progress was being made on the house. He went into the large salon. The library was hardly used since Stanley Wallace's body had been found there. Steve Donlon wandered off without saying where he was going and Penny was left to herself with the prospect of a long lonely evening in front of her. Outside it was still light and for once it was not raining. Perhaps a walk would cheer her up, she thought. She had not been out of the house today.

As she walked down the drive towards the road, Penny looked about her, noting that the leaves on the trees were slowly turning green and a few stray primroses were starting to show their faces. In the clear evening air Ardnabrone looked dark and brooding and almost close enough to touch. Penny recalled the story Mrs Quinn had told her of the mountain claiming three lives a year. Somehow it did not seem so fantastic. Two people had been murdered, one close by and the other in Ballyamber House itself. Would there be a third murder? Penny shivered suddenly, then took herself to task. It was just a legend. Steve Donlon had told her that the Irish loved ghost stories and often embellished them for the benefit of gullible tourists.

She continued on her way down the avenue with no clear idea of where she was going. The light wind blowing off the mountain felt refreshing on her face and her spirits lifted almost in spite of herself. Now that the prospect of leaving Ballyamber House was becoming real, she acknowledged that it was in a beautiful setting, surrounded by its grove of trees and with the mountain as backdrop. But she could never feel at home here. She had never wanted to live in the country, especially not with her father-in-law. The city was where she felt at home. However breath-taking the view across the valley to the mountains might be, it was not for her. Perhaps if things were different, if Stanley Wallace had been less dominating and Gregory more his own man, she might have come to terms with the loneliness of the place but as it was, she had begun to see it as a prison. Now she had reasonable hopes of returning to London. Would she and Gregory get together again? That was the question which tormented her.

At the end of the avenue she paused, debating which way to turn. To her left lay Agnes O'Toole's cottage, to her right the road led through the village and away across the mountains before joining the main road to Killarney. She had no wish to encounter Agnes and was about to turn right when she suddenly changed her mind. Why should she be scared of a nasty old woman and her silly superstitions? She squared her shoulders and turned left, walking briskly. Agnes' cottage was only a few metres away. To her surprise, the front door was slightly ajar and she hesitated a moment at the garden gate. The curtains had not been pulled and yellow lamplight spilled out onto the path. She was about to continue on her way when she heard a crash and then a sound like the moan of someone in pain. Her heart gave a thump then started to race. Had the old woman taken ill? Before she knew it, she was running up the garden path.

Cautiously she pushed the door fully open and stepped into the kitchen. 'Mrs O'Toole? Are you there?'

She stood for a moment, holding her breath and listening. The little moan came again and now she could see that one of the doors leading off the kitchen was ajar. It appeared to lead to a bedroom, she could just make out the outline of a bed, and was in darkness.

'Mrs O'Toole?' Even in an emergency she could not call the old woman by her first name.

There was no answer and all was quiet again except for her own quick breathing, sounding loud in the stillness. As she stood there she could almost feel a presence in the cottage. Her heart started to beat wildly as if it wanted to break out of her ribcage. Stifling the desire to turn and run, she stepped gingerly towards the bedroom. She reached out a hand to push the door wider and at that moment it swung inwards and the figure of a man loomed in front of her. He was dressed in dark clothes with a stocking mask over his face.

Penny froze in her tracks and stood there like a mesmerized rabbit. A few seconds later and she opened her mouth to scream but before she could make a sound she felt a searing pain as something hit the side of her head and then she was falling into blackness.

Chapter Forty-Five

'I wonder where the charming Sophie Winslow is right now,' Murray remarked as he and Flynn waited for their flight to be called at Alicante airport. 'A pity we'll have to interview her in rainy Killglash. I'd have preferred a cosy little chat on the promenade at Torrevieja with a jug of sangria thrown in or failing that a little trip to the fleshpots of London.'

'I wonder what she could have to do with anything,' Flynn said for around the tenth time. 'Ginger claims he never met her, he got this envelope with the address and the key and that's all he knows. He might even be telling the truth.'

'We should know more when we've chatted to the sister in law of Señor Geraldo Butler del Rosario this afternoon. Ginger is not someone who is closely acquainted with the truth, if you ask me. I hope he doesn't realise we've got that wallet. He'll be completely off his guard when he arrives off the ferry.'

'His fingerprints are bound to be all over Maike's wallet.' Flynn said cheerfully. 'I can't see him coming up with a credible answer to that.'

'He already has the wind up so he might do us a favour and come clean. The press will be calling this the Spanish connection and you can play the hero, Jim.'

Flynn laughed. 'What did you think of the dinner at Felipe's last night?'

'I don't like Spanish food. Italian yes, paella no. The sangria was good though.'

'Yes, I noticed you tucking in to that. He's a nice guy is Felipe.'

'If we play our cards right Percy might let us come back to do a follow up.' Murray grinned at his companion. 'I think they're calling our flight, Jim. Grab your sombrero and let's go.'

Mrs Charlotte Lewis, the sister-in-law of Geraldo Butler del Rosario, lived in a large modern house on Howth Head in Dublin. Murray had already arranged a suitable time for their visit. Mrs Lewis opened the door to them herself. She was a tall athletic looking woman with suntanned skin and a mass of jet black hair. She reminded Murray of black and white publicity photos of film stars from the 1950's.

'Do sit down. I'll just fetch the coffee,' she said, as she showed them into her elegantly furnished sitting room. She was back in a moment bearing a tray with three steaming mugs of coffee and a plate of chocolate chip cookies which she set down on a small table. 'Do help yourselves to cream and sugar.'

Murray took an appreciative sip of coffee – it tasted almost as good as what he had enjoyed in Torrevieja – and started the interview.

'Yes, I commissioned Ginger Ford to deliver a table and two chairs to my sister's place in Torrevieja,' she said in answer to Murray's question. 'My great-aunt died a few months ago and we were disposing of her furniture. Sarah, that's my sister, said she'd like to have some of the old stuff and so we agreed she'd take the table and chairs.'

'How did you decide to use Ginger Ford's services?' Flynn asked, notebook at the ready as always.

'He was recommended to me by someone at the bridge club. She'd used him when her daughter moved to Barcelona last year. I don't know how she got hold of his name, I think perhaps through her daughter who's a student, but she said he was very reliable and he didn't charge the earth.'

'And you arranged for him to get a key to an apartment where he could stay the night,' Murray prompted.

Mrs Lewis looked surprised. 'A key to an apartment? I don't know how I could have done that! I don't know anyone in Torrevieja except Sarah and Geraldo. Is that what Ginger Ford has been saying?'

'He claims that he received an envelope containing a key to an apartment in the *Calle Leandro* in Torrevieja. The envelope was put in the mailbox of your brother-in-law's villa.'

'This is most extraordinary,' Mrs Lewis said. 'My sister and her husband are in Argentina and won't be home for another month. Jorge, that's the caretaker, was there to receive the furniture. He pops in once a week to keep an eye on the place while they're away. I know nothing about an envelope with a key in it. Good heavens! Has Ginger stolen things from this apartment?'

'You are absolutely sure that you did not promise to find accommodation for Ginger for the night of his arrival?'

Mrs Lewis stood up and went to a small writing desk at the window. She took a sheet of paper out of the drawer and carried it over to the two men.

'This is a copy of the agreement I had with Ginger Ford,' she said. 'It lists here the items he was to transport, the address in Spain and the price he was charging. As you can see, there is nothing there about finding him accommodation. Good heavens, his fees will have covered that.'

'Are you thinking what I'm thinking?' Murray settled himself more comfortably in the passenger seat as they set out on the road back to Killglash. It was early evening and already the dusk was seeping across the landscape. 'A white van seen on the night of Maike's murder. Ginger drives a white van. Ginger goes to Spain and ends up in an apartment with two guys who are wanted by the Spanish police. No one knows who gave him the key. And to top it all, enter the Queen of Hearts, Sophie Winslow. A patchwork quilt of question marks.'

'It might just be pure coincidence that she owns that apartment,' Flynn said. 'Felipe told us that it is rented out to tourists by an agency, so she probably won't know who the tenants were.'

Murray gave a gusty sigh. 'It's all too much of a coincidence. Steve Donlon went to Spain the day after Stanley Wallace was killed. He was in that area, he told me so on the phone.'

'What about motive?'

'I'm beginning to think that Maike Bloem saw something she shouldn't have on that night. She intended having a cigarette before she walked down to the B&B. If you stand there at the supermarket you have a pretty good view of Agnes O'Toole's cottage and according to Vanessa Ryan a white van pulled up near there as she and Rod Kirwin were driving off. I've seen Ginger come out of Agnes' garden late one night and something was stored in Agnes' shed. It all ties in to something illegal going on and Agnes is up to her neck in it.'

'Maike was killed because she disturbed some kind of operation down at Agnes' cottage?'

'I reckon so. It'll be hard to prove it without a shred of evidence but we can put Ginger under pressure now.'

'Do you think that Ginger killed Maike? Somehow I don't see him doing something like that. Smuggling stuff, yes, but it's a big step from that to killing someone.'

'Who knows what he'd do if the stakes were high? What was he storing at Agnes O'Toole's cottage? If we knew the answer to that question, we'd probably be able to figure out of he's innocent of murder or not.'

'But what has Donlon got to do with it? He was at a party all night when Maike was killed.'

Murray passed a hand wearily across his face. 'I don't know. What I do know is that we have the major players connected somehow in Spain. If Ginger drives back and forth to the continent it's more than likely he's smuggling. He's just never been caught.'

'But there's no connection that we know of between Sophie Winslow and Ginger Ford, apart from him staying in her apartment of course,' Flynn pointed out. 'Or come to that no connection between Stanley Wallace and Ginger Ford or Steve Donlon and Ginger Ford.' He sounded tired. 'Loads of checking up to do, Alan.'

'We still have to have a cosy chat with our witch in residence,' Murray peered at the luminous dial of his wristwatch. 'It'll be too late tonight, she's probably hung up her broomstick for the day, but first thing tomorrow morning I think we had better have a long chat with Agnes.'

Chapter Forty-Six

It was dark by the time they reached Killglash garda station.

'I'm just going to check if anything new has come in,' Murray said as he unlocked the front door.

Flynn followed him into the main office and they looked over the various updates on both the Maike Bloem and Stanley Wallace murders. Felipe had sent the contact details for the agency which had rented out the apartment in Torrevieja with a note which said that the names used to rent the apartment were false. The rental agency was a respectable one, he added. He would forward the details of the purchase of the apartment by Sophie Winslow in a day or so.

Another message stated that Sophie Winslow's agent had confirmed that she would appear at Killglash garda station in two days' time. And there was still no news on Steve Donlon's car being seen on CCTV on the night of Stanley Wallace's murder.

'Nothing here to keep us,' Murray said. 'We'll go and talk to Agnes in the morning and I think after that we'll spend some time at Ballyamber House but I want to go over all their statements first. See you bright and early in the morning.'

'OK. Goodnight, Alan.' Flynn stifled a yawn.

On the drive from Killglash over the lonely mountain road to Ballyamber village, Murray deliberately shelved all thoughts of the two murders. He and Flynn had thrashed out all possible theories on the drive back from Dublin and his head ached from trying to second guess the motives of the key players. He needed a decent night's sleep, something he had not been getting too often lately. The morning would come soon enough and he needed to be alert and concentrated. All the extra hours of work were adding up and he was afraid he was losing some of his sharpness. What he needed was a few days off to recuperate but until these murders were solved this was out of the question.

A sheep crossed the road in front of him, looking like a white blur in the gathering darkness. Murray braked and mouthed a curse at the animal which scampered up the mountainside. He slowed down again as he rounded the bend near Agnes O'Toole's cottage at the beginning of the village. To his surprise light spilled out from the open door. Agnes had been locking up and practically barricading herself in for the past week, so why leave the door open at this time of the evening?

Despite his weariness some instinct made him stop the car just before the cottage. He switched off the engine, cut the lights and got out, closing the driver's door very softly. He was only a few paces from the garden gate when a dark figure loomed in the open doorway and came running down the path towards him.

'Stop!' Murray roared, leaping forward into a run.

The two of them met at the garden gate and Murray made a lunge for his man. A blow to the arm with a heavy object momentarily paralysed him. He let go his grip. The next moment lights exploded in front of his eyes as he received a blow to the side of his head. The last thing he remembered were more lights then the sound of a thud.

Voices and lights roused Murray. He struggled to sit up and put a hand to his head which was throbbing violently. He could only have been out for a few minutes, he reckoned, as memory came flooding back. Someone was shaking him by the shoulder and calling his name. He struggled to get to his feet then winced at the pain the movement cost him.

'Alan,' said the voice again. 'Oh my God, are you all right?'

It was Nicola Ryan.

'I'm OK,' he told her. 'Where's that fellow gone? What are you doing here?'

'Thank heavens you're all right.' She was sobbing. 'Oh Alan, it's so awful. I think I killed someone.'

'Killed someone?' Murray gingerly moved the arm which had sustained the blow from his assailant. He was starting to recover his wits now.

'I ran in to someone with my car,' she said between great tearful gulps. 'He's lying over there in the grass. I've – sort of covered him with my jacket.' She pointed to a spot which was illuminated by the headlights of her car.

Murray walked slowly in the direction indicated, his head throbbing at every step. The figure of a man lay in an awkward bundle in the grassy verge, legs spread-eagled, arms half buried under his body. Murray reached down and tried for a pulse on the side of the neck. He thought he detected a faint beat but it was hard to be sure. Gently he turned the man on his side and removed the homemade face mask to reveal the identity of his attacker. It was Steve Donlon.

'I've called the gardai and an ambulance. They should be here any minute.' Nicola had come to stand beside him. He could hear her breath coming in ragged gasps. 'Is he – is he dead?'

'He's alive. Suppose you tell me what happened?'

'I was driving home and I got around the bend in the road and there was this car stopped with no lights and I nearly crashed into it. I swerved to avoid it and he just ran out in front of me. I couldn't stop in time.' Her words came out in uneven jerks. 'Do you know who he is, Alan?'

'Steve Donlon.' Murray put a hand up to his head, feeling the stickiness of blood on his fingers. 'He came out of Agnes' cottage. Stay here while I go and see what's been happening.'

He walked up the short path leading to Agnes O'Toole's cottage and cautiously entered the kitchen. It was deserted but the door leading to her bedroom was wide open. Penny Wallace was lying in a crumpled heap just inside the room and nearby was another body, that of Agnes O'Toole. Murray went from one to the other, checking for a pulse. Penny was still alive though judging from the blood matting her blonde hair she had received several blows to the head. When he checked Agnes he found only a faint flutter of pulse. She too had been subjected to a savage attack.

The sound of an ambulance siren was a welcome relief and a moment later a squad car arrived and behind it another ambulance. After that things happened very quickly. Murray gave a quick summary of events to one of the garda while the ambulance crews tended to the injured. Almost before he realised it, his head was bandaged and he found himself being led to Nicola's car.

'I'm to drive you to the hospital,' she told him. 'You need medical attention.'

'Are you sure you can make it? You've had a bit of a shock. I can drive myself.'

'I'm all right now.' Her voice still sounded a little breathless. 'I'll be very careful.'

Murray was suddenly too weary to argue. His head was throbbing and his left arm felt as if it might be broken. He obediently got into the passenger seat beside her. Thoughts crowded through his mind and he tried to make sense of the last hour or so. Steve Donlon had tried to kill Agnes and Penny Wallace, that much seemed obvious. Agnes had known she was in some danger judging by her efforts to barricade herself inside her cottage. But what was Penny Wallace doing at the cottage? Had she come there with Donlon and if so why had he apparently attacked her? What was the connection, for connection there had to be, to the murder of Stanley Wallace? He felt a sudden impatience that he was not able to get his thoughts straight, that other officers were now investigating whereas he would like to be in the thick of it. Nicola was driving very slowly or so it seemed to him and in the end, almost imperceptibly, he succumbed to the grey mist which descended on him.

Chapter Forty-Seven

'I was going to bring you some red roses, Alan.' Flynn grinned, barely hiding his relief that Murray was not seriously hurt. 'Only I heard you were being discharged this morning.'

Murray sat, fully dressed, on the side of his hospital bed. He had been kept in over night much to his disgust. 'What's been going on, Jim? What's the news on Agnes and Penny Wallace?'

'Agnes and Penny Wallace are both in intensive care. It's touch and go with Agnes.'

'And Steve Donlon?'

'He'll pull through, concussion and a few broken bones. Nicola Ryan must have been going at a fair lick and he got a right smack from her car.' Flynn gave a short laugh. 'I didn't get much information from that battle-axe Dr. Schulz. Remember her? She treated me like I was a kid who hadn't said his prayers.'

'The beautiful Inge,' said Murrray. 'I'll be lucky if she lets me out of here today, I expect.' He got to his feet. 'So I'm going to discharge myself. We have a lot of work to do. How soon do you think Donlon will be ready to be interviewed?'

Before Flynn could reply, the door to the private room opened and Dr. Inge Schulz entered. Her cool blue eyes took in the fact that Murray was already up and dressed. 'We are not ready to discharge you as yet, Sergeant Murray,' she said. 'Patients are discharged at 11 a.m. and not before. We must make sure that you do not have any ill effects from the blow to the head. You will need a few days' rest before you return to work.'

'I appreciate all your care and I'm delighted to tell you that I feel fine and that my colleague Garda Jim Flynn is driving me home now.' He gave her what he hoped was a winning smile.

'I would prefer if you remained here.' From the look she directed at both him and Flynn, she was not impressed. 'Concussion is not to be treated lightly at any time.'

Murray decided to change the subject. 'How soon can we talk to Steve Donlon?'

'He will need a day or two. I will let you know.'

'Good. Now, if you have any papers that I need to sign, I'll be on my way. Hospitals make me feel a bit queasy, I'm afraid, Dr Schulz.'

'If you have made up your mind, there is nothing I can do.' She gave the ghost of a smile which Murray thought suited her far more than her usual stern expression.

'It would be interesting to have the beautiful Dr. Schulz on your side,' Murray said thoughtfully as he and Flynn drove away from the hospital. 'There's a woman in there somewhere behind all the starch. I could get used to that smile of hers.'

*****

Penny's experiences at the hospital were very different from Murray's. When she finally surfaced from the darkness which had descended on her with the hammer blows dealt to her head, she found her husband Gregory sitting by her bedside. She had been half-conscious for some time, hearing the murmur of voices, someone – probably Greg she realised now – had held her hand for a while. It felt so safe and comfortable that she did not want to wake up properly.

Gregory was alert for any movement and as soon as her eyes focused on him he leaned over and kissed her very gingerly on the cheek. 'Darling, you're awake. How are you feeling?'

'All right, a bit groggy.' She put a hand up to her head and felt the bandage there. 'What happened? I know that man hit me with something hard. And Agnes O'Toole, too. Where is she? Is she all right?'

Greg took her hand again. 'Relax, you're safe now. You're in the local hospital. Agnes O'Toole is here too.'

'Did they find – who did it?'

Gregory hesitated for a moment. 'Yes. Steve Donlon. He was hit by a car when he tried to escape. He's here as well. He's under police surveillance so you don't have to be frightened.'

Her head was starting to swim again, her thoughts becoming blurred. 'Steve? But how? Why?' Her voice was scarcely a whisper and before Gregory could give an answer she had sunk back into sleep.

Chapter Forty-Eight

Ginger Ford was arrested as soon as he drove off the ferry at Rosslare. He was taken immediately to Killglash garda station where Murray and Flynn were waiting to interview him. Sophie Winslow had already arrived at Killglash station but upon consideration Murray decided to see Ginger first.

'Come clean, Ginger,' were his opening words. 'We've found Maike Bloem's wallet and your fingerprints are on it. You might as well get it off your chest and tell us what happened.'

Ginger sat huddled in his chair, facing the two officers. He looked like a man who has seen his safe and happy little world disintegrate in front of his eyes.

'I didn't kill her,' he said. His voice was hoarse and he had to clear his throat a few times before he could continue. 'She just popped up out of nowhere and we all got scared.'

'Just tell us what happened that night.' Murray said. 'Make sure it's the truth.'

'They told me in Rosslare that the Spanish police might have me sent back to Torrevieja,' Ginger's eyes darted from one to the other, trying to gauge their reaction. 'I'm ready to do a deal if you can get me off. Interested?'

'No.' Murray stood up. 'You're wasting our time, Ginger.'

'Wait a minute.' Ginger put up a hand. 'You don't know what I have to say.'

Murray remained standing. 'You'll have to do a lot of explaining. We're a bit slow down here in Killglash. We can't see how Maike Bloem's wallet could be found among your possessions with your fingerprints on it. Help us out here.'

'I might know who was involved in killing her.' Ginger licked his lips and cleared his throat again. 'I'd need your help. I don't think I'd get a fair deal from the Spanish police. I'd be in gaol with some of that gang and they'd kill me if they thought I said anything to the cops. If you help me I could tell you a few facts.'

'I can't make promises,' Murray said, even though it was the first he had heard of Spanish police interest in having Ginger back. Herrerra had been more than ready to let him go whatever the gardai in Rosslare had intimated. But he was not going to tell Ginger that, not if the fear of being shipped back to Spain helped to loosen the man's tongue. 'No deals. So let's have it. The truth, all of it.'

'Well,' Ginger started to fidget in his chair. 'I sort of helped out a few fellows. I stored things for them. I've no idea what it was all about. It wasn't drugs, I can tell you that,' he added virtuously. 'Anyways, things got nasty. I'm no saint, but I wouldn't harm a fly, you can ask anyone that knows me. Harold Brannigan will tell you the same thing.'

'Now we're getting somewhere.' Murray sat down. 'You and your friend Harold Brannigan were smoking Muratti brand cigarettes. Very sophisticated.' He watched Ginger for his reaction. 'My guess is that you were storing cigarettes in Agnes O'Toole's shed and paying her for the privilege. Don't answer until you're prepared to tell the truth.'

Ginger looked pained then gave up the pretence. 'Like I said, I just helped them to store the stuff. I did all the arranging with Agnes. It wasn't a big operation, just a small gang. They'd tell me when a boat was coming in or when a truck would arrive and I'd go out and collect the goods and I'd help them to load up or do a delivery afterwards. That's all, I swear. They'd only just started operating down here.'

'And the Dutch girl?' Murray's voice hardened. 'Tell us about that.'

Beads of sweat started to form along Ginger's forehead and he brushed them away with the back of his hand. His eyes were fixed on Murray now. 'Like I said, I had nothing to do with that. You can't get me for what happened to her.'

'Just tell the story and it had better be the true story.'

Ginger wiped his forehead again before speaking. 'That night, I was helping two of them load up at Agnes' cottage when this girl appeared from nowhere. We were using torches with no lights on the van and we were as quiet as we could be. We were just about finished.' He looked at Murray then away again and fixed his gaze on some spot on the floor at Murray's feet. 'So, like I said, she came up to us. She had a cigarette in her hand and she asked us for a light. I think she got a bit frightened when she saw what we were doing and she started to run away. They grabbed her and one of them strangled her with a cord or something from the back of the van. They didn't want to leave the body too close to Agnes' place, but they had to hide it fairly quick, so they dumped her body down the road a bit and pulled a bit of bracken over it. They told me to keep my mouth shut or I'd be next.'

It had the ring of truth to it, Murray reflected. According to what Rod and Vanessa had said, Maike wanted to smoke before returning to the B&B and she had blundered into a gang of smugglers who could not afford to let her live. The wrong place at the wrong time. A sad epitaph for a pretty girl who, according to family and friends, was full of life and who had looked forward to a few days of hill walking in Kerry.

'Who is this gang? I need names. How did you get involved with them?' It cost him an effort to keep his anger from showing.

Ginger shifted uncomfortably in his chair again. 'I'm not rightly sure who they are. I got a message to pick up these two fellas in Killglash and they told me to drive to Agnes' place. I'd done things like this before for them. They'd phone me and give me times for pick up or delivery of stuff. I never had any trouble. Mostly that was for stuff in Spain off the ferry from Ceuta or Tangier or what's that other place? Melilla. I did a bit here too and a bit in the North.'

'Someone must have approached you in the first place?' It was Flynn who spoke. He had been quietly taking notes in addition to the voice recording which Ginger had agreed to.

'It's run by people in Spain. A couple of years back this Dublin family asked me to transport a few boxes of household stuff to their apartment in Spain and when I was having a drink on the ferry this Spanish fellow came up to me and asked if I wanted to make a bit of extra money.' He looked defiantly at the two officers. 'I know a lot of lorry drivers do it. I said I would. He said cash on the nail, no names, no pack drill. I said OK but I wouldn't do heroin or stuff like that. That's how I operated. I picked up the stuff and the money landed in my letter box in Dublin. No questions asked.'

They would have to believe him for now, Murray thought disgustedly. 'Who killed Maike Bloem? You said two men. We need names.'

'I don't know the names. Only their first names. Like I said, I got a phone call to say they needed help picking up stuff from Agnes' cottage. They were foreigners, Spanish I think. One of them was called Jose and the other fellow was Tony.' Ginger's face took on a hunted look. 'They said they'd kill me if I ever ratted on them.'

'Tell us how you came to stay in Sophie Winslow's apartment in Torrevieja.' It was very probable that the men arrested with Ginger in the apartment in Spain were responsible for Maike's murder. Comisario Herrera had been very confident of smashing the gang when Murray had last spoken to him.

'I moved some stuff for Geraldo Butler del Rosario. I was to pick up a few cartons on my way back and I was told on the phone that I could stay in that flat. It saved me looking for a hotel.'

Nothing had been discovered in his van when it was searched at Rosslare, Murray knew. He had obviously been spooked by the events in Spain. He stole a glance at his watch. It was time to interview Sophie Winslow. She might provide a few answers which could be used to put pressure on Ginger. He was probably telling them what he knew. He was a small cog in a big smuggling wheel. 'We'll need descriptions of those two men,' he said. 'And we'll be having another chat with you later on today.'

'I can put up bail,' Ginger said quickly. 'And I'd want a solicitor to sit it on my next interview.'

When he had been taken away Murray looked across at Flynn and grimaced. 'There are times when I think there's a lot to be said for countries with no human rights.' He stood up and stretched, careful of any sudden movement which could bring back the headaches he had been suffering from over the past few days. Although he would never admit it, Dr Inge Schulz had been right; he should have taken a few days off work to recover.

Felipe Herrera had provided them with the details of Sophie Winslow's purchase of the apartment in Torrevieja. Everything seemed to be above board. The letting agent confirmed that Sophie visited Torrevieja from time to time – three times last year – but never actually stayed in her own apartment. It was really half of a house, Herrera explained, as customary for summer residences of this type, with Sophie owning the lower half. There were three bedrooms, a sitting room and a small kitchen. The upper half was let out in the summer at irregular intervals and was owned by a native of Torrevieja, who was an honest, hardworking businessman with no connection to Sophie.

With this information under his belt, Murray felt only curiosity as to what he could learn from the interview with Sophie. There was nothing wrong with owning an apartment in Spain and renting it out. The one thing which did not quite fit was the fact that it had been rented to Ginger Ford and two other individuals wanted by the Spanish police on drug trafficking charges.

Sophie was accompanied by her lawyer, who she introduced as William Taylor. Despite her carefully applied make-up she looked haggard. There were deep shadows under her eyes.

'This is all most shocking,' she said. 'I have never had any trouble with that apartment. The letting agent is excellent.'

Flynn, who had been reading text messages on his mobile now looked up. 'We've just received information from Torrevieja that the apartment has often been used by various criminals in the past, including the two men arrested there a few days back. It seems to be a safe house. Could you explain that to us, please?'

Sophie's mouth opened in surprise. She looked helplessly at Taylor who immediately responded. 'My client does not have to answer that question,' he said primly, 'she can have no control over who rents the apartment from the letting agent.'

'Right,' said Flynn, who was flicking through the messages on his phone. 'We also have confirmation from police sources that in fact the apartment was bought in your name but the person putting up the money was Steve Donlon.'

'Well, yes, he did give me the money for it.' Sophie ran a pink tongue over her lips. 'Steve and I are old friends, old flames if it comes to that. So he helped me out.' She looked from Flynn to Murray then back again. 'That's not against the law, is it?'

'Nice work, Jim,' Murray said when Sophie and her lawyer had left. 'I expect Donlon was doing a bit of money laundering.'

'Felipe says they're digging into that,' Flynn told him. 'It looks like the caretaker at the del Rosario residence is mixed up in it. He's admitted to getting the key to the apartment for Ginger. He says a woman left it with him and he identified Sophie Winslow as that woman.'

'So Sophie was in Spain and everyone thought she was in Dublin? Come to think of it, she only visited Ballyamber House when Donlon was staying there. We're getting somewhere at last, Jim. We should be able to nail Donlon for Stanley Wallace's murder. His modus operandi seems to be hitting people over the head. I hope he enlightens us about his motive for killing Stanley.'

'I always thought that Agnes would get herself into hot water with all those threats,' Flynn said slowly. 'Donlon must have got wind of what she was saying about knowing who killed Stanley Wallace and knew he had to silence her. He must have panicked when Penny Wallace showed up out of the blue.'

'There's one piece of evidence which could tie Donlon to Stanley Wallace's murder. If we have confirmation of that before we interview him, we can nail him for sure.' Murray's head was starting to ache and he reached for the pills which Dr. Schulz had prescribed. He had stopped smoking since his admission to hospital and a sudden craving overtook him. 'It's nearly lunch time,' he said, 'suppose we pop down to the Italian and have a snack before we get stuck in the paperwork?'

Flynn looked slightly embarrassed. 'Sorry, Alan, I have a sort of standing date with Kay for lunchtime these days. With all the overtime, we don't get to see that much of each other.'

'When this is all over I think we'll both need a holiday.' Murray swallowed one of the painkillers and forced a smile. 'We'll make Percy an offer he can't refuse.'

Steve Donlon's condition improved enough for them to speak to him the day after the interviews with Ginger Ford and Sophie Winslow. He had suffered several broken ribs and a fracture to his left foot. Murray and Flynn interviewed him at his bedside. He did not ask for a solicitor to be present which surprised Murray. Judging by his reaction to their questions, he had been doing a lot of thinking.

'Everything just got out of hand,' he said. 'I had these contacts in Spain, we were doing a bit of smuggling, mostly counterfeit money and cigarettes, and the idea was to start our own forgery workshop in Ballyamber. Stanley Wallace wanted a live-in caretaker and I jumped at the chance. We planned to buy Agnes O'Toole out and have me live in that cottage – fully modernised, of course. The old witch was proving stubborn but I was pretty optimistic she'd change her mind.' Here he paused in his story and looked earnestly at Murray. 'I've never hurt anyone in my life before. And I'd never do drugs.'

'What happened? You killed Stanley Wallace, didn't you?'

Donlon shook his head but showed no other reaction.

Murray waited, letting the silence stretch out for a few minutes before he spoke. 'You remember that you kindly gave us DNA and fingerprint samples when we interviewed you last week?'

Donlon still said nothing but his eyes were watchful as he looked at Murray.

'Stanley Wallace was hit over the head by a heavy cut glass vase,' Murray went on in a conversational tone. 'He was hit with such force that a piece of the glass broke off. There was a partial fingerprint on that piece of glass and we have now been able to identify it. It matches your thumb-print.'

'My prints are bound to be on that vase and all over the library. Stanley and I worked in that room lots of times. It doesn't prove anything.'

'It just so happens,' Murray said, still speaking in that conversational tone, 'that there was a tiny drop of blood on that partial print. In other words, your thumb was cut when you hit Stanley with the vase. Your print could only have got on there after you had hit him and the glass broke.'

There was another complete silence. Donlon, propped up on his pillows, appeared to be mulling over his options. To Murray's surprise he did not immediately clam up and ask for a solicitor. Instead he nodded his head slightly as if he had come to a decision.

'I lost my temper,' he said. 'Stanley discovered I was having an affair with Penny and he was furious. Told me he was cancelling our agreement and that I'd only get some of the money he owed me for the work I'd put in on Ballyamber House. I already owed quite a bit of that money. All my plans would have come to nothing.' He passed a hand across his eyes. 'I didn't intend seeing him before I left that night. I'd made up a file with all the quotations we'd received from various building companies for work on Ballyamber House and I wanted to take it with me. I didn't want to do the old bastard any favours by leaving it behind. I couldn't find it anywhere and I was just about to give up and leave when I thought I'd give one last try at finding it and that's when I went into the library for a last look. Stanley was there.' Donlon paused a moment, remembering. 'He told me he had the file and had no intention of returning it to me. Not only was he not going to pay me, he'd make sure that my reputation was so tarnished that I'd never get another day's work. Before I knew what I was doing I picked up that vase and hit him with it. I never meant to kill him.'

'And Agnes O'Toole and Penny Wallace? What happened there?' Murray gave Flynn a quick triumphant glance. This was going better than either of them had hoped. They had not expected Donlon to crack so easily. Perhaps he realised that the game was up or was so shaken by the accident that he did not have the energy or will to keep protesting his innocence.

'Agnes is going to be OK, isn't she? I know that Penny is all right.'

'Just answer the question,' Murray said. 'We're not here to do medical bulletins.' In fact, the latest information he had receivedon Agnes was that she was still in a very critical condition and remained in intensive care.

Donlon took a deep breath and winced at the discomfort this movement caused to his fractured ribs. 'I heard that Agnes was talking in the village about having seen my car driving away from Ballyamber House the night of Stanley's murder. I knew you'd get to hear of it. I had to shut her up. I took a hammer from the garden shed and went down to her cottage. I think I planned just to frighten her at first but she was pretty sure of herself and I lost it. For some reason Penny came in and I had to – ' he broke off. 'I must have been mad,' he said. 'I can't account for what I did any other way.' His voice broke slightly.

Murray gave him time to collect himself before he asked the next question. 'And then you heard my car, I take it?'

'I didn't know it was you. I hit you a couple of times with the hammer. I'm sorry about that. I'm glad you're not badly injured.'

There was a flash of the old smooth-talking Donlon for a moment then he went on in a sober tone. 'I ran into the road and something hit me. I don't remember anything after that until I woke up in here.'

When they had finished with Donlon the two men went to find Dr Inge Schulz. She was just getting ready to leave her office.

'Ah, gentlemen, I am glad you are here. I have some bad news.' Her German accent seemed more pronounced today. 'I'm afraid that Agnes O'Toole passed away an hour ago. There was nothing we could do to save her. I'm sorry.'

Murray stifled a curse. 'Thank you, doctor. I know you did your best.'

'So now it's two murders at Steve Donlon's door,' Flynn said softly.

Chapter Forty-Nine

'You'll be pleased to know that I've found a buyer for Ballyamber House,' Gregory said as he escorted Penny from the hospital ward to his car.

'A buyer? Really? That's a bit sudden, isn't it?' Penny couldn't keep the surprise and satisfaction out of her voice. She half feared the news to be premature.

'It was a bit of luck in a way,' Gregory said. 'Because of all that happened there, with father and everything, I was looking for ways to sell the place without making too great a financial loss. He wouldn't have wanted that. I was approached by a hotel consortium who're interested in turning the place into a hotel and spa. They reckon there's plenty of potential for something like that around here.'

'I'm glad,' Penny said soberly. The questions about their marriage, what would happen, if there was any hope of Greg forgiving her, trembled on her lips but she kept silent. Gregory had visited her every day in hospital but they had not discussed either Steve Donlon or anything else that had happened in the past. Visiting times were restricted so that he normally checked his watch after a quarter of an hour and took his leave ostensibly to give Rod some time with his sister.

Neither of them spoke on the drive back to Ballyamber House. Gregory attended her into the small salon where Mrs Quinn had a welcoming fire going. She had come to see Penny in hospital a few times and proved invaluable by bringing toiletries, fresh clothes and glossy magazines. 'Sure I know what you'd like,' she had said waving Penny's thanks aside. 'Men haven't a clue what we need when we're in hospital.'

'It's lovely to see you back,' she said now with a big smile as she set down the laden tea tray on the little table by the fire. 'You're looking much better.'

Penny wondered briefly if she had heard about the place being sold and if she were worried about the likelihood of losing her job. She would miss this gossipy woman, she realised with a pang.

Gregory waited until the door closed behind Mrs Quinn before sitting down in the armchair opposite Penny.

'Now that everything is sorted, we don't need to stay here in Ballyamber,' he said, speaking as if he had rehearsed what he wanted to say. 'The gardai agree to us going back to London. I've given a guarantee that we will come over any time they need to see us and I've engaged a local solicitor to represent us, so that end of things shouldn't present a problem.'

Penny nodded. She did not know what to say. She was glad they were leaving but what awaited her back in London?

'Rod is off to New York fairly soon,' Gregory continued. 'Let's hope he makes full use of this fresh start he's been given and doesn't fall back into his old ways.'

'I'll always be grateful for what your father did for him,' Penny said. 'Maybe I never made that clear before.' Her voice trailed off. Even mentioning Stanley Wallace was painful. She would forever associate her brief affair with Steve Donlon with the murder of her father-in-law.

'I think that Ballyamber House will always have bad memories for both of us,' Gregory said after a pause. It was almost as if he had read her thoughts. 'We have to try and get on with our lives, pick up the pieces somehow.'

Penny had been crumbling one of Mrs Quinn's scones in her plate, now she looked directly at him. It was better to know the truth, she thought with sudden resolve.

'What about us, Gregory? Are we ever going to be able to move on from – what I did?'

'I'd like us to have some counselling.' He met her gaze straight on. 'I love you, Penny but I'm not sure that I can get over what happened between you and Donlon. I trusted you and you broke my heart. It's going to be hard for me to – 'he searched for a word -'to feel right again with you.'

'If you hated me, I could understand it. I think it's worse if you say you love me but you're not sure we can get over it.'

'I think we can, if that's what we both want. Do you want to? That's the question that's been haunting me. You must have fallen out of love with me in order to have an affair. Maybe when you're back in London and fit again you'll want to leave me.'

'You don't want to leave me?'

'No. I know I was at fault. I've been too much under my father's influence.' He swallowed and looked away for a moment. 'I've thought about this a lot. I want you back. I think we can make it, we'll need help, counselling like I said, but if you love me, it will all be easier.'

'I do love you, Greg. I think I knew that the moment I started this affair with Steve. I've been incredibly stupid, insensitive, you can't call it any worse names than I've been doing ever since it happened.'

'That's it then. We'll make it.'

Although they still sat on opposite sides of the fireplace, there was suddenly a warm glow in Penny's heart. She was beginning to realise that this crisis had deepened and strengthened their relationship. Perhaps it was a very high price to pay, but she had the feeling it was worth it.

Chapter Fifty

'Time to call it a day, I think, Jim.' Murray popped a folder into his Out-tray and leant back in his chair. It was some weeks later and things were slowly returning to normal at Killglash garda station. Steve Donlon was in prison awaiting trial. He had made a rapid recovery from his injuries and had apparently decided to continue being cooperative with the forces of the law. Perhaps he was hoping that this would have a positive effect on his sentencing for the murders of Stanley Wallace and Agnes O'Toole and the attempted murder of Penny Wallace.

Fingerprints from the two men who had been arrested in Spain with Ginger Ford were found to match prints on Maike Bloem's wallet and also on one of the buttons of her jacket. They were duly charged with her murder and were awaiting trial. They both attested to the fact that Ginger had no part in Maike's killing. Their confessions resulted in the destruction of Steve Donlon's smuggling operation. Sophie Winslow's role in the operation was also brought to light. She had helped to launder money by purchasing and selling villas around Spain in her own name with money provided by Donlon. Despite protestations of innocence and many tears and pleadings about the effect this would have on her career, Sophie was to stand trial on money laundering charges. No one had much sympathy for her. She had known what Donlon was doing and was happy to go along with it in return for a generous share of the profits.

Now that both murders had been solved and her brother Rod was in the clear, Penny Wallace finally told Murray about the noises she had heard overhead in her bedroom. Although both Gregory and Donlon had dismissed this as the creak of wood expanding or the scurrying of mice, she had never quite believed them. A forensic examination revealed that part of the attic had been used to store boxes of cigarettes. Donlon admitted that when Stanley Wallace hired him as estate manager, he had thought it a good way of hiding contraband until it could be collected and distributed. He had disguised the cigarettes under some junk items which were being stored in the attic. However, as Stanley had become interested in the possibilities of converting the attic space into bedrooms, Donlon had deemed it better to get rid of the them. The noises that Penny had heard were made by a member of the Spanish gang getting the boxes ready for transfer to Agnes O'Toole's cottage when the household was thought to be asleep.

There were changes too in Murray's life. Nicola Ryan had come to see him a few evenings before. 'My sister and her husband have asked if I'd help them run their business in Galway,' she said. 'They rent out cottages to tourists and they want me to take over the management of it. They've just invested in a new hotel nearby and they can use my help, they say. It's an exciting challenge and it will be nice to have family close by.'

'I'm delighted for you,' Murray said and meant it. He had the feeling she was hoping he would protest or say something which indicated a romantic interest. He was sorry to disappoint her but it couldn't be helped. She was a pleasant neighbour but that was all.

'It will be good for Vanessa,' she went on, looking slightly downcast. 'As you know, Rod Kirwin is moving to New York shortly. He seems to have forgotten that he was ever in love with her. She's heartbroken. I'm hoping a change of location will do her good.'

'It sounds like the best thing,' Murray said. 'She's bound to meet lads of her own age. She's a very pretty girl.'

He realised that Nicola was making him feel guilty about not being able to return her feelings and was therefore secretly glad that she was moving away. She deserved better, he told himself, but that was a subject he did not want to embark upon with her. Heart-to-hearts were not always advisable.

'I'm finished for the day,' Flynn said now in answer to his remark. 'It's good to have the desk clear at last.'

'I expect you've got a date,' Murray said. Normally he would have sneaked out for a cigarette but he had not smoked since he was attacked and the craving was no longer acute. To his satisfaction, Flynn had not yet noticed or at least not commented on his success in this regard. Perhaps he thought his chief might start up again as had happened a few times in the past.

Flynn nodded. 'Yes, I'm meeting Kay for dinner. We plan to go away for a few days soon. I'm due a bit of time off.'

'I'll have to meet her some time.' Murray's smile was genuine. 'Make sure you're not throwing yourself away.'

Flynn laughed. 'We'll do that.'

'Old Percy nearly gave us a medal for solving the Stanley Wallace case,' Murray went on. 'Did you see that interview with him on RTE? I think some of it was even shown on Sky news which makes old Percy world famous.'

'He'll be taking up politics next,' Flynn remarked.

'Good prospects for a promotion,' Murray said. They worked well together and he would be sorry to see him go. At the same time, he acknowledged that Flynn deserved more than being second in command in a backwater like Killglash and it was only fair that he should get promoted.

'We'll see,' Flynn said. 'Judging by Percy's hymns of praise, we'll both end up being Superintendents.'

'And Killglash still won't get its refurbishment, as he likes to call it.' Murray laughed. 'I've often wondered what Percy means by that word.'

'We'll be lucky to get a new door mat,' Flynn said and both of them were laughing loudly as they left the building.

Before parting, Flynn turned to his chief. 'It's Saturday night. Are you doing anything special, Alan, to celebrate cracking our two murder cases?'

'You'd be surprised,' was all Murray said.

On his drive home, with Ardnabrone standing out clearly against a pale blue evening sky, Murray was reminded of the legend which said the mountain claimed three lives a year. The deaths of Maike Bloem, Stanley Wallace and Agnes O'Toole all occurring within weeks of each other would revive that story, he reflected. There were times when he half believed it himself.

Later that evening he drove to Killarney where he had booked a table at one of the most expensive restaurants in the area. He stood for a moment in the doorway, savouring the tantalising smell of food and wine and the buzz of conversation, then he headed towards a table for two set discreetly by the window. Dr Inge Schulz looked even more attractive when she was wearing a clingy black dress in addition to a warm smile, he thought as he sat down opposite her.

THE END

Made in the USA
Charleston, SC
15 January 2017